Starfall

by

R.M. Anderson

Starfall: Starfall Chronicles Book One
Copyright ©2018 R.M. Anderson / Rhonda Mix Anderson

All rights reserved. The author guarantees all contents are original and do not infringe upon the legal rights of any other person or work. No part of this book may be used or reproduced, stored in a retrieval system or transmitted in any form or by any means without prior written permission of the publisher.

This is a work of fiction. Names, characters, businesses, places, events and incidents are either the products of the author's imagination or used in a fictitious manner. Any resemblance to actual persons, living or dead, or actual events is purely coincidental.
Cover design and artwork by Bythos www.bythos.com

ISBN: 9781983168772

Dedicated to Arielle.
May you always find the beauty and light in life,
and especially, within yourself.

Table of Contents

Star Fall	2
Discovery	6
Questions	18
Leaving	28
Another Unprecedented Meeting	39
A Strange New World	53
Eustasia	63
The Center	74
Snorg Territory	80
Sandalia	88
Confessions	103
In The Jungle	114
The Floppersnogs	125
Into The Desert	138
Where Scorpions Dwell	153
Desert Dogs	162
Sand Trap	175
Into The Darkness	181
Abandoned	195
Escape	203
Between Worlds	219
Last Hope	228
Reflections	236
Until We Meet Again	246
Home	255

Part I

-1-
Star Fall

On one fateful evening, two young stars named Wink and Blink chased each other around the vast night sky, spinning around in circles amid thousands of twinkling bodies of bright and radiant light.

The Man In The Moon sat and nonchalantly watched them all, lost in his scattered thoughts about time and space. After awhile, he yawned and pulled a blanket of stardust tightly around his shoulders, curling up inside a deep crater. His eyes grew heavy and he drifted off into a dreamless sleep, completely unaware of what would come to pass during the next few moments.

Wink was a bully. It thrilled him to pick on the younger and smaller stars. On this particular night, he chose Blink as his next victim. Glancing out of the corner of one eye, Wink noted that his mother was oblivious to his misdeeds, as usual. She was chattering on about something nonsensical to Blink's mother, so he thought the timing was perfect. Smiling mischievously to himself, he turned his attention back to Blink.

"Take that!" He shoved the young star.

Blink frowned. "Leave me alone. I don't want to fight with you." He zoomed back a few paces.

Wink laughed with delight at Blink's cowardice. "What a little starlet you are," he sneered, proceeding to hurl himself full force once more in Blink's direction. As he crashed into Blink's shimmering body, rays of light radiated out and scattered. Blink screamed in pain, and, for a brief moment, all stars in the vicinity stopped talking and stared with both wonder and horror at the pulsing, radiating light that suddenly surrounded them.

A terrible event then followed.

Due to a strange force spiraling out of his control, Blink felt himself being torn – violently – from the sky.

"Help! Help!"

His shouts rang out loud and clear as he fell, the frantic words echoing through the galaxy. His energy faded as he spun crazily out of control. As Blink descended rapidly into the inky blackness and void below, he gazed up helplessly and watched as his twinkling brethren completely disappeared from his line of vision.

While Blink fell into territory unknown, Wink watched with a mixture of horror and a surprising sudden, newfound sense of shame. He hung his head. For the first time in his life, he felt terrible.

"I've caused a falling star," he moaned, and – to add to his disgrace – his mother stared at him with disbelief and disappointment as tears streamed down her face.

A few stars moved in to console her as she wept. The others began to whisper and dart dirty, fiery looks in Wink's direction.

Amid all the commotion, The Man In The Moon woke up. "And what is the meaning of this?" he bellowed, rubbing the sleep from his yellowed eyes. "Why has my slumber been disturbed?!"

All stars halted conversation and accusingly flicked their eyes over to Wink, who darted behind his mother and waited for the judgment to come.

She nudged him forward. "It's time to pay for your crime," she whispered harshly, forcing him out into the open to own up to what he'd done.

Gazing up at The Man In The Moon with wide eyes, Wink cleared his throat and confessed. "I have caused a falling star," he mumbled. "Blink is no longer with us. I'm sorry."

The Man In The Moon scratched his graying bearded chin and pondered the unfortunate and unexpected tragic turn of events. It was not good news. Fallen star children rarely returned. Such a thing had not happened in this corner of The Outer Space for a long time.

After what seemed like an eternity, he shed a large golden tear. The shimmering orb trailed down his cheek and sparkled as it fell noiselessly into the black abyss below.

"Ahhh, the sorrow of it," he sighed. "Another of my star children, gone forever."

Glancing at Blink's tearful mother, he shook his head sadly. "There is only a very small hope of his return," he said. "Another shooting star, this one gone all too soon. Too soon before his time."

Sighing once more, The Man In The Moon turned his attention back to the perpetrator of the crime.

"Come now, young Wink," he said, stretching out a long and luminous arm toward the assailant. "Come sit in a crater for an age, and think about what you have done."

Plucking up the star, The Man In The Moon carried Wink across a great expanse of moonscape, setting him on a lonesome crater somewhere out of sight on the dark side. There, Wink would remain to ponder his rash actions.

As the bully star's mother turned away in embarrassment, Blink's mother wailed, her sobs echoing through the galaxy. "Not again," she said, her heart breaking. She thought of another star she had once loved who'd been taken from her in a similar manner.

But the Man In The Moon could offer no comfort.

"I believe it is too late," he said again, sadly. "Nothing can be done now."

With those final words, the stars joined together and formed a vast constellation of dimmed lights, bowing their heads in grief.

-2-
Discovery

Below the world of the mourning stars, the land of Eugladia, in the world of Veildom, was silent. Most of its inhabitants were fast asleep.

The land was an enchanted place full of creatures humans in the Other World – also known as Earth – had never seen, and probably will never see. Eugladia was one of those places people often feel but can never quite reach – one of those worlds that exists just beyond the veiled curtain; a land people in the Other World can only dream about.

It was a land graced with soft, undulating green hills and lush emerald valleys flowing with plants in hues all the colors of the rainbow. It was a place of clear rivers and magnificent, wondrous creatures – creatures such as the Thunderfeet – the blue skinned elephants who protected Eugladia from all intruders and harm.

Rich, wild vegetation dotted Eugladia's hills. The hills were home to fairies and elves and gnome-like beings.

The air in Eugladia was pure, the purest air that has ever been or ever will be – at least outside of Heaven. Beings much like humans inhabited Eugladia, though they had a slight resemblance to a combination of humans and giant, human-sized elves. The Eugladians were also different than humans in the sense that they tended to live completely off the land, and had never seen nor heard of a good amount of material things and matters that cause a great deal of stress in our world today. They survived solely on whatever natural resources they had – as they believed nature and The Creator intended them to live.

The Eugladians appreciated music, art, and even had their own form of literature. They were very fond of books. They also worked and had businesses of sorts, but their jobs were simple in nature and they exchanged goods and services instead of paper money.

Their clothing was made from natural fibers; their diet consisted mostly of fruit, nuts, vegetables, mushrooms, and fish (though some Eugladians disliked to eat fish, since the fish in that land could talk. It was, as would be expected, very difficult for one to eat a talking fish).

As previously mentioned, on the night of Blink's unfortunate descent, all beings and creatures below the world of the stars were fast asleep.

Save one.

Eugladian Radianne Timblebrooke tossed and turned in bed in her family's tree dwelling (an enormous, magnificent house carved into a massive tree) and grew frustrated with her restlessness. Not able to stand lying down any longer, she quietly crept to her window and climbed down the giant vine that waited there, easing past the winding outdoor staircase.

When her feet hit the soft grass, she made her way through the darkness and headed to her favorite spot to do some serious thinking.

Radianne was at an age, eighteen to be exact, when she was ready to forge her own path and find her own way. She wanted freedom. She yearned for freedom. She was tired of her mundane existence. She wanted adventure. She wanted to explore the worlds beyond Eugladia – worlds such as the Nether Lands – those mysterious places she'd heard about in tales as a child.

Her parents and older brother often told her she should be content with where she was in life and be happy with all she had. They would spout off tedious lectures about how wonderful life was in Eugladia and how Radianne should appreciate the simpler things in life and not want to search for more.

"Chasing the wind is foolish," her mother would often warn her. "You need to find your happiness right here, right where you were born, with your feet firmly planted on this solid ground."

And yet – when her mother said such things, Radianne had the feeling she could see a far-away longing in the older woman's eyes. As if, once upon a time, her mother too had wanted to chase the wind. And had never taken the chance.

Radianne told herself she wasn't about to let such a tragedy happen to her.

"Well *I'll* sure have the chance." She said the words out loud and matter-of-factly, narrowing her green eyes as she walked, vowing she would one day leave life as she knew it behind and explore all that lay out there beyond Eugladia's borders.

Chasing the wind sounded very exciting, she thought. She would not be afraid to take the chance her mother had never taken.

As she crossed the swaying bridge that hung precariously over the laughing river, she sucked in a breath, waiting for the giggling to start. Thankfully, the noisy waters seemed to be asleep at the moment. She was glad. She didn't feel like dealing with the river's obnoxious laughter on an already restless and irritable night.

Once she was safely on the other side of the bridge, she followed the uneven stone path to her special spot.

The tiny pond was hidden in the middle of tall golden grasses, grasses that were at that moment cast in a glowing hue in the shadow of moonlight. The spot was always a welcome retreat when Radianne wanted to be alone with her thoughts.

Something which had been happening more frequently as of late…

She brushed her long, light brown hair away from her eyes and sat down on the comfortably well-worn large gray thinking boulder. Tilting her head back, her eyes looked to the sky as they usually did, admiring the stars.

"How strange," she said out loud, noting that something about them seemed different that night. "They seem a bit dimmer somehow."

The wind picked up as she said the words, and she shivered in the darkness. The night was silent. It became too silent after awhile.

For eighteen years she had lived the same monotonous life. A mundane life, in the same village, doing the same things, seeing the same people, having the same friends. There had to be more out there.

She supposed she should be grateful. Her parents owned a Wimbly fruit tree orchard and business (a pear like nothing you've ever tasted) and they provided the best and most delicious fruit around. It really was something to be proud of. And her brother Leiden was very happy to do nothing more with his life than help out with the fruit tree farm. She wished she could be more like him. But she couldn't. There was no getting around it. She needed something *more*.

Her eyes continued to search the stars and she thought about the world above, its vastness and mystery. She wondered what secrets the stars held, what they knew that she didn't. They were so beautiful, scattered up there like holes punched through the blackness – as if revealing a diamond light within.

"How lovely it would be to be a star," she whispered. "To see far past Eugladia and to look down at all the other worlds... to shine light into the darkness. To be something beautiful and hopeful for people to look up to and admire. To see all the worlds beyond and below..."

Sighing again, she kicked at a pebble near her foot and continued to brood over the lack of intrigue and adventure in her life.

Just the same boring routine, year after year...

"It is who I am becoming," she muttered, with an air of despair. "I am also growing boring and uninspired."

Though, she thought suddenly, she would never admit it to anyone, but there was the occasional excitement when the Snorgs attempted to raid Eugladia.

The tribe of giant, evil trolls loved to attack villages at night. But their attempts to take over Eugladia always failed. Though their raids in other lands were rumored to be growing more violent, the infrequent raids in Eugladia never lasted long because the Thunderfeet would come stomping along and chase the Snorgs away, scattering them instantly. The Snorgs deeply feared elephants.

Radianne despised the foul trolls, who smelled even worse than the stink melons they sometimes threw. There were talks of late that the trolls were growing in power and utilizing new and dangerous weaponry, but Radianne found such tales hard to believe. If the whispers were true, however, it would be something to stay on alert for... remembering the last Snorg attack, she became so engrossed in her thoughts that she didn't hear the rustling at first.

A crunching sound in the bush behind her startled her out of her thinking. Eyes opened wide, she stood up and turned toward the sound. She stared at the shaking shrub, wondering what evil would emerge. Would it be a fiendish Snorg? Clenching her fists, she prepared to fight.

"Who's there?!" she demanded.

A little blonde head popped out. Tiny red lips broke into a huge grin. "What are you doing up and about at this hour?"

Radianne relaxed. It was only her friend, Piri. The fairy jumped out of the bush and she returned the smile.

"Are you doing that dangerous thing you call 'thinking' again?" Piri asked, fluttering a few feet in front of Radianne's nose.

Radianne sheepishly smiled. "More or less," she said, as Piri came to a rest on her knee. The pixie knew her too well.

The fairy's little blue dress sparkled in the moonlight as her translucent blue wings fluttered softly behind her. "Is there any way I can help?"

Radianne smiled again and shook her head slowly. No one could help her but herself, and she wasn't even remotely capable of understanding herself at the moment. "I think I just need some adventure in my life."

The fairy laughed. "An adventure? Don't you have enough adventure every day? Just the other day, Frink chased you around non-stop, declaring his undying devotion to you. Isn't that enough adventure in itself?"

Radianne waved her hand dismissively. Frink was arrogant and thought he was much wiser than his eighteen years. He claimed he had visited many lands, lands beyond her "wildest dreams."

He said he would be more than happy to show them to her. If she'd be his forever.

As if that would happen, Radianne thought.

Though he chased her around all day, every day, Radianne desperately tried to avoid Frink. He was a tall, dark Eugladian whom other women her age found very handsome and charming, but she found quite annoying. She wanted to explore other lands all right, but on her own.

All on her own.

"Frink thinks he knows it all," she sniffed. "But I find him quite obnoxious, actually."

Piri sighed. "I wish I could get Maiz to chase me around like that."

Maiz was Piri's love interest – a handsome, red-headed fairy that she'd long ago developed romantic feelings for. Unfortunately, Maiz was also very wild at heart and not looking to be tamed by any one fairy anytime soon.

Radianne was just about to tell Piri what a great couple she thought she and Maiz would make, if only she could tame his fiery spirit, when a sudden flash of white light exploded in the near distance.

"I wonder what that is?" She pointed to the strange light pulsating on the ground through a clearing in the trees up ahead.

Piri shrugged, squinting her eyes. "Hard to say."

"Let's go see. Come on." Radianne stood up and ran off into a thicket of brush.

Piri fluttered quickly behind.

The two soon came to a stop at the site of where the blinding light had fallen, in the meadow grasses of the clearing. There, on a bed of smoldering grass, lay a brightly glowing thing.

Radianne nervously walked toward the strange object as Piri lingered cautiously behind her. Crouching low, Radianne took a closer look. As she examined the strange thing, she couldn't believe her eyes. A memory flared to life. Recalling a picture book she'd seen as a child, she knew without a doubt that what was there on the grass before her was a star.

"But how could this be?" she wondered out loud. "Stars are supposed to be huge and lifeless burning bodies of fumes in the galaxy… though for the sake of children and their imaginations, in the picture book the stars were drawn much like what I'm seeing now."

The five-pointed star in the grass was small and definitely full of life. It glowed like an orb but had clear points. It even had silvery eyes and what appeared to be a mouth – all of which were currently open wide and staring at the two of them, as if in complete shock. Radianne could relate. She felt just as as stunned.

Piri peeked over her shoulder. "Well this is something I never imagined I'd see!" she exclaimed, fluttering her wings rapidly with excitement.

Radianne was tempted to poke the star to see what would happen, but thought that doing so might be a bit unkind. It was evident the star obviously was a living creature and was capable of emotion. So instead, she decided to try simple communication.

"Hello there," she offered, not certain if she'd receive a response.

The star stared at her with frightened eyes. "Hello," it said, in a small and timid voice.

Radianne gasped. "I never thought I'd see an actual star," she said, her eyes growing wide. "And never one that talked, for that matter."

She then frowned as she thought about its predicament. "It appears you have fallen from the sky, you poor little thing."

She darted a glance at Piri and then back at the strange arrival. "I'm Radianne and this is my friend Piri. Welcome to the land of Eugladia."

The star was silent for a moment, gazing at the two of them in bewilderment, as if at a loss for words. Then it spoke again.

"My name is Blink," it said weakly. "I did not fall. I was pushed – well, shoved actually, from the sky. I did not exactly fall. Only old and weakened stars fall. Or stars involved in violent confrontations…" he trailed off.

"Who would do such a thing?" Radianne shook her head in disbelief and moved forward to inspect her otherworldly visitor more closely. "That's horrible!"

"A much larger star named Wink," Blink the star said. He lifted his eyes to the dimly twinkling stars above and a shadow of sadness crossed his face. "But home is so far away now. I wonder how it is that I will ever get back."

Radianne shook her head again. "This is truly awful," she said sympathetically. "Well Blink. We are happy to meet you, if even under such unfortunate circumstances. I wonder, is there anything we can do to help you at the moment?"

Blink frowned. "I'm not sure. I would very much like to go home, but don't know if or how that's possible. From all the old tales, it seems unlikely."

Tears welled up in his eyes then and he began to cry softly, silvery droplets streaming down his face.

Radianne reached out slowly, stretching her hand. She touched him gingerly with one finger. She wanted to in some way comfort the strange and marvelous creature that had dropped into a world so unfamiliar from its own.

At the contact, an odd tickling sensation ran up her arm, as well as an odd jolt of connection. As if the moment was meant to be. She shivered.

"It will be all right," she whispered. "I'll figure out a way to help you. Will you come with me for now? It will be easier to figure things out at home, after I get some sleep. I'll just have to keep you hidden for tonight."

With a thoughtful look on his face, Blink nodded. Some of the girl's talk was confusing, but he had nothing to lose. "Why not? There is obviously no other place to go as I know nothing of your land. I suppose my situation can't get much worse."

Radianne thought things could get worse, if the wrong sort discovered him. She frowned and turned to Piri. "I'll see you later."

As the fairy flew off into the darkness, Radianne reached down and picked up the star with both hands. That odd tickling sensation flowed through her palms and up into her arms again, as if unleashing some sort of strange and vibrant energy. For a moment, the feeling scared her, and she wondered if she'd drop Blink. But the sensation went away as quickly as it had come.

The star was lighter to carry than she'd expected. She marveled at the feeling in her hands as she walked, and felt as if she were lighter too.

Blink glowed wonderfully in the darkness, casting the both of them in illuminating light as they trekked through the forest and back across the swaying bridge. The laughing river was still silent as they crossed. Blink's glow cast ripples of soft light over the water.

As she approached her house, Radianne tucked Blink into the folds of her green dress. She climbed up the steps past the front door, then shimmied up the vine and through her bedroom window, trying to be as quiet as possible. The last thing she needed right now was to wake up her parents – especially her father.

The floor creaked as she crawled into her room. She stood up and immediately walked to the woven vine flaps hanging over her doorway, pulling them tightly closed in case prying eyes were up and about at the hour.

As she pulled the star out from beneath the folds of her dress, rays of light lit up her room and nearly blinded her. Fumbling, she made her way over to one of her tree stump chairs, where she set Blink down and moved several feet away to sit on the bed so she could study her new friend more closely.

He looked around her room, staring in wonder at her purple pet bird, which was obliviously asleep on its perch. He admired the ivy and flowers that decorated the walls of her room.

"It's beautiful in here," he said softly. "It's a nice home. I never really imagined a home other than my own before."

"Thank you," Radianne said. "You'll have to tell me all about your home. But first..." she leaned back against her silkworm pillows and decided to share with him what she'd been thinking. "I have an idea about how I might be able to help you."

Blink turned his eyes toward her and listened.

"Tomorrow morning I will take you to the wisest in our land, a good friend of mine," Radianne continued. "She will certainly know what to do. If anyone has the solution to your problem, it will be her."

Blink said nothing but his face looked hopeful.

"Soon though, I have to get some sleep," Radianne yawned. Though she was tired, she did have some questions that she felt could not wait.

"Do stars sleep during the daytime?" she asked, rubbing her eyes.

"Stars sleep whenever they wish," Blink said. "It's what we do. Glow and sleep. And sometimes zoom around."

"Oh? I didn't know stars slept or zoomed. To be honest, I really didn't know you were even living creatures." Radianne raised an eyebrow. Then she laughed. "Truth be told, I thought you were just balls of fumes burning brightly in the sky."

"Well, I didn't know what to think of the creatures below," Blink told her. "We heard the tales, of course, but we thought they were all merely stories The Man In The Moon told us for fun. A sort of entertainment."

"Well what will happen to you during the day?" Radianne asked. "Will you still glow? And who is the 'Man In The Moon?'"

"I'm not sure about your glowing question," Blink said. "But I can answer the other. The Man In The Moon is our guardian. He watches over the sky and tries to keep things in order. He loves us like a great father. The Creator gave him charge over us."

Radianne listened intently as Blink described the mysterious moon man in detail, spinning an enchanting tale of his long white beard and kind yellowed eyes, and how he'd been guardian of the stars since the dawn of time.

Though delighted and filled with curiosity at his stories, Radianne soon grew bleary-eyed. Tiredly, she eased off her bed and walked across the room, holding out a small blue blanket to her new friend.

"I suppose I really should sleep now," she apologized. "Would you mind if I covered you with this blanket to dim the intensity of your glow? I hope you don't find my suggesting it offensive."

"Not at all," Blink said. "Sleep well."

"You too. If you can. "

Blink's light went out as Radianne placed the blanket over his shimmering body and she crawled back into bed.

Not long after, both star and girl fell fast asleep, the star dreaming of a far away home, and the young woman dreaming of how very close she was to escaping her own.

-3-
Questions

The next morning, Radianne woke up much earlier than usual and crept over to the blue mound sitting on her tree stump chair. Had last night been a dream? She wondered if it had all really been an absurd figment of her imagination.

Timidly, she picked up one corner of the blue blanket and cocked her head to the side, uncertain of what she'd find beneath.

It hadn't been a dream.

During the light of day, Blink the star had appeared to have lost his glow. His body was somewhat bumpy and slightly translucent and had none of the bright shimmer he'd vibrantly flashed the night before. In fact, he looked slightly stone-like in appearance. She poked him gingerly with one finger.

His silvery eyes popped open.

"Good morning," Radianne said cheerfully.

She stepped back in order to give her new friend time to adjust to his surroundings. To her surprise, he bent his five-pointed body forward and scrambled into into a sitting position.

"Good morning," he said.

"You can move on your own here!" Radianne exclaimed, clapping her hands with delight. "How wonderful!"

Blink looked down at his appendages and waved them around. He shrugged. "I suppose I can. Wasn't so sure I'd be able to move at all down here. Or if I'd even be alive. We always expected that falling stars died immediately after they descended." His face fell as he said the words. "Or, maybe, not long after."

"Well, I'm so glad that's not the case!" Radianne smiled and hurried over to a little room adjacent her own where she kept her clothing and other personal belongings. She tossed some items into a silk-worm woven bag, then disappeared into another small room and reemerged wearing a sleeveless green tunic and pants made from the soft leaves of a shimmer tree. "Just a few more minutes and we'll be on our way," she told Blink, disappearing into the little room again.

She came back a few moments later and pulled out a piece of paper, an ink pot, and a writing quill and sat at a writing desk in one corner of the room. Quickly, she scrawled a note to her parents.

"This will have to do," she said as she set the note on a wooden table next to her bed. She felt a little guilty about her abrupt decision, but, as she relayed in her note, she was leaving to help a friend in need and would return after her task was complete. Surely her parents would understand. She only hoped they would not be too angry with her, or too worried. Or send someone after her.

She could imagine her father, with his big booming voice, demanding to know why he had such a reckless and unsettled daughter. The thought of him confronting her and putting a stop to her adventure made her anxious to get going.

"We should leave now." She plucked Blink from the chair and set him on her shoulder. The electric feeling she'd felt the night before when he'd touched her skin surged once again. She shivered.

Blink settled his weight onto her shoulder and she climbed out her window and down the vine, feeling energetic and positive about the task ahead.

Warm rays of sunshine hit Radianne's skin as she walked through the dewy grass and along a winding path that led through the woods. She felt as if she were glowing from all the excitement.

"Miss Lugia lives in these trees," she told Blink, pushing tree branches out of her way as she walked. "She is the wisest in our land, as I said last night, and I'm sure she'll know what to do."

They made their way through the green and turquoise hued shimmer trees, the woods silent except for the occasional fluttering of a bird's wings or a twig snapping underfoot.

After while, a giant red mushroom appeared. This was no ordinary mushroom. The spotted mushroom was as large as a house with a cheerful yellow wooden door embedded into its enormously wide stem. Radianne approached the door and knocked three times, waiting. After a few moments, it flew open.

A Eugladian-sized ladybug wearing a white ruffled apron and matching bonnet appeared in the entryway. She was nearly as tall as Radianne.

She shrieked with delight when she saw her guests. "Hello my dear Radianne! What are you doing here at this time of day child? What is that on your shoulder? Why, it looks like a star from one of those old picture books we have at the library! But how can that be? Oh, do come in dear, come in."

Hopping up and down with joy, the ladybug enthusiastically stepped aside to let her visitors in.

The star gazed at the red and black walls of the mushroom's interior with awe as they entered the main room. Black and white polka-dotted furniture was scattered throughout as well as in the adjacent living space.

Radianne smiled at his reaction. The house did seem to have a color and life of its own.

"Come and have a seat," Miss Lugia said. "And tell me why you're visiting today."

Radianne settled onto a chair at the black and white polka-dotted table and glanced around the room with appreciation. "It seems you have acquired some new finery since my last visit, including those red polka-dotted window curtains," she pointed out admiringly. "I love your home more with each visit."

"Thank you my dear." Miss Lugia placed a carved wood tray filled with little cakes on the table. "I just made these, so eat them up!"

Radianne gladly took one of the little yellow cakes and bit into the sweet and sticky goodness. "Delicious, as always," she said as the sugary honey cake melted in her mouth.

"What about that young star? Does he want one?"

Embarrassed, Radianne realized she had forgotten to introduce her guest. Or to offer him any food.

As she properly introduced Blink, Miss Lugia moved closer, eyeing the star with suspicion and scratching her shiny black chin.

"What exactly is a star doing in Eugladia anyway? I always thought stars were bodies of burning gas..." She leaned forward, her voice lowering to a warning whisper as she raised her eyebrows at Radianne. "Seems to me like it could be foul magic from the likes of those no-good Snorgs."

Whatever a Snorg was, Blink didn't like the sound of Miss Lugia's voice. His eyes grew wide at the accusation and he became even more pale and translucent.

"Have a honey cake." The giant ladybug promptly presented the pastry to him, as if reading his troubled thoughts, seemingly forgetting her insult.

Normally a polite star, Blink did not know how to respond without sounding ungracious. "Uh, I…" he began.

"What is it?"

"It's just that I've never eaten this sort of food before. I'm used to eating moon dust."

Radianne looked at him with sympathy. He must find this world very strange.

Miss Lugia frowned. "Moon dust? Dust!" She clucked her tongue and shook her head. "There is no nutrition in that. No wonder you look so dingy. Stars are supposed to shine."

She thrust the cake at him again.

Appearing to be embarrassed at her words, Blink accepted the treat. His mouth took a small bite. Instantly, his eyes lit up. "Oooh. This is good," he said appreciatively. "Yes, much better than dust."

Miss Lugia smiled proudly.

As Radianne and Blink ate, the hostess chattered about random topics, such as the weather, the forest fruit supply, and rumors of recent Snorg attacks. After some time, the chatter stopped, and she looked expectantly at Radianne. "Well? As I said earlier, I know there is a purpose behind this visit and your new companion…"

Radianne cleared her throat. "Well," she began. "I need your advice. I figured if anyone can help us, it would be you." She leaned forward. "After all, you're the last Large Ladybug of your kind and we all know how wise your ancestors were."

"This is true," Miss Lugia said sadly, her face growing solemn. "I am the last. And our advice, of course, always brings the best of luck. It is a tragedy the others have gone." She sighed a deep sigh. "Our world could use much good advice now."

"Indeed," Radianne said, thinking of the horrible disappearances.

The vanishing of the Large Ladybugs was a great Eugladian tragedy and mystery. The Eugladian ladybugs had mysteriously disappeared from the land a number of years before, in a matter of a few days. No one knew for sure what had happened to them, though some suspected the Snorgs had something to do with the unusual incident.

Miss Lugia's family had vanished one night during her youth, and, sadly, she'd never seen nor heard from them again. It was also a mystery as to why she'd been the only one spared. But, she'd quickly learned how to fend for herself. And somehow, she'd kept a remarkably positive attitude at the same time.

"Blink was forced from the sky, he was attacked by another star," Radianne said, beginning to explain the reason for her visit. "It would seem it's impossible to get him back where he belongs. We were wondering if you knew of any way to accomplish this?"

Miss Lugia stared off into space silently for a few moments, deep in thought. She scratched her head. Her antennae twitched back and forth. She rubbed her shiny black chin and sighed a few times.

When she finally spoke, her tone was ominous. "Such an awful thing," she began. "Hmmm. Dangers there will certainly be. But I do know who might be able to help you…" She smiled and there was a sudden twinkle in her eye.

Radianne sucked in a breath. "Yes?"

"The Winged Ones."

"The Winged Ones?" Radianne let out the breath she'd been holding. She'd heard tales as a child about the magnificent winged horses of Shondalina, one of the Nether Lands. But back then, she'd thought they were the stuff of long-lost legends. Or tales made up to entertain young ones. She hadn't been quite certain they were even real.

"Of course." Miss Lugia stood up and waved her hands around excitedly as she paced back and forth around the room. "It would have to be them. Only they could do it. Their wings are powerful, enabling them to soar to unfathomable heights. However, the only Pegasus who would truly be capable of such a feat as to reach the stars would be The Queen," she said, nodding her head. "She has the greatest wing strength. Though I'm not sure how willing to assist others she is these days. From what I hear, the Winged Ones are trying to keep a low profile."

Filled with excitement at the prospect of traveling to Shondalina, Radianne didn't bother to ask Miss Lugia why The Queen of the Winged Ones would be unwilling to help out or how she knew the Pegasus were trying to keep a low profile.

"I remember the tales from my childhood," she said instead. "The stories that told of kind-hearted, winged horses. I'm sure they would help us! Please, Miss Lugia. Tell me how to get to Shondalina."

"I think I have an old map somewhere around here," the ladybug murmured. "Let me check." She scurried from the kitchen and left Radianne and Blink sitting at the table.

"This sounds very confusing to me," Blink admitted. "My world is very different from your own. Maybe I should just resign myself to a life here in Eugladia. At least I'm still alive. That's a surprise and that's something."

Radianne frowned. "Your mother will miss you. And as much as I do already like you, you don't belong here, in such a boring place. You are a shining star, who rightfully belongs in the sky. Eugladia is no place for such magnificence. You deserve more! It will turn out for the best Blink. You'll see." She patted him.

Blink wondered why Radianne didn't appear to be very fond of her homeland, but he didn't have time to question her. Miss Lugia ran back into the room at that moment, waving something in her hands and wearing a triumphant smile.

"I found it! Now let's take a look, shall we?" The giant ladybug unrolled an old and yellowed map and spread it gingerly across the table. Girl, star, and ladybug studied the faded parchment and tried to make sense of the print and images.

"We are here," Miss Lugia pointed to one spot on the map. "And Shondalina, the land of the Winged Ones, is here." Her fingers trailed across the printed images and came to rest upon what appeared to be a mountainous region with deep valleys, surrounded by clouds.

From what Radianne could gather from the markers on the map, the journey would take many weeks or, perhaps, even months. The route would lead them through several of the Nether Lands. There would be dangers for sure. Her heart quickened at the thought.

"The going will be long and treacherous," Miss Lugia warned, looking up at Radianne with concern, as if reading her thoughts. "The way will be difficult. Please don't tell me you are attempting this on your own?"

Radianne smiled, trying to reassure her. "My dear Miss Lugia, I will not be alone." She gestured to her new star friend. "Of course, I'll have Blink with me. I *have* to get him home. I have no choice as it is the honorable thing to do."

"Ahhh!" Miss Lugia shook her head and rubbed her antennae vigorously, obviously stressed. "Going it alone would be ridiculous and unwise. You should have more sense, young lady. The Nether Lands are ever-changing, and quite mysterious as well. It will be easy to get confused, lost, or much worse. I would accompany you myself… but in my old age now…" she trailed off.

"I think I'm up for a little danger," Radianne countered. "I know I'll be fine. Please don't worry."

At least, Radianne told herself, she would act confident until she believed it. "May I have this map?"

With an eyebrow raised, she waited for Miss Lugia to challenge her. While she was grateful for the ladybug's assistance, now that she knew how to get Blink home, nothing would stand in her way.

Sighing, the ladybug reluctantly rolled up the map and handed it over. "I suppose no amount of trying to talk you out of this foolhardy endeavor will change your mind."

She shook her head again."I know you can be quite stubborn when you put your mind to something. But you're not a little girl anymore, that's for sure."

"I'm not. Thank you. I will return it when I myself return."

"Do you plan on leaving today?"

"Yes."

"I suppose your parents don't know about this either." Miss Lugia wrung her hands nervously. "They'll have my shell for this! The very least I can do is pack you some food. I feel so guilty for my encouragement."

"That won't be necessary." Radianne waved her hand dismissively. "You've been so helpful already. And don't worry, this is all my choice. No one is forcing me into anything. You'll never be to blame."

"Nonsense! I'm packing you food and a large flask for water." Miss Lugia bustled around the spotted room, throwing random items into a sack. "You must promise you'll be careful. I've known you since you were a child and I also know how daring you can be. You must be sure to use your intelligence."

"Of course." Radianne smiled, feeling a bit of pride well up at the idea that Miss Lugia thought she was intelligent. Most of the time she felt like her own family thought she was foolhardy and dimwitted.

The ladybug handed her the sack of food and embraced her.

"Thank you so much," Radianne said as she kissed Miss Lugia's cheek.

"I should have never shown you the map! If anything happens to you I will be to blame!" Miss Lugia wrung her hands again, her large and heavily-lashed eyes growing wide with fear.

"Again, this was all my idea," Radianne assured her. "Besides, nothing is going to happen. Just an adventure!"

Laughing, she tucked the map securely into her bag. "I suppose we should be on our way now," she said, placing Blink on her shoulder. "There is no time to waste. Thanks again for all your help, Miss Lugia. Wish us luck!"

They said their final goodbyes and Radianne and Blink left the giant mushroom house and its ladybug occupant behind, venturing off on the first leg of their quest, into the great unknown.

Miss Lugia watched the way the girl and star had gone long after they had vanished into the woods.

-4-
Leaving

The sun was hot. *Very hot.* Scorching, unrelenting rays stretched out across the land, striking out at whatever crossed their path with claws of searing and suffocating heat.

Radianne wondered, fleetingly, how far along the day was. She'd walked many miles and slept under trees for several days, Blink sitting on her shoulder the majority of the time. She knew they were still in Eugladia. She'd also stopped to eat, refill her flask, and rest several times – Blink hadn't been inclined to eat any food since Miss Lugia's and seemed to be fine – but had mostly kept on walking, trying to leave Eugladia far behind. However, it seemed to her that leaving was taking forever. She was done with Eugladia and was growing very impatient.

Up ahead, she spotted a lake. "Let's stop over there," she said to Blink, pointing toward the shimmering body of water.

Walking over to a soft patch of green grass near the water's edge, she sat down and removed her boots. The water felt wonderful as she lowered her feet into its refreshing depths. "Oh, this is nice," she sighed contentedly, wiggling her toes in the coolness.

Blink hopped down and scampered off, settling himself a comfortable distance away, eyeing the strange substance nervously. He knew very little about large bodies of water or what they would ultimately do to stars. There were legends, of course. The older stars would often tell the younger stars horrible stories about ancestors that had fallen from the sky and had instantly turned to smoke when they'd touched watery elements in the world below. Blink didn't want to take any unnecessary risks in this strange new world he had fallen into.

Radianne examined the map closely. If her calculations were correct, she speculated they would arrive in the land of Eustasia very soon. She recalled that the heart of Eustasia was also the home base of the Snorgs. "Hopefully we don't run into them," she muttered.

"Who?" Blink asked.

"The Snorgs." Radianne glanced at him and noted his confused expression. "I suppose I should explain who they are."

She told him the tale as she trailed one hand slowly in the water. "The Snorgs are awful, evil creatures who have tried to conquer our land numerous times. Ogres of sorts, with some troll mixed in as well as something else. Though I don't expect you would know much about such creatures. And supposedly, they've been destroying many other lands as well. Those could just be rumors though. Anyway, as nasty as the Snorgs are, I'm not really afraid of them."

"It is true, I don't know much about other creatures or all the dangers of your world here below," Blink said. He looked out at the water and shuddered a little. "But I do know what it is to be afraid sometimes. So if you are not afraid of these ogre creatures, what is it you are afraid of then, Radianne?"

"Well," Radianne thought carefully for a moment.

"I'm starting to think I am afraid of living an empty life. You know, one without true meaning or adventure. I'm tired of doing the same thing every day. I really do want to help you, which is, of course, the main reason for heading out on this quest. But… "

She paused and looked away, feeling a little uncomfortable with what she was about to say next. "I'll be honest with you and also say that my life is desperately in need of a little adventure. It is quite dull, actually. So there you have it. This is also exciting for me," she blushed. "I also know it is difficult for you to be here, away from your mother, and I'm sorry."

Blink was quiet for a moment. He thought Radianne seemed much too young to be so disappointed in the life she lived. However, he also had an inkling of understanding. There were many moments he himself had wistfully wondered what lay beyond the world of the stars. Now he wondered if he'd ever be able to get back to his world again.

"I think I understand what you mean," he told his new friend. "But I also believe there is something good and comforting doing the same routine, day after day. You do come to appreciate it after awhile. The things we take for granted…"

He looked away from her then, a faint smile on his face as his eyes focused on something far away, a distant memory.

"Stars live for ages you know. I am quite young in my world. We remain with our parents for a long time. My mother and I, we have a nightly routine. We slowly spin around in circles, round and round, amid the other stars. It is quite lovely and we've done that for as long as I can remember. I can't imagine ever growing tired of such a routine."

Radianne looked at him a little thoughtfully and said nothing for a few moments as she reflected.

There were things she did like about home… one being her family, of course. But she had to admit she felt she was outgrowing her life in the family tree. And if she was being completely honest, she was also curious about something else. Something she had yet to find and knew she probably wouldn't find in Eugladia...

Her cheeks flushed as she thought of it. Well, perhaps she could tell her new friend. He probably wouldn't know much of such things anyway. She opened her mouth to speak.

"I suppose if I'm being completely truthful, I'm also afraid of never finding true love," she admitted to Blink. "Do you know what true love is? Do stars fall in love? The kind of love I'm talking about is the love I've seen between my mother and father. Or that I've read about in books."

"I don't know much about that kind of love personally," Blink said, staring up at the sky, a little wistfully. "Stars leave their parents when they find their mates. I know my mother and father were in love. But my father was a falling star, like me, and vanished when I was much younger. I never had the chance to really talk to him about such things."

The star grew solemn and lowered his eyes sadly. "He never came back you know," he added, with a whisper. "I don't know your love stories. But we stars do have our own beliefs about love. I know what love is. In the sky, certain stars are automatically drawn together, in a force that spirals out of their control. When this happens, they align. The magic begins when they find their mate. That's how stars fall in love. That's all I know."

Radianne was saddened to hear of Blink's father and thought it was such a terrible tragedy that the same fate had befallen Blink. Had his father been pushed as well? She asked him as much.

"No," Blink said. "He caught a rare star illness and grew too weak to stay. It was from natural causes, you could say. "

"I am so very sorry to hear about your father Blink," Radianne said softly. It was tragic. "But hopefully, at the end of this journey, you will be home again, see your mother, and have the chance to fall in love with some lucky star."

As they sat together, Radianne solemnly thought about what Blink had revealed to her about his father and star love. His description of stars in love was fascinating and sounded so romantic. She sighed dreamily and imagined his world, again, a world so completely different from her own. How lovely it would be to travel there…

"Well I have another question for you," she said wistfully, as she looked down at him. "What's it like to be up there and see for an eternity, beyond and below? And how does it feel to know that you yourself shine your light over it all? What a lovely thing to light the world. "

Blink smiled. "It *is* a nice life. But we can't see anything below except a dark void. Beyond, we see the vastness of The Outer Space. That is quite nice, but stars often do talk about what the land and water rumored to be below are like. Now I know! Or at least, I know a little." Blink smiled sheepishly."Even though I do want to go home, I'm actually having a good time being here with you. Seeing new things I never imagined I'd see…"

"It is nice to experience different things, isn't it?" Radianne grinned. "I never imagined I'd be having a conversation with a star!"

"And I never imagined I'd be having a conversation with a life form other than another 'burning ball of gas'," Blink joked.

Radianne laughed with him and thought about how suddenly her life had changed. She had already experienced something unique and special in finding Blink. He was a friend unlike any other.

Lost in their conversation, Radianne and Blink didn't notice the lake mermaid leaning up against the grassy rocky river bank and scrutinizing them. That is, until until a melodic voice interrupted their discussion.

"Hello," the mermaid said, popping up near Radianne's submerged feet.

Radianne gasped and jerked her legs back in fright. As her eyes focused, however, her frown relaxed into a smile.

Leaning forward, she studied the mermaid. The creature was beautiful. Her long dark hair swirled in curls around her shoulders. Aqua eyes framed thick, black lashes – lashes Radianne coveted. She suddenly felt a little jealous and self-conscious about her own looks in comparison.

"If only I were so beautiful," she thought. But she pushed the thoughts aside.

"Hello," she said.

"My name is Pearl." The mermaid extended a delicate ivory hand to her.

The siren's hand felt cold and clammy, exactly as one would expect a mermaid's hand to feel.

"I'm Radianne."

Pearl smiled and eased herself up onto the grassy bank beside the young woman, her greenish-blue tail scales sparkling brilliantly in the sunlight.

Blink stared at the jewel-like scales, fascinated. The mermaid flipped her tail in the water, sending little droplets scattering around like gems. Blink gasped, hoping none of the water would land on him.

Radianne motioned to him. "This is my friend Blink."

"Hello." Pearl studied the star quizzically. "You appear to be a star, from what I can gather. Though it seems very strange, and nearly impossible to comprehend."

Her mouth formed a slight frown. "What is a star doing in Eugladia?"

Blink felt small and insignificant under the mermaid's gaze. She intimidated him. Never had he seen a more strange and beautiful sight than the lovely creature that was before him at that moment.

"I was pushed from the sky by another star," he said, lowering his eyes in shame. He did not like to admit to the defeat.

"Well that's horrid." Pearl tilted her head to one side. "I hope the other star was punished. And I do hope you can find your way back. I do wonder though, as this is my only opportunity to ask… how is it that we can see the stars, as small as you are, from way down here? I always imagined stars to be so much larger. And burning balls of fumes, of course. This is very mysterious and difficult to understand."

Blink blinked. These quick questions from the Eugladians confused him as well. He was also very surprised. Everyone kept referring to stars as burning balls of fumes and he did not really have an answer to such things. He had also never considered his size before. "I suppose some things just cannot be explained," he offered. "Maybe there are some questions better left unanswered? I don't know. I also suspect a star's glow is supposed to be a mystery, like many other things The Creator made in life. Some things just don't have simple answers."

Radianne smiled at her new friend's response. He certainly was wise. But however wise he was, she could also tell some of the conversation was making her new friend a little uncomfortable. Clearing her throat, she tried to change the subject.

"We are on a quest to try and find a way to return Blink home," she told Pearl.

"I wish I could help," the mermaid said wistfully. She sighed and then pouted and pointed to the water. "But I'm trapped. That's my cage. My life is so boring down there in those depths. If only you knew… it's not even the ocean!" she wailed. "That would be something. Oh, the life of a lake mermaid!" she moaned again, bringing her hands up to her forehead dramatically.

Radianne could relate. She nodded. "I know how you feel," she said sympathetically. "Of course, I do want to help Blink get home. But, there is another reason why I'm so excited about this journey. My life, up until this point, has been pretty uneventful."

Pearl stared at Radianne with envy. "But you can move about wherever you wish on those legs of yours," she said. "Even if it is just in your homeland. I'm confined to the water, forever."

Sorrowfully, she flipped her tail. The two females talked about their seemingly confining lives for some time, as Blink sat quietly and listened, until the day grew older and Radianne knew it was time to be moving on. She stood up.

"It was nice meeting you Pearl. I've always wanted to meet a mermaid."

"Nice meeting you as well." Pearl brought one hand up to to her ivory neck and tugged at the strand of pearls she wore there, unclasping them. "Here," she said, holding the necklace out to Radianne. "Take these. Perhaps they will bring you luck on your journey."

Speechless, Radianne took the shiny white beads in her hands and slipped them around her own neck. Mermaid pearls were rumored to bring good fortune to whomever possessed them. Never had she worn something so beautiful... the beads sparkled like the mermaid's tail in the fading afternoon sun.

She wished she had something to offer Pearl in return. "Thank you," she said after a moment. "Thank you very much. And I hope you find your own adventure someday soon."

Pearl smiled sadly and slid slowly back down into the water. Waving goodbye to Blink, she sank into the mysterious depths, disappearing from sight. Radianne watched her descent a little longingly. Even though she was having her own adventure – finally – she did think it would be wonderful to visit Pearl's world.

She told Blink as much. "I know she doesn't think so, but I think it would be amazing to be a mermaid and see all the sights under the surface of the water," she said. "But to not be able to escape it at all, I suppose, would be miserable too. So I do pity her. I suppose she's right. An ocean mermaid's life probably is more interesting, as they have much more world to explore."

Though he had only just met Radianne, Blink thought she should really stop and think about the good things in her own life instead of pining for more. He wanted to tell her she should be grateful for what she had and should stop pining for things she couldn't have. Or the impossible. He should have told the mermaid the same as well. He personally believed life was precious and could change drastically in an instant… his fall had already proven this. Sometimes life could spiral out of control, as it had with him. One never knew what would happen from one day to the next.

But he said nothing to his young new friend. He hoped she would learn in time.

The hot air began to cool down as day gave way to night. After awhile, Radianne stopped to eat a few bites of Miss Lugia's honey and acorn cakes. She felt guilty eating in front of Blink, as there was, of course, no moon dust on hand, but he seemed to be doing well enough and didn't care to have another helping of Eugladian food.

As late afternoon faded into early evening, the darkness fell fast and Blink's glow returned, lighting up the path before them. Radianne hoped the glow would not warrant too much attention, but she was grateful for its warm cheer. As they walked, the electric feeling that seemed to come from Blink also returned.

She would have to ask him about that later.

Radianne walked on until her legs threatened to give out. Stopping under a large tree, she looked around and tried to gauge the security of the area. All appeared well, but one couldn't be too cautious.

She may have led somewhat of a sheltered life up until that point, but she still had common sense. Settling into the grass with her back up against the tree, she glanced up at its shadowy branches. She supposed she could climb up if necessary.

Chirps, creaks, and eerie howls sounded off in the night air. For awhile, she and Blink gazed up at the moon and the array of stars scattered across the sky.

"Do you think your mother can see you?" she asked him.

"No."

"Why not?"

"As I said before, when you're up there, all you can can see is a void below and my own world beyond."

"Oh yes. Sorry, I forgot." Radianne was growing tired. "I remember now," she said, yawning as she adjusted her body into a more comfortable position. "So, tell me again how you know about life below and have some knowledge of the creatures that live in my world."

"The Man In The Moon." Blink lifted his eyes to Radianne. "He was put there by The Creator. He knows a good number of things."

Radianne smiled. "Oh yes. The Man In The Moon," she said dreamily. "One day I would like to meet him," she murmured, and covered her friend with a small blanket she'd stored in her bag, shutting out his light in order to avoid attracting unwanted attention as they slept. "Tell me more about your world Blink. Tell me about life among the stars."

Blink began to talk in a gentle and quiet voice, whispering tales about his life in The Outer Space, sharing his lovely memories of home.

As Radianne listened, she imagined his world – a place of talking, living stars that were not big balls of burning fumes – and her eyes grew heavier. She was lost in a land of dazzling lights that dreamily twirled in the heavens. And she danced with them, spinning Blink high above her head. It was a glorious feeling. She felt a powerful glow, as if she were shining completely from within and the light had overtaken her.

As she lost herself in Blink's far off world, she fell into a deep, deep sleep. And slept more soundly than she had in a very long time.

-5-
Another Unprecedented Meeting

Radianne woke to the sensation of something tickling her eyelids. Slowly opening one eye, and then the other, she gazed up into the smiling face of Blink. He was tickling her face with the leaves on a twig he held firmly in one of his points. She smiled back, and slowly sat up.

"Good morning," she said.

"Good morning," Blink said, and turned his eyes toward the sound of the river ahead. A thick forest of trees surrounded the body of water on one side. He had yet to tell Radianne about his fear of water, but being so close to it continued to make him nervous.

Radianne pushed herself into a sitting position and followed Blink's line of vision to the sparkling water. "That looks refreshing," she said, wondering why he seemed to be looking at it with unease. "Care for a swim? Can stars swim?"

When he didn't answer, she stretched and stood. She made a mental note to also ask him about his obvious aversion to water later. "Well, I think I will. I need a bath and I also need to fill up the water flask. If you don't mind, please turn your head for propriety's sake."

Blink was not sure what Radianne was talking about but he did as she asked.

Radianne stripped off her clothing and ran straight for the water, jumping into the flowing, shallow river with a loud splash.

"Oh, it feels wonderful!" she called out, laughing. "At least come sit nearby."

The star scampered over to the riverbank and sat in a patch of grass at a distance he deemed safe enough.

Radianne sang as she bathed, her voice echoing loud and clear in the quiet morning air.

Blink listened and stared off into the distance, lost in his own thoughts. He didn't understand all the words coming out of Radianne's mouth, but he enjoyed the sound. Stars never really sang, though when they were at their brightest in the evening, the sky resounded with the hum of their contentment. He closed his eyes, trying to imagine what his mother was doing at the moment.

****

Watching from his hiding spot behind the tree, the young man wasn't sure whether to reveal himself just then or wait until the girl was finished bathing. Sighing, he weighed his options. He had been walking along, minding his own business, trying to plan his next course of action. Then he'd heard the singing, and as if pulled by a force of magic, was drawn to the source of the sound.

Shocked indeed was he to stumble upon the sight of a young and beautiful woman bathing in the river. Even more unusual though was the sight of what appeared to be a strange creature – a creature that seemed to resemble a picture book depiction of a star, sitting near the riverbank, watching her.

Maybe he was growing dehydrated and delusional, the young man thought. Surely, his eyes must be playing tricks on him.

"How odd this is," he said to himself as he leaned against the tree and watched the strange scene play out before his eyes. He also wondered what the young Eugladian was doing out in the middle of nowhere by herself.

And if he wasn't seeing things, how and why was a star on land? It was very peculiar. He supposed he could leave then, unnoticed. Pretend as if he'd never seen anything out of the ordinary and put the incident behind him. However, his curiosity won out, as it always did.

"Perhaps I should go introduce myself," he grinned and stepped out of the shadows. "Yes. Yes, I think I shall."

****

Radianne dipped her head under the cool rushing water, shaking her long wet hair out of her eyes as she surfaced. The river felt so nice and freeing.

Humming to herself, she continued to bathe with her eyes closed. When she opened them again, she looked toward the shoreline to check on Blink. She screamed.

A man stood next to the star and was staring at her.

She lowered her body deeper into the water, feeling terrified and humiliated. The man smiled, looking like a mischievous boy. Radianne waited for the intruder to say something – she certainly wasn't about to.

An odd moment of silence passed and she felt her face turning hot under his uncomfortable gaze. She wrapped her arms tightly around her shoulders.

Finally, he spoke, in a deep and somewhat gruff voice. "Hello there," he said loudly.

Radianne said nothing in response. She shot a look at Blink, who also appeared to be at a loss of words as he stared up at the strange man.

"My name is Henrick Longfellow." The intruder bowed and flashed a wide, toothy grin. "Sorry to disturb you, but I could not help myself. After all, it is not every day one sees a beautiful lady such as yourself out in the wild, on the edge of Eugladia. Even rarer to find a beautiful lady in the company of a star." He looked down at Blink and raised an eyebrow. "Which is very hard to believe actually. I suppose my eyes were not playing tricks on me after all."

Radianne stood fast in her muteness. She wanted the man to leave and didn't want to encourage him to linger by saying anything to him. Plus, the situation was very uncomfortable and embarrassing.

"Well, I was just passing by and I heard your singing," the man who called himself Henrick continued. "I decided to follow it and now here I am."

He paused and waited. When he received no response, he began talking again. "Though the singing I heard wasn't exactly kind to the ears. All high pitched and shrill, really."

Those words ignited the fire. Temper flaring, Radianne frowned as anger overtook over her resolve to stay silent.

"And I suppose your singing voice sounds glorious, when you aren't spying on young women bathing in the wild," she retorted, her brow forming into an angry line.

She turned her attention to Blink. "Blink, can you please bring me my clothes – those coverings I had on my body – and set them where I can reach them?"

As the star did as she asked, Radianne averted her eyes away from the man. He was still staring at her and it was making her increasingly uncomfortable.

When Blink dropped her clothes to the grass, she cleared her throat. "Now both of you, turn around," she commanded.

She didn't mean to speak so harshly to Blink, but, at the moment, her temper was getting the best of her.

Blink automatically turned, but the man flashed a mischievous smile before he did so, causing Radianne to wonder what his intentions were. She nervously swam quickly to her clothing laying on the shoreline, jumped out of the water, and threw the garments on. Out of the corner of her eye she watched the man. Embarrassed, she stalked back over to the tree and sat down. Blink quickly followed suit.

The man named Henrick sauntered over.

Radianne tried not to notice how handsome he was, and was angry with herself for noticing that fact at all at a such a time. He was of muscular build, tall, and wore clothes made from gray sheepskin. His wavy light hair was streaked with gold.

She knew that moment was not the time to be admiring his physique. He had been spying on her, she reminded herself.

"What's your name?" He asked the question with an amused look on his face.

"Why?" Radianne plucked up a piece of grass and fidgeted with it between her fingers, still feeling humiliated and angry. A man had never seen her unclothed before. Not that she was sure he had seen everything, but still. She felt his spying had been a violation of privacy.

"It is very rude to spy on people bathing, you know," she told him. "I think it's best if you just leave me alone now."

He bowed. "I apologize for my intrusion. I did not mean to offend you. And just so you know, you were properly hidden from my view."

Pausing as she blushed, he took a breath. "Well, you already know my name. It would be nice to know yours as well."

Apparently, he wasn't going anywhere at the moment. Radianne scowled. But then, before she could stop herself, the words came out of her mouth. "Radianne Timblebrooke."

She wanted to kick herself. Though she spoke the words in an unfriendly tone of voice, she wasn't quite sure why she had decided to give him the courtesy.

Henrick leaned against the tree and stared down at her. "Radianne, huh? Such a pretty name for someone with such a dreadful singing voice," he said, laughing.

Flushing angrily, Radianne stood and picked up Blink. She forced herself to make direct eye contact with the intruder. She wouldn't let this stranger intimidate her. "What exactly do you want with us?"

Henrick sobered. "Only trying to be polite and say hello in passing. And, of course, wondering about that star…"

Well that was none of his business, Radianne thought. Not willing to talk to him a moment longer, she bent down and quickly gathered up her belongings. "We should be on our way Blink," she said, placing him on her shoulder.

As she began to walk, Henrick fell in step beside her and chatted. "What is a young lady like you doing out here all alone anyway? And why do you have a star? I'm really curious as to how this is possible?"

Her mouth betrayed her again.

"I don't see how or why that is any of your concern," she said, pushing a few stray strands of light brown hair out of her eyes impatiently. The sun was growing hot again. And her temper still hadn't cooled, which made her feel even more flustered.

"Well one doesn't often see young ladies wandering about on the outskirts of Eugladia by themselves, as I said before. Not with the Snorg issues of late. And it's quite strange to see a star on land," Henrick said. "No one probably ever has. They are supposed to be burning balls of fumes, after all. Anyone would be curious…"

Radianne tried to focus on anything – the sound of the branches crunching under her feet, the chirping of birds in the trees, her breath coming out in angry puffs – anything but the irritating stranger walking next to her.

"You can't be much more than seventeen," he continued. "You're too young to be out here by yourself. You have no idea what has been happening in these parts or even just beyond."

Radianne stopped walking and glared at him, hands on her hips. "Eighteen," she countered. "You don't look much older than that yourself. So what are YOU doing out here, all by yourself?"

Henrick seemed amused. "I'm twenty. That's quite a bit older than you. Of course, I left home behind years ago. And I'm a man, though this is stating the obvious. You're definitely not."

He flicked his eyes over her appreciatively as he said the words, as if to make a point. "As I said, it's not that common to see young women wandering around Eugladia without travel companions."

"Ha. That is an outdated view." Radianne turned on her heel, walking away from him again.

"So at least tell me this then…" Henrick quickly caught up with her. "Why do you have a star with you? At least explain that mystery."

She sighed, exasperated. He probably wouldn't let up unless she offered some sort of explanation. She supposed she had to, if only to get him to stop pestering her.

"If you must know, he has a name. His name is Blink. He fell from the sky. We are setting out to return him home. And honestly, none of this concerns you!"

As they walked, Henrick continued to question her. Even though she didn't want to talk to him, and perhaps it wasn't wise, for some reason after awhile Radianne found herself telling the young man about the Winged Ones and how the flying horses were probably Blink's only hope of seeing his world again.

Eventually Henrick did listen – surprisingly, without interrupting too much. After a few moments however, he interjected with his input. "And you think you're going to get to Shondalina all on your own, without any outside help? Without anyone to help you find the way?"

He began to laugh, a deep, throaty laugh that instantly annoyed Radianne. She felt like he was mocking her. She had an urge to step on his foot but thought better of it at the last minute. "I can handle it myself, thank you very much, despite what you think."

How dare he mock her this way! She picked up the pace. She should have known it was a bad idea to tell a strange man about her plans. Perhaps she was not as grown up or as wise as she thought.

"Not all women are weak and helpless you know," she retorted as she walked. "Your viewpoint is very ancient."

Henrick slapped his hand against his forehead. "Oh! Forgive me," he said. "I must be so very foolish to think that a beautiful young woman can't handle herself in the wild lands to come."

He stopped walking and suddenly reached out and grabbed her arms, holding her in place.

Radianne jumped. He wasn't hurting her and was holding her gently, but the fact that he'd touched her at all frightened her. A ripple of alarm raced through her body. Blink, picking up on the negative energy, tensed on her shoulder. Shocked and irritated, Radianne struggled against Henrick and her heart began to pound furiously. Blink nervously hid behind her hair, peeking out timidly between the long strands. He would bite if he had to...

"You don't know me!" she shouted, pushing Henrick away. He stumbled back a few steps. "How dare you put your hands on me like this!"

"Now you listen to me." Henrick narrowed his eyes and took a step forward, moving his face, which suddenly looked travel-weary, much closer to hers. "You're right. I don't know you. But I do know something of the world. The roads that lead to Shondalina are treacherous. You have no idea. I think it's best you turn around and head home. There has to be some other way to figure this situation out."

Radianne couldn't believe his rudeness and nerve. She knew he probably truly believed the journey would be too dangerous for her. But she also knew the time had come for her to venture out on her own; it was her time to explore. To have her own adventure. Most importantly, it was time to make a difference. To do something with her life. To be strong. To chase the wind and take a chance. He would not stop her. He didn't even know her!

Though his words unnerved her a little, she knew she was tougher than he thought. Tougher than Miss Lugia thought. It was time to make her own way in the world, and what better way to start doing that than by helping a new friend? She would not fail Blink and she wasn't about to let this man named Henrick sway her decision to help him.

"I have made up my mind," she said firmly, easing her way around him and walking on ahead.

"Soon you will enter the Eustasian border." Henrick said the words ominously as he trailed behind, as if he were trying to scare some sense into her. "You know what that means, don't you?"

Radianne laughed. His scare tactics wouldn't work. She knew every well what threat he was referring to: the Snorg's base in the center of Eustasia.

"I'm not afraid of the Snorgs. I don't care about them."

"Well you should. They are more dangerous than you know."

Radianne kept walking without looking at him, but could feel his eyes on her back studying her. Probably trying to assess her fear levels, she thought.

A small part of her was a little scared, of course. But she would never admit that to him. She wished he would just leave her and Blink alone. They had been moving along just fine until he showed up.

"It's not just the Snorgs," Henrick continued. "There are those other lands to come too – Sandalia for example. Have you heard of the cruel giant hermit crabs that live there? They will not hesitate to take you in their claws and drag you away to their dens where they will torture and devour you – piece by piece – for dinner…"

Radianne half listened with annoyance as he rambled on and spoke with apparent confidence of all the dangers of the lands she would have to travel through in the coming days. She truly wished he would stop talking. She wanted to experience the world for herself and his revealing all this information – whether it was factual or not – was ruining the mood of her expedition. She picked up the pace again, deciding it would be best to put even more distance between them.

"The endless Jungle of Vancor… I'd like to see you get through that place by yourself!" Henrick exclaimed. "And the Ongoing Desert, the place where people lose themselves, and, more often than not, their sanity…"

He continued to prattle on, easily keeping up with Radianne's stride and paying no attention to her obvious disdain.

"The Ongoing Desert is also raging hot during the day and frigid at night. How do you suppose you'll survive all that on your own, without any knowledge or survival skills?"

Radianne stopped in her tracks and turned to glare at him. "I have faith in The Creator, as well as confidence in my abilities," she retorted. "However feeble you think they may be. I can handle things myself."

With that, she walked on, trying to concentrate on Blink's dire situation and the goal ahead. Blink's energy tickled her shoulder once more, the sparking feeling encouraging her.

She tried to shut the stranger's voice and negativity out. After all, she thought, he couldn't possibly know everything.

And why did this man named Henrick speak so matter-of-factly anyway? How did he know all these things? Despite the fact she wanted him to be quiet, she gave in again and decided to ask him as much.

"How do you know so much about these places," she muttered, casting a sidelong glance his way while pushing tree branches out of her path.

Henrick rolled his eyes. "I know this, because, if you haven't figured it out already, I'm a Wanderer. I have spent a good amount of my days roaming through the Nether Lands, and have explored them all. I have even been to Shondalina once, long ago."

The intrigue was starting to grow, though Radianne didn't like it. She wondered, fleetingly, why he had chosen the life of a Wanderer – a person notorious for being strange and best avoided.

Wanderers were the outcasts on the fringes of Eugladian society… mysterious and elusive, they most often lived alone and did not take part in ordinary aspects of Eugladian life. It was even often whispered that they were dangerous and unpredictable. Some Eugladians feared they may even be spies for the Snorgs, though Radianne always thought that idea was highly unlikely. She couldn't imagine any Eugladian, Wanderer or not, aligning with a Snorg.

Didn't he have family somewhere? He certainly was strange. As she glanced over at Henrick again, she felt heat rush to her cheeks. She was unhappy with herself for wondering about him, talking with him, and for allowing him to continue to walk with her in the first place. He was rude, improper, and arrogant.

To complicate matters, she was still angry that she couldn't help but notice he had a much more appealing look about him than any other man she'd known. His attractiveness was unsettling. Not that she had much experience in that area…

He caught her staring.

In that instant, their eyes connected and a strange flicker of something sparked between the two of them. It seemed to crackle in the air.

Two strangers, caught in a moment, instantly spellbound and unable to look away.

One of them was more uncomfortable with the exchange than the other.

Radianne flushed again and looked away. She had to stop turning red. She focused on the path ahead. Her nerves were probably getting to her. She had counted on this journey being her and Blink's. She tried to figure out ways to get rid of the newcomer. Blink sat quietly on her shoulder, and she wondered what he was thinking.

Henrick reached out and touched her arm as they walked. "I know I don't know you," he said. "But… I really do think I should help you. Put your pride aside and let me join you on your travels. You can't go alone. I'm not going to hurt you or the star, I promise."

Radianne jerked her arm away. "Don't touch me! Stop touching me! Don't you have anything better to do?!"

She had a sudden urge to slap him, which surprised her. Usually she was pretty level headed and didn't get so enraged over small things. Yet, she had known this man for less than a day and he was already making her furious.

"You most certainly should not go with me," she added, sharply, as she tossed her hair over her shoulder, inadvertently covering Blink in the mound. "I don't even know you, as you said. We just met! You're a Wanderer, after all. And you have to know that your kind have a strange reputation among normal Eugladians. So what makes you think I'd let you continue to follow me, anyway?"

Blink peeked out from the mound of hair, taking in the verbal exchange silently. He was starting to think Eugladians were very complex creatures. Stars always got straight to the point about things. He thought the two of them were certainly dragging the conversation out.

Henrick shrugged. "Even if you say no, I'll follow you. It's the right thing to do. I consider myself a man of principle, despite my being a *Wanderer*. A life which you also apparently know very little about." He narrowed his eyes.

"Now that you've crossed my path, I can't have it on my conscience that you are somewhere out here, attempting this ridiculous quest on your own," he continued. "Wanderers may be odd to you, but most of us are honorable and misunderstood. You're bound to run into trouble at some point. And besides, I don't have anything better to do with my time at the present."

Radianne sighed, not doubting his determination. But she was equally as determined not to give in.

"I don't need any help," she said, exasperated.

Her heart sank a little as she realized the conversation was going nowhere. The man had seemingly invited himself indefinitely on her adventure.

"You will need my help." Henrick gave a firm nod. "As I said, I'll promise you this – I know I'm a stranger, and a Wanderer – and I'm well aware of the connotation that comes with that title. But I won't hurt you or the star. I'll just follow, quietly. Like a shadow."

Scowling again, Radianne sighed and headed off into a thicket of trees. The last thing she wanted was a strange man glued to her side for the duration of the journey. She didn't want a shadow.

But a small part of her – admittedly, a very small part and one that she was presently annoyed with – was for some reason not entirely upset about meeting her new acquaintance.

-6-
A Strange New World

It seemed like they had been walking for hours. Relentless, never-ending hours. The one saving grace was that Henrick had kept true to his word. He had acted like a shadow and kept his mouth closed as they journeyed on.

Radianne stopped by a blue willow tree and sat down next to a cluster of wildflowers colored in the same hue. Blink scampered down from his shoulder perch and sat beside her. Opening up her bag, she took out one of the bean sandwiches Miss Lugia had packed. As she glanced into the sack, she made a mental note that the food had already dwindled down significantly.

Draping one arm around Blink, she pulled him close for comfort. She knew it must be hard for him, forced into a strange new world, with even stranger beings that were so different from stars. She couldn't imagine how he must feel.

Shielding her eyes against the late afternoon sun, she looked over to her other companion – the unwanted one – cautiously.

Henrick leaned against a tree and was staring out at the horizon. She supposed she should try to tolerate his presence as best as she could for the time being. And that might mean being pleasant when she didn't really want to be… and trying to make a temporary peace offering.

"Would you care for anything to eat?" She raised the bag.

He turned to look at her and his eyes widened. "Are you actually being nice to me? Lowering yourself enough to speak to me?"

Radianne snorted. "It wouldn't be right to let you starve while I ate in front of you. I am at that decent."

Henrick smiled and walked over, taking a seat next to her in the grass. "Well in that case… what do you have in that bag of yours?"

She handed it over.

He rummaged around in the sack for a moment, pulling out another sandwich. "Thanks," he said, and took a bite.

They ate silently for awhile and he studied Blink with interest. After some time, he cleared his throat.

"Forgive me if I'm being rude, but do stars eat?" he asked.

Blink proceeded to explain star diet while Radianne pretended not to watch Henrick.

Unfortunately, it seemed she was drawn to his face. So she chose to focus on her misgivings about him instead.

She again wondered why he'd been passing through the river area that day. What were his real motives for helping them, and where had he been going? Was he on his way to visit a friend? A family member? A love… she chastised herself for even thinking that.

He caught her staring and she looked away quickly. She had to stop doing that too, she thought.

As he and Blink chatted, her thoughts drifted to home. She wondered what Piri and her parents were thinking, if they had gone to

Miss Lugia seeking answers. They both knew how much time she spent with the ladybug. But she hoped they hadn't gone to her. She didn't want or need anyone else coming after her now.

"Soon," Henrick said, suddenly speaking directly to her and snapping her back to attention, "we will be in Eustasia. Then we'll have to be on high alert for Snorgs. But their fortress is in the heart of the land, so we probably won't have to worry about seeing them right away. For a few days, anyway."

Radianne didn't know what was she supposed to say. Should she thank him for providing unwanted advice? Congratulate him on his expertise?

Daylight began to fade into early evening as they continued on their way.

Soon, the moment Radianne had been waiting for had finally arrived. They passed a shadowy grove of trees, one of which had a rickety wooden post and a sign with the word EUSTASIA affixed to it.

She was surprised at how simple the marker was. She'd expected the boundary markers dividing lands to be much more magnificent, as if making a grand announcement. But there it was – a simple marker carved roughly into old wood.

"Well here we are," Henrick announced. "Grand welcome sign, huh?"

He grinned at her, then glanced up at the sky and at the fading sun. "We should find a place to sleep before night settles," he suggested. "Nasty things will be about soon. I know of a place, actually. Follow me."

Reluctantly, Radianne trailed him. And as she took her first steps into the new land, her excitement grew and she looked at her surroundings with interest.

In the shadowy light, silhouettes of gigantic, mysterious flowers towered up toward the sky. Plants sprung from ghostly-looking grasses, and in the distance, the jagged and somewhat foreboding outline of the central mountains loomed.

Her spirits lifted at the thought of the lands beyond that awaited her. Who knew what wonderful secrets they held?

Her excitement was short-lived, however.

Henrick touched her arm, trying to get her attention. "We have to go this way."

Recoiling from his touch, she frowned again. She wished he would stop touching her. What she really wanted right then was to head off in the opposite direction, away from him. But since it was nearly dark, and she knew it would be unwise, she had no choice. With Blink sitting on her shoulder, she reluctantly followed Henrick's lead again.

He trudged along a narrow dirt pathway to a cave hidden amid a cluster of the enormous flowers. The shadowy shapes of the giant plants looked strange and feral in the darkness. As if they could eat a whole person. Radianne shivered.

"I've stayed here many times," Henrick said as he stepped forward into the dark and gaping hole. He motioned for her to follow. "It's safe."

Radianne wasn't so sure, but she followed him into the darkness anyway. At first, she couldn't see a thing, as the interior of the cave was filled with a void of empty blackness. Soon, however, Blink began to give off his soft and ethereal light, brightening the room enough for her to make out shadowy shapes and objects.

She looked around with wonder.

Clumps of large rocks were scattered around the domed cave interior. Jagged, dangerous-looking formations hung down like daggers from the top of the cave. A few drops of water trickled down rhythmically, making soft pit-patting sounds. The remnants of a fire long burned out were arranged within a stone circle in the middle of the room.

"I made a fire here last time I passed through," Henrick said. "I'll get it going again. It will be cold soon."

He walked over to the circle and Radianne and Blink watched as he sat down and began to arrange wood, stones and brush. He worked for some time, until a brilliant flame roared to life.

Radianne shivered as the heat enveloped them. Her father and brother always made fires back home, and in that moment, she wished she would have paid more attention and learned how to do so herself.

Moving closer to the growing flickering orange and yellow flames, she rubbed her hands together and reveled in the warmth.

Blink sat near her and stared at the fire, transfixed. "This is quite extraordinary," he said. "Wait until I tell the others."

Radianne smiled. She was glad he was finding some joy in her world even though he was so far from his own.

Unbidden thoughts of her own home came to mind and she remembered and how eager she'd been to leave. She thought of the endless sunny days she'd spent exploring the acres of fruit tree orchards… following her brother around dutifully helping out… having picnics with her parents. She frowned. She'd ended up in her current location with a stranger. Had she lost her mind? Perhaps she really was a foolish young girl after all for wanting to chase the wind. Perhaps it would have been safer to stick to those orchards, the comfort of home.

Darting a glance at Henrick, she caught him staring and she quickly looked away again.

That had to stop happening.

Her thoughts drifted back to home again. She wondered if her friends and family were worried. What if she couldn't trust Henrick?

She tried to shake the doubts and believe she'd made the right decision. She had to focus on Blink and getting him home.

All these new worries were tiring. Sullenly, she told herself they had only seemed to increase since the second she'd met Henrick. It was his fault.

Sighing, she leaned back. She knew she had to find a way to enjoy the present in order to keep her confidence high. Maybe she just needed some sleep.

****

Henrick was lost in his own thoughts. He stared at the beautiful young woman before him and figured she must be frightened, sitting in a cave in the dark in a strange land with a Wanderer.

He knew all too well what was said about Wanderers and had experienced his share of insults and shunning from other Eugladians over the years.

At that moment, however, he simply wanted to learn more about Radianne. Perhaps he had been a little too pushy in following her. But he did feel an odd responsibility toward her for some reason.

Though she was young and naive, he admired her determination to get the star back to the sky where it belonged, even if the idea seemed like an impossible and somewhat ridiculous task.

He wondered what her family was like. He wanted to tell her how important family was and how she should appreciate the people who loved her while she had the chance. He wanted to tell her to hold them close and never let go. Because everything could change in an instant.

But he figured that would be a strange thing to say to someone you'd just met.

Radianne truly was interested in helping the star, but he also suspected she'd been eager to leave home for some other reason as well. He wouldn't ask why. Not just then. He was a stranger and he knew that questions would come in return. And then he would have to open up about his own lonely life – something he wasn't willing to discuss with anyone, any time soon.

****

Radianne could feel Henrick's gaze on her again and forced herself to feign ignorance. Being indifferent and aloof to the man was a must, she told herself. She didn't want him there. She wasn't weak or incapable of taking care of herself. She and Blink would be completely fine without Henrick's assistance.

Though – she also couldn't help but admire his determination to stay. Determination was an attractive quality. Admittedly, she thought he was annoying and had imposed on her adventure, but he did seem to know a thing or two about travel, from what she'd seen so far. Perhaps the knowledge would ultimately be useful, in the end. Even if she would hate to admit it.

Blink certainly seemed fascinated with him. Remembering how joyous the star had been when Henrick made the fire moments before, Radianne looked over at her friend. To her horror, she immediately noticed something wasn't quite right. In the darkness of the cave, Blink's light was pulsating.

"Blink!" she cried, lunging toward him. "What's wrong?"

The star curled up into a ball. "I don't feel well Radianne," he moaned, his points clutching at the center of his body. He was obviously in pain.

Radianne gently picked him up, cradling him in her arms. The electric sensation pulsed through her as well, keeping time with his erratic light. Her eyes filling with tears, all she could do was watch as he writhed in agony. Something terrible was happening…

"I… my light. There's something wrong," Blink whispered. He closed his eyes and sighed deeply. "I remember now. I remember those old stories about fallen stars…" He looked up with wide eyes. "The Man In The Moon once said that if a star ever fell to the world below – if it didn't die on impact – starlight would soon be taken. And if given enough time, a fallen star would become like a stone in appearance. I don't know why I forgot that. What if that's happening now?"

Radianne drew him closer. She refused to allow her new friend to become a stone! His body was still glowing. There was still hope…

"I think it means I will eventually stop shining and never shine again unless I find my way back to the sky somehow," Blink said quietly.

Radianne continued to hold him and waited until his light settled down, until it returned to a still and calming glow. The electric feeling soon became gentle waves.

"At least we will always have the glow of fire," he told her, closing his eyes to rest.

Radianne cuddled him in her lap. She didn't understand all that was happening. Afraid for Blink, she made a vow then and there that she would do whatever it took to get him back to his family. As soon as possible.

The strange currents that seemed to flow through her body whenever she touched him were also confusing. In the morning, she would have to remember to ask him about it.

"One day," she whispered to him, "you will shine your radiance on the world once more. I promise."

Blink smiled at her words, his eyes still closed.

Henrick stood and walked over. Crouching beside her, he examined Blink. "I will do what I can to help you get him home, Radianne."

A sharp retort began to form on Radianne's lips. He couldn't know about stars. He couldn't possibly know everything there was to know about everything, even though he certainly thought he did...

But as she glared at him, and saw the look in his blue eyes, her frown faded. She held her tongue. He genuinely seemed concerned.

Whatever reason this stranger had crossed her path and had agreed to help them, she realized then that perhaps she need not be so harsh.

Maybe, she thought, maybe she should be more trusting in her fellow Eugladian and have faith that the meeting could possibly be meant to be.

As he looked up at her again, her heart skipped a beat. But he was still a stranger, she told herself. Brushing all of the troublesome feelings and thoughts aside, she mumbled "Thank you," and curled up into a ball near Blink, resting her head on her hands.

****

Henrick took out the light he carried in a hidden pocket at all times. It was made by glo-worms and had been given to him by his father. With Blink's glow being present, he hadn't needed to use it, but the treasured light would come in handy if the star's light completely faded. He turned the switch off and on, playing with the patterns the beam made on the cavern wall, lost in time and thoughts of his family.

He remembered how beautiful his mother had been. How brave his father… Beautiful and brave. Like his new friend…

His thoughts trailed back to the girl. Though moments before, she seemed extremely upset, she now looked peaceful as she lay asleep in the firelight. He wondered if she'd dream tonight, and what about. He also wondered again why he had been so intensely determined to help her. She wasn't the easiest person to get along with.

Even though he knew he'd made the right choice, he'd also avoided spending too much time with other Eugladians over the last several years and was out of practice with how to behave. He knew he would ultimately be better off on his own. Most of them had no clue about Wanderers. They wouldn't understand. Only time would tell where the new and unexpected path was going to take him.

Leaning back against the wall of the cave, he stared into the dying fire for awhile and then again at the sleeping girl and star. As he watched them, a frightening – but welcoming – feeling washed over him. The change was a good thing, he decided, contradicting his thoughts of just moments before. He was no longer alone.

For the first time in a long time, a small flame of hope sparked to life inside his soul.

-7-
Eustasia

Radianne was fascinated with how much the scenery in Eustasia differed from Eugladia. It had changed so quickly. The air in Eustasia seemed crisper and more fragrant... a delicious scent wafted on the breeze. The smell seemed to be coming from the mammoth flowers she'd spotted the night before.

In the morning light, Radianne looked up at the giant rainbow-colored flowers with delight. They were no longer eerie. "They're so beautiful!" she exclaimed, happily tossing Blink into the air. She caught him in her arms and danced, feeling that electricity again.

Earlier, with Henrick out of earshot, she'd asked Blink about the strange feelings. She told him that whenever she felt the current, she felt more energized and alive. Powerful. Unafraid.

But unfortunately, there hadn't been much of an answer to her question. Blink said it just must be a star thing and left it at that. Radianne decided not to question it for the time being.

She was especially happy because her friend also seemed to be feeling better and was in good spirits.

He laughed as she twirled around a purple rose towering above her head. Her long hair spiraled out in waves around her shoulders as she danced.

She thought of him dancing with his mother in the sky and all the wonderful things he could tell her and the other stars when he returned home.

Though Radianne hoped he would remember the dance under the giant rose forever.

Smiling as she whirled him past a giant blue daisy, she even dared flash a grin over to Henrick. She momentarily forgot she was supposed to be angry and unhappy he was traveling with her.

"Aren't they some of the most beautiful things you've ever seen?" she asked as he leaned against a giant flower stem and watched her gush over the flowers.

He smiled back and shook his head, as if confused.

Radianne supposed men didn't really appreciate the true gloriousness of flowers.

Happily she turned her attention to Blink again and whirled with him once more. When she stopped spinning, she dizzily paused for a moment or two and then proceeded to examine her surroundings more thoroughly.

It was hard to believe that Snorgs dwelled somewhere in Eustasia. She thought the land was enchanting – much too beautiful for the likes of them. The idea of such ugly creatures living in such a pristine place didn't make much sense to her.

Pale brown mountains rose up in the distance, jutting toward a perfect blue sky lined with puffy white clouds. The scene seemed serene, untarnished.

Could Snorgs really inhabit such a place, and if so, why did they want to conquer other lands? It seemed they had everything they could want, right there in Eustasia.

She hoped there wouldn't be a Snorg encounter any time soon. After the incident with Blink the night before, there wasn't any time to waste. Growing solemn again, Radianne thought of his pulsating glow. He did seem to feel better, though he also looked even more pale and slightly rock-like in appearance.

She worried about what the changes could mean, but she had to have faith that once he returned to the sky, he would be completely back to normal. No time to fret about it just then. They had to keep moving.

The trio set out in the morning light and walked until they came to a field full of enormous white mushrooms.

How astonishing, Radianne thought. What had moments before seemed to be an endless field of fragrant flowers was now a forest of giant, odd-looking fungi. Rays of sunlight filtered down over the hooded tops and around the towering stems of the giant mushroom forest.

"What's this?" She raised an eyebrow and looked to Henrick. He would certainly have an answer, she supposed.

"One of the first things you'll learn as we travel along," he said, taking a few steps closer to the mushrooms and making a wide gesture with his hands, "Is how the scenery changes very quickly in The Netherlands. Things are often unpredictable and don't always make much sense."

As he said the last words, a shadowed look came over his eyes, as if he were remembering something he'd rather forget. He shook it off.

"This is where the Oodles live," he continued.

Radianne frowned. "The who?"

"The Oodles." Henrick walked forward into the forest of fungi without offering further explanation.

Blink looked at Radianne from his position on her shoulder. Shrugging, she trailed along after Henrick and quickly discovered that navigating though the forest of fungi was not at all an easy task.

Repeatedly, she tripped over their bulky stems and the stench in the air from their spores made her choke. The air smelled awful, like wet mold and other nasty unpleasant things. The putrid odor only intensified and the mushrooms grew darker and crustier in appearance the deeper the trio progressed into the dank forest.

And then there was a voice. "Good day!"

Then another. "Good day!"

And another. "Good day!"

Radianne paused to listen. She turned her head this way and that, trying to find the source of the sound.

What was that? Was she hearing things?

But Blink heard the voices too, so she knew she wasn't losing her mind.

"Good day!"

There they were! Turning quickly to her left, Radianne spotted three slimy worms in little black hats, sitting on a smaller brown mushroom.

They were somewhat difficult to see. She had to squint her eyes to get a good look at them.The creatures grinned at her and bowed, then proceeded to argue about something indecipherable amongst themselves.

Radianne reluctantly looked to Henrick for an explanation. Standing several feet ahead, he motioned her forward, simultaneously mouthing something.

"What?" Radianne asked, not understanding.

"We said GOOD DAY!!" the worms screeched in ear-splitting unison.

For such little creatures, their voices were completely horrible, Radianne thought.

Henrick sighed loudly. "Oodles," he grumbled. "Ignore them and just walk on."

But Radianne could not help but gawk at them. They were very peculiar little creatures and, as annoying as they were, she was also amazed by the capacity of their vocals.

"Very, very rude!" one of the worms screeched.

"No morning greeting!" another said with a sniff.

Blink stared. He too had no words for this situation, so he just sat, silent, on Radianne's shoulder as they continued to express their dismay at not being greeted by the forest crossers in their midst.

Radianne decided to try to appease them as she walked.

"G-Good day," she stuttered, trying to untangle her leg from around an especially rancid giant mushroom stem. A chunk of it broke off around her foot. The foul smell instantly wafted up and almost knocked her over. Even Blink covered his eyes. Radianne gagged and pressed on.

"Good day!"

"Good day!"

"Good day!"

The three worms jumped up and down and excitedly shouted their greetings.

Radianne, Henrick, and Blink picked up the pace, but as they walked, more of the worms popped up.

They all continued to shout. "Good day!"

The sound soon became deafening. The mushrooms seemed to vibrate with each Oodle scream.

Radianne's head began to throb. Greetings were coming so fast, left and right, from above and below. It all culminated to a ear-splitting unison and she knew if she didn't get out of the mushroom forest soon, there was a good chance she could very well lose her mind.

Clutching at her head, she tried to run, as if the action would help block the sounds out.

Henrick turned to see what was holding her up. He noted the mass of Oodles surrounding her, shouting out their greetings relentlessly.

"I suppose you've had enough," he called to her, laughing.

"Good day! Good day! Good day!" the Oodles sang out.

The forest hummed with their greetings, giant mushroom stems shaking violently from the deafening song.

Radianne pressed her hands against her eyes and fought back the urge to scream. The urge started welling up in her throat... Blink still had his eyes covered. She was just about to open her mouth and let loose when –

"GOOD NIGHT!" Henrick shouted.

Immediately, the chaotic chorus stopped. The Oodles sank to the ground at once, sulking and creeping away, murmuring "so rude," as they disappeared.

Radianne and Blink sighed with relief.

"That's it?" Radianne turned to Henrick with a raised eyebrow. She couldn't believe how easy it had been for him to quiet the nasty little creatures down. "You should have done that sooner! What was wrong with them?"

Henrick laughed. "I don't know. Just one of those many strange sights you will come across in your travels. I figured you should experience it. I think they just love to be annoying," he said, and kicked a rotten mushroom stem out of his way as they walked on. "I figured out the key to quieting them down one day when I was passing through. I got tired of them saying the same thing over and over, and, finally, I told them 'good night!' That ended it."

"Well I'm glad that's over with," Blink announced. "Very strange creatures in a very strange land. The strangest beings I've met yet!"

"I'll take that as a compliment," Radianne said with a laugh. She was also completely relieved the Oodles had gone, though she didn't like how helpless she'd felt and how Henrick had to come to her rescue.

What would have happened if she'd been alone? She wondered. She would like to think she would have made it through, but given the fact that she'd just felt on the verge of insanity, she wasn't so sure. The thought depressed her a little.

But, she decided not to make a fuss about it. She didn't want to seem childish and ungrateful for Henrick's help. Even if she still really didn't want it.

They walked away from the monstrous fungi forest and crossed into a meadow. The giant flowers reappeared and were a welcome sight. The meadow was also full of tall, white, lovely grasses.

"Sometimes, in this area," Henrick said, "there are tremendously large butterflies that pass through. They seek the nectar from these flowers you love so much." He turned with a smirk to Radianne. "The butterflies are known as the Gentle Giants. You know what would be a good idea?" he smiled. " We should ask them for a lift. They could easily fly us to the heart of Eustasia, saving us some valuable time."

Radianne froze. The heart? Wasn't that where the Snorgs lived? She'd almost forgotten because she'd been too taken in by all the pretty sights. Though, she did suppose they would have to pass through The Center at some point – it was inevitable.

As for Henrick's new revelation... she had never seen a giant butterfly and once again, didn't feel happy about him making all the suggestions, as she still felt confused about their situation. At a loss for words, she didn't comment.

Henrick thought her silence a little rude, but intuitively knew she probably didn't want his input. After all, he'd somewhat sabotaged 'her adventure,' though he was only trying to help. He too grew silent as they walked along.

Blink and Radianne eventually began to talk between themselves, laughing and telling funny stories about things that had happened to them when they were very young. They were so busy chatting that they didn't see the Gentle Giant appear.

Henrick noticed the butterfly first as it alighted on a gargantuan tulip. "What luck!" He pointed. "Look up there you two! There's one of the butterflies now!"

Radianne and Blink stared in awe as a mammoth orange and blue butterfly with black, heavily lashed eyes smiled and slurped up nectar from a gigantic turquoise tulip, seemingly oblivious to their presence. It was as big as a horse.

Not wasting any time, Henrick ran over to the giant flower and quickly shimmied up its stem, scaling it. Momentarily, he was face to face with the magnificent creature.

Radianne and Blink craned their heads and watched in amazement as the Gentle Giant twitched its antennae and studied Henrick with a slight look of dismay on its face. It apparently did not appreciate having its dinner so rudely interrupted.

"I am sorry to disturb your feast," Henrick said humbly, bowing. "I do apologize, but you see, we have a favor to ask of you."

Brushing his hair away from his eyes, he smiled, charmingly, and took a deep breath. "It would be most helpful to my friends and I," – he gestured toward Radianne and Blink standing below – "If you would do us the honor of carrying us to The Center of Eustasia. I know that is as far as you will go, because of the Snorgs. But it would be most helpful to us. And we would be very appreciative and would certainly return a favor in the future."

The butterfly continued drinking, seemingly unmoved by his speech. Henrick sat down patiently and waited, holding up a hand at Radianne's inquisitive look.

Offended by his curt dismissal, she pursed her lips.

Some time passed before the butterfly finished its meal. Then, with one final slurp, it slowly lifted its massive head and turned to Henrick. Just as slowly it opened its mouth to speak.

"You are correct. I will not travel across The Center," it said in a melodic and sleepy voice. The creature narrowed its giant eyes and studied Henrick carefully. "However. Since I was heading near the location anyway, I will fly you and your friends there. It is not often we have friendly visitors of late."

Henrick grinned. "Thank you very much! We truly appreciate your kindness. If any of the Gentle Giants ever need a favor and we are able, we will be sure to come to your aid." He lowered his voice. "I know things have been difficult for you."

The butterfly nodded, frowning a little. "Indeed."

Henrick looked to his friends down below. He waved. "Come on up!"

Radianne had somehow managed to hear some of the conversation between Henrick and the butterfly and wondered what difficulties the Gentle Giants had faced, but she couldn't waste time asking such questions. It was time to get moving again.

Blink attached himself to her hair as she began the ascent up the tremendous flower stem. She realized it was not an easy feat, climbing the stalk, and was a little envious that Henrick had managed to scale the mountainous flower so gracefully. He'd made it look so easy, she thought as she strained upward.

Henrick offered no assistance from up above as she climbed. Instead, he rolled onto his stomach, smiling down from the top of the flower, watching her with apparent pleasure as she struggled.

After observing her battle with the stem for a few moments, he let out a laugh. "Need a hand?" he asked, reaching down.

Radianne shook her head and ignored his outstretched fingers. She could do this herself. Never mind him, she thought. She had to prove to Blink, and to herself, that she was more than capable of all this journey required. Mentally and physically, she could do it.

After what seemed like an eternity, she finally made her way up and over the giant tulip, panting heavily. Her face was red with exertion as she stood up and smoothed out her tunic. Blink climbed off her shoulder as she readjusted herself.

Henrick smiled a mischievous smile. "Fantastic."

Radianne ignored him and focused her attention instead on the beautiful butterfly before her, taking in its large head and lovely eyes. In Eustasia there were such strange and marvelous creatures, so different from Eugladia.

"I believe we are ready to go," Henrick said abruptly, shattering her thoughts, as he nodded to the Gentle Giant.

Radianne felt a slight surge of irritation. She'd barely caught her breath nor had a chance to admire the Gentle Giant and properly introduce herself, and there he was, already dictating the next move.

Pride welling up, she desperately wished she had demanded he stay at the river where she'd met him. She should be able to do things on her own terms. The joy she'd felt earlier in the day, when she'd danced around the flowers with Blink, was fading fast. She didn't like how moody she was becoming in Henrick's presence, nor did she fully understand why it was happening. Never had she met a man who irritated her and yet so intrigued her at the same time.

As if sensing her unhappiness, Blink patted her on the leg. "Good job climbing up that obstacle Radianne," he said as he congratulated her.

At his touch, Radianne felt that electric surge of energy again. Her anger faded and her confidence rose. She smiled down at her friend, thanking him. Then she looked once more at the Gentle Giant.

"It is very nice to meet you," she said. "It truly is an honor. I wish I had more time to speak with you. Thank you very much for your kindness in helping us."

"You are most welcome," said the butterfly. "Get ready to climb aboard. And remember to hold on tight!"

Crouching down, the Gentle Giant flattened its wings so the passengers could climb onto its velvety back.

Radianne lifted one leg and then the other onto the butterfly's soft back and Blink attached himself once more to her hair.

Henrick climbed up next, grinning.

"You know," he whispered, "you probably should let me sit in front. It would be nice that way, to have you hold on to me." He moved closer. "Besides, I'm stronger, and probably could maintain a steadier grip. We don't want anyone plummeting to their deaths today."

What nerve he had, Radianne thought and frowned. A shiver ran down her spine at his ominous words. No one would die. She would not listen to him. She forced the negative remarks from her mind.

"Fine," Henrick continued. "When we fall off because of your weaker arms, don't blame me."

At that moment, Radianne felt like pushing him off and leaving him behind. But then, the butterfly began to ascend.

-8-
The Center

She knew Henrick was grinning behind her back, probably delightfully imagining the fury his words were igniting in her. It seemed as if it were already becoming a fun game to him, seeing how easily he could get her temper aroused.

As he wrapped his arms tightly around her waist, knowing full well she probably hated it, Radianne stiffened and fought back the urge to say something harsh. The shiver she'd felt seconds before had turned to hot anger. But she didn't want him to know how much he was getting to her.

Still, the thought of forcefully removing his hands from her waist was tempting. The vision of him blowing away, back to where he'd come from, made her feel a little better. She smiled at the thought.

The Gentle Giant flapped its great wings and slowly continued its ascent into the air. Radianne tightened her grip on the soft velvet, just as Henrick tightened his arms around her waist. She tried to enjoy the fact that she was riding a giant butterfly and ignored his embrace.

Blink also tightened his grip on her hair, but she didn't mind. The electricity from his touch seemed to flow through her hair strands and, as they soared higher, her mood lifted once more.

As they climbed toward the clouds, her anger toward Henrick faded and she focused on the wonderful experience she was having.

A thought suddenly came to her... perhaps the butterfly could fly to the stars?

Would that be an option for them, one Miss Lugia hadn't known about? Maybe Blink could get home sooner than they'd thought...

But she soon had her answer when, a moment later, the mammoth insect gasped for air.

"This is as high as I can go," the butterfly said, panting. "Gentle Giants are not meant to fly higher than this."

Radianne gazed down at the fields and flowers below, noting how far away everything seemed. The rivers appeared to be mere slivers of shiny silvery water. No wonder Blink couldn't see much from his star world above – everything was so small even from this vantage point. Still, the view was marvelous. She could only imagine what a speck she must look like in the grand scheme of things.

As they flew through the clouds, the sun's rays illuminated them, casting the group in a brilliant and ethereal glow.

Radianne closed her eyes and relished the moment – the grand view she'd just seen and the feel of the wind in her hair. Life had gone from mundane to magical in such a short amount of time, without warning. Who knew what dreams would reveal themselves next...

Her private moment was soon interrupted, however. Henrick must have been staring at her with her eyes closed and assumed she was afraid, because he wrapped his arms around her a little more tightly.

"Relax," he said with an annoying air of confidence. "You're safe with me."

She wanted to laugh at him, but instead chose to focus on the exhilaration she felt as they flew.

Blink loved the feeling too as it reminded him a little of home. He said as much.

The group seemed to float quickly and effortlessly over the miles they would have been forced to walk if it had not been for the assistance of the Gentle Giant.

But then, as they descended a bit lower, things began to change. What had mere moments before been a beautiful, lovely scene, now grew ugly.

Green fields gave way to great expanses of what appeared to be dark nothingness. Dismal black mountains jutted up on all sides, towering above the vast and darkened dusty wasteland. Slivers of brown murky rivers snaked through the desolate and dreary terrain.

"How could things suddenly change so drastically?" Radianne asked in horror. She couldn't believe her eyes. Blink shuddered next to her.

The butterfly also shuddered, its furry back rippling. "It is not all that difficult, when evil takes hold," the Gentle Giant spoke quietly. "Light can then be snuffed out. Sometimes painfully slowly.

"The heart of Eustasia was once a thriving place full of joy and life," she continued. "Once upon a time, luscious, tasty flowers and vibrant and plentiful gardens grew all throughout this land. It was a favorite place among my kind, the Gentle Giants. But the Snorgs destroyed it all. They devoured all that was good and beautiful, sucking out life, turning the land into this place of despair."

The Gentle Giant shuddered again. "One day I believe they will destroy all of Eustasia – and maybe the lands beyond too – with their vileness and devastation. They hate hope. They do not want it. I do believe that is part of their ultimate plan."

Radianne's heart sank. How awful! What if what the Gentle Giant said would ring true? What if the festering ugliness would one day extend to other places., and snuff out the light where beauty once flourished? The thought of such things happening to Eugladia and beyond was sobering.

Perhaps she should have been more fearful of the Snorgs all along. Perhaps she had somehow underestimated them.

"This is as far as I go," the butterfly suddenly announced. She descended slowly, eventually coming to a stop in a field of brown and shriveled lifeless grass. With a worried expression and twitching antennae, she looked around nervously.

"I would take you further, but many of my kind have been ensnared by traps the Snorgs set up in the mountains," she whispered, sadness filling her eyes. "Many of my friends have been lost."

"What could they possibly want with your friends?" Radianne asked, horrified. She eased off the butterfly's back and looked up at the Gentle Giant with concern.

"Oh, my dear. Dreadful, unspeakable things," the butterfly whispered again, looking around with agitation. "I dare not say too much here. Like the land, all goodness that once existed in the hearts of those captured is stripped away..." she fidgeted and lowered her voice so it was barely audible. "There are rumors that the enslaved ones now help the Snorgs drain the life from the land, just as they once sucked nectar from flowers! It is some sort of dark magic at work, you see. The Snorgs are using us – and countless others – to help destroy all that is pure. And this is only the beginning."

Radianne shuddered at the images the Gentle Giant's revelation had conjured up in her mind, wondering what had become of other creatures the Snorgs ensnared. What countless others was she referring to? Who were these others? Where did they come from? Did they all truly become evil?

"I must go now." The butterfly looked at her three passengers solemnly. "Good luck in your travels. You will need it."

The trio gave their thanks and watched respectfully as the beautiful creature flew away.

As they turned to examine their surroundings, Henrick made a disgusted face.

"I haven't been here for many years," he said. "It is unfortunate we have to pass through The Center to get to where we need to be. There were other ways, but the roads have recently been destroyed by the Snorgs. Last time I came through this route was on my way to visit Shondalina."

Radianne started to ask him about that journey, but stopped herself. Now was probably not the best time for questioning, as talking too loud and lingering in one place for too long would be dangerous.

She also had to pretend that she was not interested in Henrick's life story – not that she really was, she told herself.

As she gazed out at the forlorn landscape, a sense of cold despair clawed at her. An ugly darkness stretched on far beyond what her eyes could see. The despairing feeling welled up inside, seemingly unstoppable, like water breaking free from a dam.

Rotten and stinking vegetation covered the ground beyond the dead dark grass for miles. The eerie black mountains formed a circle on all sides, as if trying to keep everything – and everyone – in.

There was a cold and foreboding air about the place. Radianne tried to shake off the feelings of doom. Just then, Blink patted her shoulder, as if sensing her distress. The electric feeling returned. She felt a comforting little surge of light and hope.

At that precise moment, she also happened to notice a small yellow flower near her feet, poking its way up through the rocky soil.

"Look there, Blink and Henrick," she said, pointing.

"How strange, but how wonderful too! This goes to show there is still hope amid the ugliness. That's a good sign." She patted Blink and smiled at Henrick. "The flower survives, even in the middle of such poor conditions. Maybe one day beauty will return to this place again. Yes. There's always hope…" she trailed off, smiling as she said the words.

Turning her head, she looked to the star on her shoulder and spoke to him softly. "Thank you for reminding me. And thanks to the flower too."

As she smiled at her friend, Henrick wore a frown. He gave Radianne credit for her positive speech, but he personally knew all too well that it would be a long time dark in this land before a new dawn would come.

He knew things she didn't. He'd heard the stories from other Wanderers. Terrible, frightening stories. Worst of all, he'd experienced some of them firsthand. The girl was a little too naive. Maybe one day he'd tell her. But in that moment, she was oblivious to what the Snorgs were truly capable of.

"It's time to go," he said abruptly. "We can't stay for long. This way." He began walking.

Radianne followed and whispered to Blink sitting on his perch on her shoulder. "Trailing behind him is getting a little old already."

"I wouldn't worry about that," the star said softly, as they followed Henrick through the wasteland. "The faster we leave these parts, the better. I don't like this place Radianne."

Radianne placed a comforting hand on her friend. "Neither do I Blink. Neither do I."

-9-
Snorg Territory

Though the center of Eustasia was riddled with obvious signs of their foul presence, the Snorgs were nowhere to be found. For that, Radianne was grateful, though she did wonder when the fiendish creatures would make an appearance. She realized for the first time that she did not have any weapons to use for protection and chided herself for not being better prepared. So caught up she'd been with leaving. She made a mental note to come up with some ideas soon.

They all needed weaponry to protect themselves. She wondered what would happen if Snorgs found Eugladians – and a star of all things – in their midst.

The scenery went from bad to worse. More of the putrid, stinking mushrooms began to pop up, but this time they featured ugly large flies sitting all over them. The flies did not talk as the travelers passed by, but they still caused Radianne to cringe with disgust at their sheer number and eerie, unsettling stillness.

After some time, a vast lake of steaming black ooze appeared in the distance.

"We have to stay away from that," Henrick said, gesturing toward it. "It is one of the numerous terrors of this place."

Radianne looked at him with curiosity and a little bit of dread. "Oh?"

He flicked his eyes to her and away again. "There are horrible creatures lurking in there," he continued after a moment of silence. "Get too close, and we will all be dead." Shadows crossed his face as he said the words.

They veered away from the path of the treacherous black sludge and walked on.

That deep melancholy she'd been feeling was growing in Henrick; Radianne could sense it. Blink and the flower had helped remedy the same feelings in herself for the moment, but she knew they would probably return if they didn't get out of The Center as soon as possible.

The feelings didn't really seem to be affecting Blink – perhaps he had too much light within himself to think on dark things, she thought. It must be nice to always feel that way. Her own management of the feelings certainly must have had something to do with the strange energy he seemed to be giving her.

She noted Henrick's pained expression again and wondered if there was something more spurring on his feelings than the hopelessness and darkness lingering in the air. She felt the urge to talk to him about such things, but her pride wouldn't allow it.

The trio continued to trudge along in the desolate landscape, lost in their own thoughts, sometimes stumbling on pieces of rotten vegetation. The vegetation soon gave way to dusty black earth and eventually, vacant trails, void of plant and animal life.

Then came the shrill voices.

"The last of those beastly, nasty butterflies will be ensnared if they come near our mountains!" one voice growled. "What great and wicked slaves they are!"

"Yes, yes! They will ALL one day become our vessels of destruction," another voice sneered. "Just like those disgusting Eugladians!"

There was an evil laugh. "That will be a fine day! I look forward to it!"

The voices echoed out from a cave that sat ahead to the right. Not speaking to one another, Radianne and Henrick came to a stop and listened.

"All in due time!" an angrier voice bellowed. "Now GET BACK TO WORK!"

Grumbling followed, as well as a scuffling noise and a terrific crash, and then there were stomping feet, as if a giant herd of animals were fast approaching.

Henrick and Radianne looked at each other with terror in their eyes, both thinking the same thing. Time to go – quickly!

"Hurry!" Radianne grabbed Henrick's hand without thinking, and they ran full speed ahead past the cave, Blink once again attached to her hair.

Kicking up clouds of black dust as they fled, they ran down one of the long and snaking trails and headed toward a thicket of decaying trees that would provide adequate shelter for the time being.

That is, if there were no Snorgs lurking about in the shadows.

No sooner had Henrick and Radianne found safety in the cover of the trees than five ugly Snorgs emerged from the cave. The dark-haired, giant lumbering creatures wore scraps of brown leather over their bumpy, prickly bodies. Even from the distance, their stench was nauseating.

The fiends each held two squawking chickens in their hands. They narrowed their soulless black beady eyes at the birds as they walked.

"Stop your yapping!" one Snorg growled, shaking a chicken. "It will do no good. You're done for. "

Peering out from the shadows, Radianne swallowed nervously and watched as the Snorgs approached the steaming black lake. It was difficult to see exactly what was happening from her vantage point, but it was obvious the chickens were intended to be a meal for whatever lived in the bubbling sludge.

Henrick clenched his fists in anger as the scene unfolded; Blink stared with horror etched across his face.

"What sort of creatures are these?!" he exclaimed.

"These are those Snorgs I told you about," Radianne whispered.

As the trolls came to a halt on the bank of the lake, they shouted out something unintelligible. A few moments later, the black water began boiling and smoking, and a two-headed fire crocodile the size of a Thunderfoot surfaced. Smoke flared from its nostrils and it let out a shrill scream.

Radianne bit her lip to keep from screaming herself. The beast was hideous. It snapped its massive jaws against the air, revealing rows of dagger-like teeth. Angrily, it turned both its heads toward the Snorgs, staring them down with four bulging, yellow eyes.

"Here you go Morga! More chickens to feed your belly," one of the Snorgs shouted as it tossed two chickens into the air.

The poultry were promptly scorched as blasts of flames shot out from the creature's two mouths, instantly cooking its dinner. The enormous jaws snapped shut around the birds and swallowed them in one gulp.

Radianne couldn't believe her eyes. A fire-breathing, two-headed crocodile! She wondered where the thing came from. The sight was terrifying.

"Here's more!" a second Snorg shrieked. Feathers flew as the next group of poor, unfortunate chickens were tossed up to their violent and fiery fates.

After the Snorgs fed the chickens to the beast, they stood watching and laughing as the creature slunk back into the blackness. Then they turned and walked back to the cave. They had almost all but disappeared when one fiend paused and looked toward the trees where the trio hid. It sniffed the air.

"Get down!" Radianne said quickly.

She and Henrick squatted and peered through the dark foliage, waiting to see what the troll would do.

It took a few steps down the dusty pathway and and sniffed the air, pausing again.

Holding her breath, Radianne prayed to The Creator that the creature would turn and return to where it came from. After what seemed like an eternity, the Snorg grunted and retreated, disappearing into the black abyss of the cave.

"That was close!" Breathing a sigh of relief, Radianne stood. She turned to look at Henrick. His eyes were full of rage – and, curiously, what seemed to be grief as well. He stared at the lake, transfixed.

Radianne knew in that moment that Henrick's anger and sadness were influenced by much more than the bleakness of the land and the fact that the unfortunate chickens had been sacrificed in such a violent manner.

It was something personal.

Tension was rife in his body. Her eyes trailed down to his hands, one of which was curled tightly around a wicked looking curved dagger.

"Where did you get that?" she demanded, taken aback. Had she known he had been carrying such a nasty looking weapon, she may have really put her foot down at his traveling with them.

Then again, if she was being honest with herself, she was glad –

and a little envious – he had the dagger. She felt a little relieved. Though she would feel even more comfortable with her own weapon...

"Never mind that now," Henrick muttered. "There are much more pertinent matters to worry about."

"Poor little creatures." Blink shook his head sadly, shaken up by the fate that had befallen the chickens. "I've never witnessed such an awful thing in all my life."

Radianne patted and comforted her friend. Stars were such innocent creatures, she was quickly learning. It was a shame his innocence was being ruined in her world. She only hoped his light was strong enough to carry him through all the negative moments.

"Yes, poor chickens," said Henrick, narrowing his eyes. "Yet, that creature has also had many other victims. And it is spawning children in the water with a mate as well, no doubt."

He faced Radianne and Blink. "The Snorgs have to appease the beast or it won't bend to their will. It and its offspring are going to join their army of dark warriors and mind-warped slaves one day in the very near future. May The Creator help us when that day comes... and who knows how many more of these creatures exist."

"How do you know so much about such things?" Radianne questioned, raising an eyebrow. She knew Wanderers did tend to live secret lives and probably could spy and collect a good deal of information, but she was curious.

"Some things are better off not mentioning, at least not for now."

Henrick didn't make eye contact as he said the words; only continued to stare at the lake with hatred in his eyes. After a moment, he turned away.

Though Radianne was not satisfied with his answer, she decided to leave the subject alone. For the moment. As he hadn't known her that long, she knew she couldn't expect an instant explanation when it came to his apparent strong emotions. He didn't owe her that.

Confused by how quickly her feelings toward him fluctuated, she patted Blink. The gesture comforted them both. The electric hum instantly ran up her arm and filled her with warmth. She relaxed a little.

As soon as it was safe, the trio came out of hiding, scanning all directions to make sure there were no Snorgs wandering about.

Radianne continued to fight the battle within herself as they walked, the desolate ambiance of the place relentlessly trying to defeat her own spirit. Shadows and sadness lingered in Henrick's eyes, which didn't help things.

The ugliness of the land didn't change. Bleak and despairing scenery loomed up at every turn, around every corner. It was as if the life and soul of the world had been sucked away.

It was a place, Radianne thought, that seemed without The Creator's touch. As if it had been forsaken and left to the darkness.

Much to her surprise, by nightfall, they arrived at the edge of the center. There were no Snorgs in sight and they had miraculously escaped an encounter.

"We should find shelter, quickly, before Blink's light attracts unwanted attention," Henrick said, as the star's first soft glow began to light up the early evening.

They decided on a small cave – one they thoroughly checked out for Snorgs before entering – and noted how fitting it was that the cave was so much more foreboding than the last one they had spent the night in.

Ugly and bleak seemed to be the theme of the land. There was a sort of blackened fungus growing on the interior walls, and a foul stench filled the cavern air. Blink's soft glow filled up the cave and the flickering condition that he'd previously experienced thankfully did not return.

Radianne supposed Snorgs had spent some time in it not too long ago. Shuddering, she knew there were few additional options, they had to spend the night somewhere, but she didn't like the nearness of their newest quarters to the enemy.

Henrick turned his glo-worm light on for awhile, but when the bouncing shadows made the night seem even more eerie and unsettling, he shut it off.

Radianne watched Blink as he rested in her arms. She reminded herself of the real reason for her journey.

Yet... the doubts crept in. What if she failed in her quest? Her heart sank. What if she let her new friend down? She fought against the negative thoughts as she closed her eyes.

They all had difficulty sleeping that night.

At the first rays of morning light, they were up and eager to move on. They finished crossing the center of Eustasia in a day, without encountering another Snorg. Several more uneventful days were spent in a somewhat healthier looking part of Eustasia. The excitement returned when they came across a lovely river which proved valuable for bathing and filling up the water flask. The shadowed mood and atmosphere began to lift.

It was time to leave Eustasia behind.

-10-
Sandalia

The food ran out the day they crossed into Sandalia – a land of palm trees, sand, and a beautiful clear ocean that stretched on for miles. Radianne felt her spirits rise up completely again, being away from Eustasia, even if the food supply was gone.

"Things do change quite often in the Nether Lands!" she exclaimed with wonder as she watched a bunch of white sea birds squawk and dart into the nearby ocean, splashing around as they hunted for fish.

"This doesn't look like such a bad land, Henrick," she said pointedly, as she took in the sweeping, lovely views of the sea. She turned to her companion. "What about those giant crabs you mentioned before?"

"Well wait until you meet one of those giant Hermits," he shot back teasingly, with a raised eyebrow. His spirits had also seemed to improve. "You'll not mock me then."

As the sun rose high in the sky and the day grew hot, Radianne ran along the beach, kicking up the sand as she went. The run took her back to her younger days, when the charms of Eugladia had been enough for her. When her family had been enough. Back then, her land had seemed to have its own special magic. Everything about her world had seemed interesting in her youth. She smiled and thought of her family as she sifted through the memories.

As she recalled one glorious day spent with her mother picking wildflowers, she wondered when it had all changed.

Discovering new lands and experiences seemed the only thing that would make her happy now.

Would her world ever be the same again? How could she go back to the life she'd lived before? It would seem so boring compared to this... it would seem so unbearable compared to this.

She stretched out her arms and came to a stop. Closing her eyes, she reveled in the feeling of the warm breeze across her face. She opened her eyes and glanced down at Blink, who smiled up at her as he hopped along by her side. She smiled back.

Radianne vowed that after she helped her new friend return to his rightful place in the world, her own journeys would not come to an end.

The adventures were only just beginning.

Maybe she'd become a Wanderer, like Henrick, she thought. Though she still wasn't quite certain of all that a Wanderer was, and, admittedly, she'd criticized him a bit unfairly for having the title. She for one would have to visit her family from time to time...

She wondered how many female Wanderers there were... and if Henrick had befriended any of them. Turning her head, she looked at him then.

He stood a distance away, watching her and Blink walk along the shoreline. His hair blew in the breeze and her heart skipped a beat as she could not help but notice how handsome he looked standing there in the sunlight. How wild and free...

She knew she shouldn't be worried about him, his occupation, or become overly concerned with what he was thinking or doing. Because after all, this was her newfound freedom and adventure. And after all this was over – or maybe even sooner – they'd part ways. This was her time. What she had been searching for. No more simple days in Eugladia, with the same boring routine day after day. Now she had the chance to become something more.

A rush of energy suddenly flowed through her body. Embracing the feeling, she took off running again, nearly leaping into the air, heading straight for the rolling waves of the ocean. Crashing through the cool water, she enjoyed the feel of the spray hitting her legs.

She suddenly thought of Pearl, the mermaid she'd met in Eugladia, and wondered if she would meet one of her ocean sisters. Her fingers trailed along the necklace the lake mermaid had given her and she wished Pearl could be there with her to experience the joys of this particular ocean firsthand. The sea back home was not nearly as beautiful Sandalia's. Pearl would love it...

As Radianne touched the pearls, the waves seemed to suddenly come to life. The water curled up and swirled around her knees in caressing tendrils, as if they were the hands of the ocean itself.

How strange, she thought. It was as if the necklace were somehow connected to the flow of waves.

She dived under the salty water and surfaced, not caring that her clothes were thoroughly drenched. Shaking her wet hair out of her eyes and licking the salty water from her lips, she guiltily searched the shoreline for Blink. Her emotions had overtaken her.

She knew she shouldn't have left him just standing there on the shore, as he seemed to have an aversion to water. But then, there he was.

Henrick stood at his side and she waved.

"Why don't you come in? The water's great!" she shouted.

Henrick shook his head and frowned at her. Blink followed suit.

Radianne thought she was being nice to extend the invitation – and she had thought Henrick's mood had improved, but maybe she was mistaken. It was difficult to understand his feelings.

Shrugging off his downtrodden demeanor for the moment, she went back to swimming. When her limbs grew weary of working through the waves, she trudged back to shore and plopped down on the sand next to Blink. He inched out of reach as the droplets of water fell from her skin.

"That," she said breathlessly, wringing the salt water from her clothes and hair, taking note to do it away from her friend, "was amazing."

"I'm sure." Henrick rolled his eyes.

Radianne didn't like his attitude. "What's wrong with you?" she demanded.

"Nothing." Henrick averted his eyes and set his mouth in a scowl.

Blink said nothing. The interaction of the Eugladians confused him.

After some time, Radianne stood up. She didn't want to be part of Henrick's negativity at the moment and decided she needed time away from him.

"I'm hungry. I'm going to find food," she announced. She turned to her star friend. "Blink, do you want to come with me?"

Blink, suddenly torn between his two companions, shrugged – at least, as much as a star could shrug. He sensed something was wrong with Henrick, and, kind soul that he was, chose to stay by his side.

"OK, well, I'll be back soon," Radianne said. She turned on her heel and walked down the beach.

****

"She is quite a strange girl, you know that?"

Blink was nonchalant at Henrick's words. "I don't know much about girls," he admitted. "But I do know she's my friend. And she rescued me. That's all that really matters, right?"

Henrick smiled a small smile. Personally, he was starting to think Radianne was a little selfish and was too focused on 'having an adventure' and oblivious to dangers and maybe even reality sometimes. But he also knew she had lived a pretty sheltered life and was inexperienced in the ways of the world. That explained a lot about how excited and naive she was.

On the other hand, he had to admit, she did seem kind too and she evidently did care for the star. Blink was right about that. Friendship did matter. Such things in life did count for something, though they were things Henrick himself knew very little about.

He stood and hoisted Blink onto his shoulder. It probably would be best to trail Radianne, even though he was still feeling drained from the soul-sucking experience in Eustasia. Despite the fact the victims were only chickens, it was a cruel reminder. As time went on he tried to put on a happy face, but it was not working. The memories were fresh.

"Let's go make sure she doesn't get into trouble," he mumbled to Blink.

****

In a stroke of luck, later in the day, they came across a crop of trees bearing plentiful coconuts. Radianne managed to shake a few down. She handed one to Henrick and smiled, pleased with herself.

She didn't need him for everything, she thought.

Though the journey into Sandalia had thus far been uneventful, it was during the middle of their meal that the huge Hermit approached.

Radianne was lost in thought, humming a song to herself, and Henrick was daydreaming again, seemingly entranced by the waves of the ocean.

It was Blink who saw the creature appear first.

"Uh-uh-uh," he stuttered, staring at the hulking giant crustacean fast approaching, waving its claws angrily in the air.

Radianne stopped humming. "What is it Blink?"

"Look behind you!"

Radianne and Henrick simultaneously jerked their heads around and opened their mouths in shock. There, hulking above them, stood a giant red Hermit crab, snapping its mighty, murderous-looking claws. Claws that could grind bones to powder in an instant.

The giant crustacean wore an evil smile, saliva dripping from the corners of its black and gaping mouth.

Radianne could feel its fetid breath. The stench and horror of it was too much. Screaming, she stood up.

"No!" Henrick yelled, trying to silence her. "Don't do that Radianne!" He jumped up, pulling his dagger from a hidden pocket.

Continuing to scream, Radianne launched one of the remaining coconuts full force at the huge crab, hitting the beast squarely on the head. The crab made a sort of guttural sound and snapped its claws violently in warning.

Henrick grabbed at Radianne's arms. "Stop it! You're only going to make it angrier."

The words had barely escaped his lips when the giant Hermit suddenly lunged forward and plucked up Radianne swiftly in one claw. It then began waving her around wildly in the air.

"Help me!" she screamed.

"Oh no!" Blink cried. He jumped up and down, his points waving around frantically. "We have do do something Henrick!"

The Wanderer ran alongside the mammoth crab and began pounding on its tough shell with his fists, trying to get the creature to turn its attention to him and drop its prized possession in the sand.

When the assault didn't work, Henrick whipped out the dagger, took a running leap, and jumped onto the creature's back. He then brought the dagger down – hard.

Roaring in pain, the monstrous crustacean bucked as the weapon pierced through its shell. A crunch could be heard as the knife made its way through to the soft flesh beneath. Dropping Radianne onto the beach, the beast furiously shrieked and turned and focused its beady, vacant eyes on Henrick.

Radianne rolled off to one side and and watched in horror as the crab snapped its lethal claws dangerously close to Henrick's head.

It would not happen, she thought. As annoying as he'd been, and even though he'd sabotaged her journey, she had to help. He would not die this day. She had to do something. If only her mind would cooperate…

"Run!" Henrick shouted when he noticed her frozen in place, trying to figure things out. "Don't worry about me, just take Blink and go!"

But Radianne, and Blink – who'd scampered to her side – were immobilized.

Henrick darted through the crab's legs and quickly grabbed Radianne's arm, yanking her to her feet. Grabbing Blink with her free arm, she held him close to her chest as they ran, the giant crab trailing close behind.

"Head for the water," Henrick panted. "For some odd reason, they don't like water. I think because they sink. Ironic, isn't it?"

As they approached the ocean, Blink suddenly wrenched himself out of Radianne's grasp and hurled himself onto the soft sand.

"What are you doing?" Radianne screamed, crashing into the waves. "Come back here!"

But Blink stood his ground on the shore. "I can't go into the water!" he cried.

The beast came to an abrupt stop near Blink and stared down with curiosity at the star.

Radianne and Henrick watched the scene unfold with terror on their faces, knee-deep in the ocean and out of ideas.

Time seemed to stand still. And then...

Blink bravely looked up at the crab and raised his voice. "You can try to eat me, but I'll taste awful!" he warned.

The crustacean looked at him with confusion.

"I have no insides, only star particles," the star continued. "I don't know what will happen if you eat me. Maybe you'll turn into a star yourself, or worse. Maybe I'm poisonous and will kill you, maybe you will explode into a thousand pieces."

The crab seemed at a loss of what to think for a few moments. However, it apparently soon decided to take its chances, as if the thought of a bite of star might not be a bad idea. It lunged toward Blink, saliva dripping down its mouth in anticipation once again.

Blink stumbled as he tried to move out of range from the snapping claws.

Radianne thought quickly. *The mermaid's gift.*

Touching the pearl necklace again, she watched as the waves swirled high around her body, taking on a life of their own.

Henrick watched the scene unfold in amazement.

"My friend is in danger," Radianne said to the ocean waves, which lapped playfully around her waist. "I would appreciate it if you would help us."

She gestured to the beach, where the crab was still flailing its claws around at Blink. "Please drag that horrible monster out to sea."

She no sooner had said the words then the waves swelled and roared, flowing toward shore. As they approached the crab, Blink moved quickly out of the way and the crustacean stared in shock at the towering wall of water.

Suddenly, what appeared to be an enormous hand made of sea foam rose out from the center of the waves and lunged forward, plucking up the crab by its shell.

The crustacean shrieked an ear splitting shriek as it was pulled into the sea against its will. It fought, snapping its claws into the air in protest, but to no avail. Within seconds the waves had taken it far away from shore, past Radianne and Henrick, pulling it into a deeper part of the ocean, where it soon was engulfed by foam and sank out of sight.

Everything had happened so fast that the three travelers were left completely in shock. The ocean returned back to normal almost instantly and Radianne gazed at her pearl necklace with wonder. She touched the waves in gratitude.

"Thank you," she whispered. "And thank you, Pearl."

Looking up, she found Henrick staring at her, also apparently awestruck for the moment.

"A gift from a mermaid," was all she said. She laughed and quickly made her way back to the beach, back to Blink.

"You are so brave, you wonderful star!" Radianne scooped him up into her arms and planted a kiss on his top point. "I was so worried about you! I'm sorry we fled into the water like that."

"It is understandable, you were scared," Blink said. "I'm just glad that thing around your neck came in handy!"

"But I'm a little confused," Radianne continued. "What happens if you go into the water, Blink? You should have told me your concerns before."

The star frowned. "The Man In The Moon said that if a star became water bound, he would automatically disappear in a puff of smoke. I don't want to to find out if that's true!"

Radianne held him close. "I'm sorry we didn't know that," she said apologetically.

She then turned her attention to Henrick, who had joined them. "And I'm sorry I screamed like I did when we first saw the crab. We could have all been killed."

"I did the same thing the first time I saw one." Henrick ran his fingers through his wet hair, still feeling a little stressed and amazed from the ordeal that had just transpired. "And almost met my death in the process. We were lucky this time. Let's just move on."

As they walked, he pointed out huge holes in the beach – dark, foreboding, and mysterious caves where slumbering giant hermit crabs probably lurked. But thankfully, by nightfall, they hadn't encountered another of the unpleasant species.

"Last time I was here, I had to fight off three of those things at once," Henrick said nonchalantly.

"And how did you do that?" Radianne asked him with a raised eyebrow. She wondered if he was exaggerating or simply trying to brag. "With that flimsy dagger you carry?" she teased. "That sounds a little unbelievable to me."

Henrick made a face at her comments. "Well, obviously they are too big for the dagger to do much damage, although it did seem to work at one point today, if I recall," he added. "Last time, I climbed up the largest tree I could find and then I hurled coconuts at their eyes."

"Well then why did you shout at me when I threw coconuts today?" Radianne asked, annoyed.

"Because you weren't at a safe distance and you were also screaming your head off," Henrick retorted. "The sound of you screaming is more irritating than dealing with the Oodles. I figured all that noise would enrage the crab more than anything else."

Radianne put her hands on her hips. She thought he had some nerve. Sure, he had saved her, but once again, he was being rude. Maybe being a Wanderer so long had done something to his head to make him say the things he did, she thought. Maybe he lacked the skills to communicate properly.

She said nothing as they began to collect branches from ocean shrubs that grew nearby. They arranged them for the fire on a cleared area of beach.

"This will help keep the Hermits at bay," Henrick said matter-of-factly as he started up the flame a few moments later.

Radianne didn't comment.

Night fell and the trio sat by the warm flames in silence. After some time, Radianne and Blink curled up together on the sand, gazing up at the sky and admiring its beauty.

"I miss home," Blink said quietly. "I miss my mother."

Radianne thought of Blink's mother pining away for him somewhere in his world and felt very humbled and sad. She could only imagine how she must feel.

Though she didn't want to admit it, at that moment she too was starting to slightly feel a little homesick. The elation she'd felt when she'd first run along the beach had diminished. The encounter with the crab reminded her how dangerous adventures could be and how so many things could go wrong in an instant.

She wondered how long she had been away now. Time was slipping by, days were jumbled together. Was her family looking for her? She wondered how Piri was, and if her friend had managed to tame Maiz's wild heart yet.

For that brief instant, she longed for those simple, boring days and girl talk. The feeling surprised her.

But despite such thoughts, she knew she had made the right choice in leaving. She was helping a friend in need; she had to help Blink get home. *He needed her.* That was the most important thing. And, as she'd reflected on earlier at the beach, it was the first time in her life she could make a difference. *And* she was actually having an adventure. A real adventure.

"You will see your mother soon Blink," she whispered to the star, focusing on the most important matter at hand. "I promise." Bending down, she kissed him again and he closed his eyes. His light still shined; he hadn't any issues with it since that first night in Eustasia. She hoped their luck would hold.

Cautiously, she glanced over at Henrick.

The firelight flickered across his handsome, chiseled face as he stared out into the darkness, the light casting deep shadows across his skin. It seemed he was thinking about something important again – or brooding. She couldn't yet tell the difference with him. She wondered if the odd moods were always present.

Sensing her gaze, he suddenly turned his eyes to her. "And what is on your mind? You doing alright?" he asked.

His words surprised her. There he was, acting mightily interested in her well-being again. Even though he'd offended her earlier, as their eyes locked, her heart betrayed her again and skipped a beat.

For a moment, the strange feeling she'd felt with him the day they met came rushing back. Her skin felt hot under his gaze. She blushed, thankful it was too dark for him to see. She hated to admit it, but as crazy as he made her feel, her resentment of him was slowly vanishing the more time she spent with him. The acknowledgement, coupled with the irritation she'd been feeling all day at his shifting moods, left her very confused. Weary even.

"I'm fine," she said, looking away. She lay down and closed her eyes. At least she could pretend to sleep.

****

Radianne was confusing, one minute acting like she hated him, the next moment, acting like a bashful young girl, Henrick mused. *Such strange mood swings.*

As he looked at her then, in that moment it was unsettling that all he could see was how beautiful she was. Radianne looked like a giant-sized fairy. A complicated, but beautiful, fairy.

He'd met the cheeky creatures in the woods sometimes during his travels. Fairies were flirtatious, ridiculous and mysterious all at once – with a little bit of naivety thrown in. Kind of like Radianne, he thought.

He had a sudden urge to kiss her. What would she do if he tried? He'd seen many beautiful women in his life, despite being a Wanderer. He had even had wooed a lady or two, but Radianne was different than anyone he'd met. Even though she had her quirks, he was starting to think he liked her combination.

However, he also knew such thoughts were foolish. Turning his eyes to the fire, he thought about what he was going to do after this spontaneous journey he'd invited himself on was over. He'd been without friends or family for so long. He didn't really know what to do about his growing feelings for Radianne and Blink. Yes, he was starting to care for the star too. Wanderers were not made for such ties.

"You are a foolish person, Henrick Longfellow," he mumbled to himself. "What were you thinking anyway? You have no direction, no path, and nothing to offer anyone. You were born to be a Wanderer. You were born for a solitary life. Always alone. No attachments. That's a Wanderer's world. Solitude is your fate."

Looking down at the girl again, he tried to burn the moment into memory. He would one day remember in his old age a point in time when a stunning young woman lay next to flickering flames and a golden star, the firelight and the star's gentle glow casting lovely shadows across her smooth skin.

The images of Radianne and Blink would remain with him forever. They were magical.

He looked up a the sky with a quiet sigh. Staring at Blink's beautiful and far off world, Henrick wondered where fate in his own world would lead him next.

Part II

-11-
Confessions

As they trudged through the vast land of sand, another giant hermit crab walked by.

For a moment, the trio braced themselves for an intense altercation. But the crab just grunted and said "No appetite," as it passed.

Radianne stared after its retreating back, dumbfounded. "That's odd," she said. Still, it was a relief not have to deal with another battle all over again.

"It is indeed a strange day when a carnivorous crab decides not to eat you for lunch," Henrick shrugged, glancing sideways at Radianne and giving a small smile. "Maybe it's a sign of good luck to come."

The hours passed uneventfully. Radianne thought it strange, but Sandalia seemed pretty devoid of life other than the occasional giant crabs. As the air began to cool with the onset of evening, the group settled down in another comfortable looking spot to set up camp and eat. They ate more of the coconuts they'd gathered along the way.

"Sandalia is quite a small place," Henrick shared as he started the fire again. "We should be arriving in Vancor, otherwise known as the land of the endless jungle, by tomorrow morning. It is only endless to those who don't know the way. And I of course, do, so the journey through should be swift."

Radianne wanted to roll her eyes. But instead, she looked at Blink, who sat nearby. She had not assessed his physical ailments in some time and scanned him then, with a guilty conscience. He still appeared to be in decent shape, but she noticed that over the course of the afternoon his chatter had become less frequent and he seemed to be growing a little weaker and slightly listless. He sat quietly, his glow just beginning to pierce through the falling darkness. She noted there was a dimness to it and she thought back to the night in Eustasia, when his light began to pulse wildly. She hoped that wasn't about to happen again. She prayed it wouldn't.

Scooting over to him, she patted her friend as he curled up next to her side. As he closed his eyes, she stroked him gently, feeling the strange star vibrations run up and down her arm. She shivered at the warm glow and felt her spirits lifting, as they always did when she touched him.

The fact that the odd connection was still there was a good sign. She watched Blink sleep for a few moments and then glanced over at Henrick. As usual, he seemed lost in thought.

He was proving to be too much of a distraction. Irritated with herself again for wondering about him, she turned her eyes toward the stars. She *had* to think about Blink first and foremost. Her focus had to be on her friend and getting him home.

And then she could figure out what she was going to do with her life after the quest came to an end.

But she couldn't resist another glimpse. An uncomfortable feeling fluttered in her chest as she cast another sidelong glance over to Henrick, feeling guilty that her thoughts were drawn once more to this stranger she'd met not that long ago.

His hair looked ethereal in the moonlight. She'd always expected Wanderers to look rough and menacing. Nothing like that man sitting before her.

He caught her looking. Again. The flush rose to her cheeks. Feeling ridiculous, she darted her eyes away in embarrassment. The feeling was truly getting old.

"Radianne," Henrick said slowly, "your family is probably very worried about you. At their wits end most likely. How do you feel about that?"

His eyes locked on hers over the flicker of the flames.

She looked away and pretended to brush sand off her legs. It was a struggle to find the right words. She didn't want him to know that she had already been experiencing the first real pangs of homesickness. It was bad enough she'd appeared weak in so many other areas...

Clearing her throat, she opened her mouth. "Yes. Well. I'm an adult now. And Blink's family is probably worried about him too. I'm all he has at the moment, so getting him home is what I have to focus on. He is my priority."

If only you weren't complicating things, she added, silently.

They both stared at the flames, watching them rise. After a little while, the silence grew uncomfortable.

Radianne decided to be bold. It was her turn to ask the questions.

"Henrick?"

"Yes?"

"Where were you going when I met you back in Eugladia?"

He rubbed his neck and looked away.

"I already told you. Anywhere. Everywhere."

He shifted and Radianne could tell he was very uncomfortable with the conversation.

"I'm not one to sit still. I like to float around, like the wind. There's nothing like chasing the wind. I can't be tied down. No other freedom like chasing the wind."

He said the last words firmly, as if to convince himself he wholeheartedly believed in what he was saying.

Chasing the wind. Radianne's heart thudded in her ears, skipping around wildly.

All those conversations she and her mother had often shared about such things... how she'd always thought chasing the wind had sounded wonderful, though her mother would disagree. And now, someone else was confirming that chasing one's dreams could indeed be a wonderful thing. Sharing her exact thoughts.

But did he really believe that? Radianne wondered. She knew Henrick wasn't telling her a lot of the story. She was not that naive. He was trying to escape something. His moods certainly gave that away.

She was quiet for some time as her mind drifted once more to her life back home and the many nights she'd dreamed of escaping it. The idea of "floating around" had sounded so romantic and adventurous, as she'd always thought, but then again, she'd always been in one stable place and had the luxury of a family who loved her. Had she taken all of that for granted?

Henrick, on the other hand, lived a lonely life it seemed.

What if she hadn't had her family and all the comforts that a routine existence could bring? Would the thought of chasing the wind seem so appealing then? Or would the idea just seem empty and pointless?

She rubbed her hands along her arms to comfort herself and ease the confusion swirling around inside. A slight ache moved through her heart when she thought of home now.

Was that how if felt to be a Wanderer? To ache for something you couldn't have? Were they all just lost souls, looking for their places in the world?

If she was starting to feel such things after such a short time away, how must Henrick feel? How long had he felt the sting of loneliness and longing?

And yet – as she listened to the sound of the crashing waves of the ocean, she also could not deny the other powerful feelings she was experiencing at the moment. Though she truly was starting to miss the comforts of home and the familiarity of her family, there was something deeply enticing about the wildness and the unknown. She couldn't deny it. Adventure had gotten under her skin. She supposed that was a big attraction for Wanderers as well.

She'd felt such powerful freedom several times already – when she'd first found Blink, while dancing with the giant flowers in Eustasia, when riding the Gentle Giant… getting lost in a moment in the ocean waves.

Looking to Henrick again, she felt the uncomfortable feelings return. Was this part of it? Were these silly feelings and this attraction simply part of becoming an adult? Newfound freedoms and the desire for new experiences?

He was new, interesting. That's all. She could not help but be intrigued. So why was she also suddenly so afraid of him?

Maybe, she thought, maybe such things weren't to be feared. Even if she'd never had those kind of feelings for a man before. Such feelings were an experience, after all.

All the thoughts racing through her head at that moment made it hurt. And worst of all was the sudden urge to move closer to Henrick and rest her head on his shoulder. But she pushed it away.

Blink was the priority.

"Well," she said to Henrick, drawing him back into conversation once more, "what about your family? Somewhere out there, you must also have someone, or some people, missing you. Don't you?"

The words hung in the air on a question voiced with hope. She waited, praying he was not truly alone in the world.

But his face turned stony, his eyes grew hard and cold. He clenched his jaw, and she could tell that she had struck a nerve.

Heart sinking, she tried to quickly think of something to say, anything to stop him from feeling like he had to explain, but the words wouldn't come fast enough.

"You want to know a little bit about me and my past Radianne?" He lowered his voice and leaned toward her with narrowed eyes. "Maybe then you will realize not everything in this world is sunshine and rainbows. So be it."

There was a terrible pause. It suddenly seemed as if a dark shadow had fallen over their camp. Henrick did not speak for a few minutes, and then when he did, the words came out sharply.

"My entire family is dead."

Shocked, Radianne brought one hand to her mouth. Her heart seemed to drop to her toes and through the ground. She shouldn't have pried. She shouldn't have pushed him as it was none of her concern.

"They died when I was thirteen," Henrick continued, his voice hard and angry. "I've been a Wanderer ever since."

He stopped talking again and stared into the night. He was suddenly far away, lost in the past and an unpleasant moment in time, remembering.

"We were on our way to Shondalina – my mother, father, sister and I…" He paused, taking a deep breath. "My parents loved to travel, unlike most Eugladians. They thought it would be a great experience for us."

There was another pause before he continued. "It happened in Eustasia. This was back when the Snorgs were first starting to cause trouble, but before they'd really taken over The Center. There we were, laughing and walking through The Center, recalling fond memories. Then we walked past that black lake of death."

Silence again. Radianne was surprised he was sharing his story. She knew that what he was about to reveal was very difficult and she hugged herself for comfort, bracing for the rest of the terrible tale.

"The beast came out of the darkness and attacked my father, carrying him off screaming into that bubbling blackness. It was a young monster then, but still powerful."

Several emotions flickered over his face as he recalled the memories and the horror of the dark day his family had been taken from him.

"We could not help him. We could not do anything but stand there in terror, screaming his name. Then the Snorgs came, several of them," he continued. "My mother told my sister and I to run and I argued with her, but as she screamed at me to run again, some primal instinct kicked in and I listened. Like a coward. But my mom and little sister – they didn't get away quickly enough. They couldn't keep up with me. The Snorgs killed them. I heard them screaming, their shrieks piercing the air as their lives were taken."

Henrick seemed to gasp for breath for a moment. As if the mere fact he was breathing – and his father, mother, and sister weren't – was a truth too painful for him to endure.

"I left them," he choked out. "Like a coward. I left them." He lowered his head into his hands. "I could not save any of them. I failed."

Radianne slowly let out the breath she'd been holding in.

His tragic story had all come out in a rush. She felt ill as she took in the magnitude of what Henrick had just revealed to her. His life made sense now. Yet, it was more information than she'd bargained for.

She hadn't meant to bring back such painful memories... she couldn't imagine what she would have done if something like that had happened to her family... how different her life would have been.

"I traveled on to Shondalina, dragging myself forward somehow," Henrick continued quietly.

Once he started to share his story, it was as if a dam had released water that had been pent up for far too long. Henrick wasn't sure why, but when he'd started to tell Radianne the truth, he couldn't stop. He'd carried his secrets inside too long and they had been killing him.

"Though I was young, I didn't care what dangers awaited me," he said. "I thought the Winged Ones would help me wage a war against the Snorgs. After all, we'd all heard the stories of their valiant natures as children. But even though they pitied me and my situation, they would not help my cause. They said the time had not yet come for such actions."

He looked up at the stars as he continued.

"At first, I was angry with them, but they treated me with kindness. The Winged Ones told me I could stay in their kingdom for as long as I wished. But I left. I vowed I would get my revenge on the Snorgs. I would go back and kill that beast, make it pay for what it had done to my father. I would then get rid of the Snorgs, one by one, in payback for what they'd done to my mother and sister.

"But when I returned to the black lake and hid in the shadows, observing, I found I was greatly outnumbered by Snorgs," he continued. "I plotted and bid my time. I watched them gather. But their number was massive and alone I knew I couldn't handle them. I'd have to wait until I had an army, or I'd join up with an army aimed at dismantling them."

He turned to Radianne.

"To my ultimate shame, that day has not come. There are no Wanderers who wish to rise to the challenge. The Snorgs are feared more than you know. But the war will happen. Soon. Don't take the Snorgs lightly, as you seem to do. You really have no idea how many of them there are. They are like roaches. You have no idea of the things I saw when I went back…" he trailed off. "I had no choice but to run for my life, putting revenge on hold until I knew the right time had come and I could recruit an army. But I did, and still do, feel like a coward for that as well. For not exacting my revenge at that precise moment in time."

"Does that satisfy you?" he whispered, anger and hurt stirring in his eyes. "Is that what you wanted to hear Radianne? That I'm a failure without a family? A failure of a man, and not a hero? Does it help justify those first thoughts you had about me? That I'm just a strange Wanderer with no direction in life?"

He held her gaze and waited for a response, his eyes burning into hers.

As her heart pounded in her chest, Radianne found that for the first time, she couldn't look away. She was so caught up in his angry passion, and the hate and pain that seemed to radiate from his body filled her eyes with tears as she thought of his great and terrible loss.

"I-I'm sorry." She managed to tear her gaze away and looked down at the sand. Her fingers toyed with the grains nervously. "It was none of my business. I'm very sorry for prying and for the loss of your family. I cannot imagine what I would do in such circumstances."

She paused for a moment.

"But you have to know, it was also not your fault," she continued. "There was unfortunately nothing you could do in those circumstances."

"If you say so. Well, one day I will have my revenge. I will make up for my cowardice." Henrick pounded a fist on the sand, as if sealing a vow. "Mark my words. Now if you don't mind, I think that's enough of the questioning for tonight."

He turned his face and body away from her then, closing his eyes, shutting her out.

Radianne sat in the darkness, confused by the sudden turn of events.

She felt sorry for him but also knew Henrick had to deal with his pain instead of burying it deep inside. The emotions were eating him alive. It was not his fault, but he obviously had not made peace with the fact he could not have prevented the incident. She figured he probably wouldn't, until his revenge against the Snorgs and their fiendish pet was complete.

Would it even be possible, she wondered... to gather an army? He said there were no Wanderers willing. She knew the Thunderfeet probably would be willing to help, but word was that they were waiting until the right time to launch a full-out attack themselves. Just like the Winged Ones.

Everyone was waiting. Always waiting for something bigger to happen. As she had been on that night Blink fell from the sky. The whole journey had begun because she wanted to help Blink find his way back home to the stars. But she also discovered so much more was taking place along the way. There was so much more out there than the life she knew.

She was learning much more about her world than she'd bargained for... including the darkness and horrible secrets it held. She was being forced to confront some difficult life truths. *Things she hadn't wanted to think about.* Like that fact that the Snorgs were more of an enemy than she'd given them credit for.

Suddenly, she was exhausted. Lowering her body to the sand, she rested her head next to Blink. His light comforted her in the darkness.

She would help him find his way home. And then – maybe – she would also find a way to help Henrick, if it were even possible.

-12-
In The Jungle

Opening one eye, and then the other, Radianne gazed up at a perfectly blue sky. Perhaps the loveliness of it would bode well for the day ahead, she thought.

Stretching, she rolled over onto her back and tried not to let the memory of the conversation she'd shared with Henrick the night before ruin the start of her day. As dismal as it had been, she had to remain positive. Especially for Blink.

As she turned her head to look at her star friend and check on his well-being, there was a loud moan to her left. Startled, she sat up.

There was Henrick, lying right beside her.

How had that happened, she wondered? She scooted away quickly, as if burned by fire.

He had turned away, she fell asleep… wait a minute… she recalled a vague memory of Henrick crying out in the middle of the night. No doubt reliving the horrors of this past in this dreams.

She'd gone over to comfort him, to set a reassuring hand on his back the way her mother had done for her when she'd had nightmares as a child. It was the only thing she could think of to do.

Radianne supposed she had drifted off right next to him during the night. So it was her fault...

As he opened his eyes, she jumped up. She hoped he wouldn't remember the night before.

In an attempt to appear nonchalant, she raised her arms over her head and stretched again. Then yawned. She would pretend everything was normal and well. Speaking of well... she quickly looked to Blink once again make sure her friend was still in good health.

With relief, she noted he still seemed to be in good spirits, sitting and drawing star shapes in the sand, humming a song to himself. His weak states were coming and going, but at least his glow was still holding out strong.

She started to prepare some of the coconuts they'd gathered for breakfast. As she and Henrick ate, they talked about the day's plans.

Much to her relief, Henrick seemed to forget all he'd revealed the night before, for the time being. She wanted to help him but she wasn't sure how, and she was still sorting her feelings out about the matter. It was all so tragic.

"So do you suppose we will make it to the jungle today?" Radianne asked him.

Though at first his knowledge had seemed annoying and sometimes boastful, she was beginning to find all he knew very useful.

"Almost certain," he said.

And indeed, several uneventful hours later, the trio arrived in Vancor.

The jungle of Vancor was dense and humid, a tangled mess of varying green hues. It was a feral place. Lush trees grew in wild clusters amid plants that seemed to sparkle under the dimly lit canopy.

There were numerous exotic animal and insect species, and Radianne, of course, found them all to be quite fascinating.

Her usual awe was short-lived, however, when a chubby blue bug she'd thought looked so adorable suddenly sank sharp little teeth into her hand and drew out bright red droplets of blood.

"Oww!" she cried, swatting the insect away.

"Welcome to the endless jungle of Vancor," Henrick announced, as he also swatted at a shiny red bug that promptly landed on his arm. Grabbing a large branch that had fallen nearby, he began to clear a path for them to progress through the foliage, beating at the dense vegetation as they went.

"Endless Jungle?" Blink asked Henrick, as he sat on Radianne's shoulder. "Why is this place endless?"

"Endless," Henrick pressed on with another whack of his stick, "unless you are an expert in the wild, like I am. Have no fear Blink. It's just a name given to this place to strike terror into the hearts of those who dare venture in. This jungle will not get the better of us. I've come through here several times. We will be out soon enough, without incident."

Ughh," Radianne joked. "Someone is very sure of himself."

She knew it was a facade even though he seemed to have left his anger and sadness and self-perceptions of failure behind in Sandalia.

He bottled things up so easily. She supposed it was how he had to deal with things. Burying the pain, forgetting, pretending all was well. Just so he could survive one more day.

Though his shifting moods were bothersome, she was coming to understand that Henrick was really a hurting person trying to find his way in a world that had suddenly and violently left him alone. She suspected maybe not all Wanderers were so strange after all. Just misunderstood.

Henrick cast her a haughty look and raised an eyebrow. "Don't you know how utterly lost you would be without me? You should be forever grateful."

Radianne made a gagging sound. But secretly, she knew there was truth to what he said. Even though she knew he was teasing her, she did feel very inexperienced and she had to admit she would probably still be stuck somewhere barely outside of Eugladia if it hadn't been for him.

She still had yet to make her own weapon and was quite ashamed of this fact. Though she would never share the revelation with him, of course.

"Well," she said with a sniff, "I am grateful. I suppose."

"You are?" Henrick pretended to be shocked. "I can't believe I'm hearing such words come from you."

Blink laughed, apparently amused by the conversation.

"Yes. Thank you." Radianne did a little curtsy. "But don't let it go to your head. If that thing gets any bigger, it will definitely float away. Although," she paused for a moment and rubbed her chin, pretending to be deep in thought. "That might be a good idea actually. Let it inflate. Maybe then you can carry Blink home!"

Henrick chuckled and shook his head. They continued deeper into the jungle.

The world under the trees was shady and the air felt cool, warm and moist all at once. Radianne marveled at the wonders of the jungle, though did tire of constantly having to swat bugs away as she walked. A large green beetle waddled up her arm and she promptly plucked it off, tossing it to the ground. It shimmered as it ran off.

"Kind of disgusting and beautiful at the same time," she murmured.

"They're just curious," Henrick said. "Come on. A girl like you?

Such an adventurer? You shouldn't be put off my a mere beetle."

Radianne rolled her eyes and smiled.

They continued walking for hours, taking in the jungle's unusual sights as they went.

Once, they came across an odd hairy yellow tree that grew luscious pink fruit and they stopped to eat some of it. The fruit was the sweetest Radianne had ever tasted, and she would never forget its deliciousness. Even if the tree had looked unsettling.

They trod over giant tree stumps and through bright green, dew-covered brush and vines that threatened to tangle up their legs. Mushrooms in all colors of the rainbow sprouted up here and there, and thankfully, none of them were topped with ugly little insects or smelled bad.

Monkeys swung overhead, making shrieking sounds as they passed. Radianne and Blink were captivated by the creatures, and Radianne almost stumbled more than once as they stared up at the trees to take in their antics.

"We need to find a place to camp for the night, while it is still somewhat light out," Henrick said. "Never mind those monkeys. They can be cheeky little thieving beasts. And all sorts of nasty things come out and about in these parts at night."

Seemingly as comfortable in this new environment as he'd been in the others, Henrick led the way to yet another cave hidden away near a jungle waterfall, complete with a small pool.

Radianne supposed Henrick spent a good deal of his life living in caves, which was why he could spot them so easily.

The cave and its surroundings were glorious. "How beautiful," she whispered, as they walked past the sparkling blue waterfall and into the moss-covered cavern. "This is the most beautiful place!"

Henrick smirked. He had known she would say that. Every place seemed beautiful to her. He opened his mouth to say something sarcastic, as he usually did, but just then she turned to him and hugged him.

The gesture surprised both of them. They both stilled for a moment, startled. Just as quickly as she'd embraced him, she pulled away.

Radianne ignored how warm and happy she'd felt when she'd hugged him. Instead, she focused her attention on Blink. "What do you think of our new quarters?"

"Quite lovely. I will have many stories to tell of such wondrous places when I get back to the sky," the star said quietly.

They settled into the mossy cave, which came complete with a perfect view of the waterfall, and shared stories together as the day grew older.

Some time later Radianne said she wanted to take a walk before the sun set. She also wanted to fill up the water flask. She stood.

"Wait, I'll come with you," Henrick was up on his feet in a flash, before she could protest.

She shrugged. "OK." Turning to Blink, she asked him if he'd like to come as well.

"No, I think I will stay here and just enjoy the view," he said. He still hadn't gotten over his fear of water and he was trying to conserve his ever-waning energy.

Radianne and Henrick walked out of the cave and down to the grassy bank situated beside the small pool.

"Do you suppose there are giant water snakes in there?" Radianne asked, as she stopped and stared into the water. She imagined all kinds of horrible creatures that could potentially be lurking beneath. Though the waterfall was a sparkling blue, the depths were also somewhat murky where it pooled. How deep they were, one could only guess.

Henrick stopped beside her. "Yes. And they are huge. Last time I was here I decided to go for a swim and a large black snake came after me with this giant gaping mouth and razor sharp, venomous fangs. I escaped the bite of death just in time."

Eyes wide, Radianne looked at him, and then back at the water, with horror. "How awful. And here I thought this was such a lovely place."

"You think every place is lovely," Henrick laughed. "Appearances can be deceiving you know."

A devious thought suddenly crossed his mind. It would just be a little joke, he thought. Harmless, really. She wanted adventure, he thought, she was going to get it!

"The snakes especially like to eat young ladies," he continued, and before he could second-guess himself, he gave Radianne a little push into the lake.

With a giant splash, Radianne fell.

When she surfaced, she unleashed some of the most ear-splitting shrieks Henrick had ever heard in his life. She flailed around as if she were drowning, crying out about water snakes.

He stood on the grassy bank, doubled over in laughter.

"Help me! Help me!" Radianne screamed.

In the distance, Henrick could see Blink appear at the mouth of the cave, obviously concerned by his friend's screams. He waved at the star to reassure him that all was well and figured he better quiet her down before she attracted undue attention from real nefarious jungle dwellers.

Radianne felt like she was going to die at any moment. She floundered in the water, struggling to swim to the grassy bank. Panic had gotten the best of her and she was sure she would meet her doom. She screamed again at the very idea of it, her adrenaline and temper roaring to life. She couldn't believe Henrick had pushed her in. Anger giving her a sudden burst of energy, she forcefully propelled herself through the water and flung her body up onto the bank. Shaking in both rage and terror, she remained there for several moments, soaking wet in the tall green grass.

Henrick walked over and stared down at her with a huge grin on his face. He continued to laugh as she glared up at him with narrowed eyes. She could have been strangled to death and he thought the situation was funny!?

"You horrible, horrible beast of a boy! You could have killed me!" Radianne jumped up then, fists clenched, eyes flashing, hair dripping. "And this whole time, you've been acting like you wanted to help me! Maybe you actually want me to die. Maybe, you want to take Blink away from me for some corrupt reason!"

The color drained from her face as she thought of Henrick betraying her in such a manner. She knew the thoughts were probably irrational, but she felt a little out of sorts at the moment. Darting a frantic look toward the cave, she was slightly comforted by the sight of the little star waving to her.

She waved back. Then she turned and glared daggers at Henrick again. "Why did you do it? I could have been killed!"

"Calm down, Radianne." Henrick sighed and took a step closer to her, shaking his head at her frazzled and ridiculous thoughts. However, he couldn't help but also notice how especially fetching she looked in her rage. "It was just a joke. I made that story up."

Radianne scowled. He lied? That made things even worse, she thought. She wondered how she could trust him when it came to anything then. She told him as much.

"What else have you been lying about? That was horrible of you Henrick!"

Nerves had weakened her legs, so Radianne had to sit down.

Lowering herself again to the grass, she took a deep breath. She was so embarrassed for screaming the way she had, but she also knew it was justified. She sat with her head in her hands and tried to take deep breaths to calm her frazzled spirits.

As if finally realizing just how unhappy he'd made her, Henrick sat down beside her and attempted to make amends.

"I'm sorry," he said quietly. "I suppose I just wanted to lighten the mood a bit. Things have been getting too intense. What with last night's revelations and all…"

The breeze picked up. Radianne shivered as it rippled against her damp skin. Her anger faded a little, as she thought about his confession the night before.

They were both quiet for a few moments.

Henrick spoke first. "Thanks for trying to be a friend last night," he offered. "I haven't shared what happened with anyone before. In fact, I haven't talked to anyone much these last several years. So I apologize if my moods are a bit shifty and my conversational skills aren't always the best. I'm still trying to make sense of it all and figure out where my future is headed."

Radianne knew she was supposed to be annoyed with him at the moment – for good reason – but there he'd gone and changed the mood once again.

"Sure. No problem," she replied, even if still a bit miffed, and looked at the water.

Once again, she was feeling sorry for him. When just a moment before she'd been so angry she could have slapped him. She wondered how she was supposed to continue to travel with such a person when her emotions seemed to be in constant turmoil in his presence. From the moment she'd met him, he'd turned everything upside down.

"I really am sorry," Henrick reached out and touched her hand then, a gesture which surprised her and sent a kind of tingle up her arm. "I would have never let you fall into that water if I truly thought it was dangerous. And I'm sorry for lying about the snake story. I have not lied about anything else. Will you forgive me?"

She looked up and his blue eyes met her green. She blushed. Again.

Reaching out with his free hand, Henrick gently tilted her chin up with one finger and moved his face toward hers before she knew what was happening.

She froze and did not turn away as she usually did.

Henrick moved closer.

"I'm sorry," he whispered again.

As he brought his lips down to hers, Radianne melted into the kiss, all anger and confusion momentarily being shuffled to the back of her mind.

In that moment, she couldn't think of anything except how nice the kiss felt. It was like nothing she'd experienced before. It was like a dance...

Though the sun was fading and the sky growing dark, her world lit up in that moment. It was, for Radianne, another moment of pure magic and light.

Henrick pulled her closer in an embrace, encircling her with his strong arms as he held her against his chest. She could feel his heart pressed against hers, thudding loudly, matching the wild beat of her own. They held each other for another moment, and then she pulled away.

"Uh, I'm, uh sorry..." Henrick trailed off.

At a loss for words herself, Radianne clumsily struggled to her feet, not sure why, exactly. She felt dizzy.

Henrick stood as well, but he seemed equally as awkward.

"It's getting dark," he managed to say. "We had better be getting back."

He reached out a hand to her. She placed her fingers in his, timidly.

They found their balance again. Hand in hand, the two of them walked back to the cave. Back to Blink.

-13-

The Floppersnogs

Blink watched in horror as Henrick pushed Radianne into the water. She soon surfaced and screamed and he prepared himself to go to her rescue. Somehow. Even if he was afraid of water, he would save his friend.

He may not be a strong star, but he knew one thing. If Henrick was hurting Radianne, Blink would be valiant and fight! He would also bite!

But then – something strange happened.

Radianne climbed up onto the grass and was still for a time, and then she yelled at Henrick again. And then – then Blink watched as the the two of them brought their faces close together and embraced.

How peculiar, he thought. Were they in love? But how could that be? They always seemed so angry with each other.

His thoughts drifted to stars back home. When two stars were in love, they aligned. But stars had to control their passions. If stars ever got too angry or heated up, they could explode into a supernova. He'd seen it happen once or twice when a star had allowed jealousy to get the best of them when it came to romance.

Frowning, Blink studied what was happening between Radianne and Henrick more closely. He could see sparks flying between them. Hopefully, nothing catastrophic would happen because of that strange moment they'd shared.

When they began walking back toward the cave, hand in hand, Blink moved away from the entrance. These Eugladians were quite interesting, and very confusing, he thought.

****

Radianne woke up to what sounded like an angry beast growling loudly at the mouth of the cave.

Quickly, she sat up. Though she was still half asleep, she could make out the hulking, shadowy shape of the creature crouching just ahead, its form blocking out the morning light.

A scream escaped from her lips. She couldn't help it. There, at the entrance to the cave, was an enormous black jungle cat, barring the way out. The beast stared at the intruders in its midst with narrowed and evil-looking yellowed eyes.

Henrick woke at once, jumping up and ready to fight.

"Stay calm," he said, seemingly trying to prove his manliness in the situation, though it was evident his nerves were frayed.

Radianne rolled her eyes. "I think you are the one who needs to stay calm," she hissed.

Blink, also awake, moved close to her side.

She silently berated herself. She wished she could do something for once, instead of sitting there helpless and relying on Henrick to figure out the answer.

He crouched down and picked up the large branch he'd used to clear their pathway through the jungle brush. It was lying on the cave floor, conveniently very close to his feet. Radianne nervously watched as he moved slowly toward the large feline.

"It might attack if it feels threatened," Radianne warned as Henrick lifted the branch and wielded it like a weapon. She could at least give him advice, she thought. *Not that he would take it.*

"I know how to handle this."

He walked a little closer to the animal as it stood motionless and continued to scrutinize them.

Suddenly, it spoke. "You're in my cave," it said it a low, dangerous voice.

Henrick stood his ground.

"I came to sleep now," the large cat continued, arching its back and lazily stretching out its long and powerful legs. It flexed its dangerous looking claws in the process. "It was a long night on the prowl and I'm very irritable as I didn't find what I was looking for."

Pausing, the creature licked its chops as it looked at each cave intruder. "However, you all would make a tasty breakfast indeed."

Sighing, the beast then flicked its drooping tail side to side. "But as hungry as I am, I won't maul you if you promise to leave immediately. I'm quite tired. Think and move fast. For I am likely to change my mind."

Radianne darted a quick look at Henrick as she held Blink close. She hoped he would keep the dagger in his pocket hidden, as she knew it would probably just anger the cat. The threat of the branch was bad enough.

She stood. "Of course, you can have your cave back," she said, nodding sharply to Henrick, daring him to argue with her.

She raised an eyebrow at the surprised look on his face – he apparently was shocked at her taking charge. She knew that had to change. She looked back at the cat. "We will leave at once."

The feline watched with amusement as the three of them gathered what little belongings they had and swiftly made their way across the cave, staying close to the walls as they moved toward the entrance, avoiding coming too close to its body.

"And don't ever return," the big cat warned, letting out one last menacing growl and hiss as it whipped its tail around and retreated into the darkness.

It was with great relief that the trio stepped out into the sunlight.

"That was close," Radianne breathed. "Thank The Creator we're still alive."

"That cat was too tired to do much harm to us," Henrick said. "We were fine."

Radianne smirked. As brave as Henrick might pretend to be, he could not hide the relief in his voice. Apparently, big cats scared him. But she knew he would try to keep pretending he feared nothing.

Tall jungle grasses and meandering vines hanging suspended from thick trees brushed across their faces as they walked. This caused the terrain to become quite unmanageable for Blink, who once again attached himself to Radianne's hair.

She didn't mind. She was growing fond of having the star sit on her shoulder, and welcomed the positive and odd energy he gave her every time they touched. Blink seemed to enjoy his perch too.

Henrick whistled as they walked, whacking away at any offending plants that obstructed their passage deeper into the jungle.

Small, hidden animals could be heard scurrying about making rustling sounds, but none of the creatures seemed overly interested in introducing themselves.

Several hours into the journey however, a peculiar group of forest animals appeared. The creatures were small, round, and furry, with brightly-colored plumes of hair standing straight up on top of their heads. The animals had large round eyes and tiny, O-shaped mouths. Every now and then one them would run up to Radianne and Henrick, sniff the air, squeal, and run away.

"How adorable," Radianne said as one puffy blue individual darted away from her feet with a squeak. "Do you have any idea what these little ones are?" She turned to Henrick, waiting for the answer she knew would come.

He always had an answer, so she was surprised when he said he didn't know.

"Wow, for once there's something you can't explain," she teased, noting, with pleasure the flush that crept up Henrick's cheeks. She was secretly delighted. It was about time he faced his own share of embarrassment. She turned her attention back to the strange creatures.

One of the animals seemed to be quite taken with Henrick. It stared up at him with large brown eyes, apparently fascinated. But as soon as Henrick reached down to touch it, it began to shout strange words.

"Floppersnog! Floppersnog!"

The furball bounced around, yelling loudly.

"Floppersnog! Floppersnog!"

As it shouted, ten more of the little creatures came running out from under the shelter of nearby trees.

"Woggle doo snog!" they yelled back.

"Let's get out of there," Henrick muttered, quickly moving ahead. "They may be like the Oodles." He grabbed Radianne's hand and they began to run, trying to get away from the noisy, bouncing animals. Radianne was a little disappointed, as she had initially thought the creatures were a cute and harmless bunch.

She felt a sense of deja vu as they ran. "What is it with all the loud creatures we keep running into?"

She and Henrick were so focused on escaping the noise that they didn't pay full attention to where they were going.

Until they crashed into a mountain of fur. They looked up.

An angry face stared down at them from a few feet above their heads. It was a giant version of the smaller creatures and it did not look pleased with their unfortunate crash into its large and soft belly.

"Floppersnog bellow Mog!" It said the words accusingly, grimacing at Radianne and Henrick as it thrust a furry finger at them.

"We really have to stop upsetting all these creatures," Radianne whispered, taking a few steps back. "This is getting ridiculous. Worms, monstrous crabs, starving jungle cats, and now, now this thing…" she trailed off as the beast stamped its foot in anger.

"Nobber Mog!"

The giant plume upon the creature's head began to twitch. "Nobber Mog!"

Suddenly, all its little replicas reappeared. They kept their distance and cowered in the tall grasses, peeking out at the unfolding scene with fear in their eyes.

"Nobber Mog," the large one said again, more quietly this time.

"Hmm. Those must be its children," Radianne noted.

Henrick and Blink said nothing. They watched in fascination as the smaller creatures stared up at the larger creature with their eyes wide, waiting to see what it would do. The plume on the giant one's head began twitching more rapidly. The creature soon began huffing, puffing, and repeatedly stamping its large furry feet on the jungle floor.

"Floppersnog bellow Mog. Nobber Mog ubber nobber!"

Blink shifted on Radianne's shoulder. "I'm going to say something," he said. "Maybe I can help calm it down."

Radianne was a little surprised. Blink had been pretty quiet on the journey so far, but perhaps he'd been growing more comfortable in her world. And perhaps he'd had enough of the creature's outbursts. The annoying sound was getting to him.

Or, maybe, she thought, he was tired of her and Henrick making all the decisions, all the time. Maybe he wanted his turn.

She expected her star friend would be polite and could possibly indeed calm the situation.

"Floppersnog to you!" Blink shouted at the giant furball.

Radianne's eyes went wide.

The large beast stopped stamping and turned to look. When it spotted the source of the sound, its eyes also grew large with amazement.

"Soppernog!" it exclaimed, clapping two furry paws together in apparent delight. A huge grin broke out across its big-eyed, purple puffy face.

The little ones jumped out of the grass. "Soppernog!" they chanted.

At that precise moment, the large creature lunged forward and grabbed Blink in one swift move from Radianne's shoulder. It did a little dance of celebration as it did so.

Blink screamed.

All the furry creatures turned and began to bounce away in formation, the large one leading the pack.

"Help me! Help me!" Blink cried out.

Radianne and Henrick gave chase, following the beast and its babies as they bounded through the jungle. Their little arms flailed up and down as they bounced.

When Radianne and Henrick finally managed to get close enough, they launched themselves onto the bigger creature's burly back and grabbed fistfuls of its fur.

Henrick decided the creature didn't seem dangerous enough to warrant a stab from the dagger. Not at that moment anyway.

"Let go of him this instant!" Radianne commanded as she forcefully pulled at a tuft of hair.

"Floppersnog! Floppersnog!" the creature screamed, arching and bucking its back in protest of the assault.

As Radianne and Henrick attacked, the smaller creatures began to cry. They all sat down in the grass and began moaning with deep and pitiful little sobs, rubbing their eyes.

Blink cried out again as the larger creature shook off its two assailants, sending Radianne and Henrick rolling to one side. The creature held him high in the air and waved him around with pride, triumphant. It would not give up its prize that easily.

Radianne stood up quickly, prepared to fight. She had to act fast. She was afraid of what the stress of the situation would do to Blink.

But it was Henrick who attacked first. Launching himself at the lumbering creature, he yanked on the plume twitching violently on top of its head.

Howling in pain, the giant purple ball of fur dropped Blink to the jungle floor. The battle was won.

The star quickly ran for cover behind a tree and Henrick rejoined Radianne. They watched with fascination, and admittedly, a little pity, as the giant furball began to cry, its sobs soon matching the sounds the little ones were making. It sadly sat down with a big thud, next to its children.

"Soppernog, soppernog," they all wailed.

The sight was very pathetic to Radianne. She began to feel guilty for her actions. The strange animal probably wouldn't have hurt Blink, in the end.

"I hope we didn't hurt it," she whispered to Henrick.

As the creatures all cried, Blink ran out from his tree and joined Radianne and Henrick.

"Why do you suppose they are crying and saying that strange word?" he asked.

Henrick shook his head and shrugged. "Perhaps I was too rough. I'll go speak with them and see what this is all about."

"They probably won't understand you," Radianne said and raised an eyebrow. "In case you haven't noticed, they are speaking their own language."

"Worth a try." Henrick shrugged again.

He walked to the circle of crying creatures and sat down in the center of the bunch. They continued to cry, but their sobs began to fade as they sniffled and studied his face.

Henrick sat up straight. He raised his shoulders and lifted his palms upwards in a shrug, trying to get them to understand he was confused.

One little green creature stood up and bounced over to Blink, waving its small furry arms around.

"Soppernog," it wailed sadly.

Radianne suddenly thought she understood. The creatures must have recognized Blink as a star and they wanted to keep him in their group for themselves, for some reason. Maybe they were just lonely, or, more likely, they were as fascinated by Blink as everyone else who had come into contact with him. He had that magnetic draw and sense of mystery about him. She wasn't sure what the creatures would do with him, exactly, but she was certain he was what they wanted.

"I think they must want Blink to be part of their little tribe," she suggested. "Maybe you should explain where he comes from."

Henrick stood. "They probably know that already. I'm not sure that makes much sense."

It made perfect sense to her. Radianne picked up Blink and walked directly into the circle. All the creatures watched with great interest as she held Blink up against the sky.

"Soppernog must return," she said, jabbing the index finger on her free hand toward the clouds. "Home."

The creatures stared silently for a moment, seemingly awestruck, before they began nodding in apparent understanding.

"Soppernog. Home. Soppernog. Home," they repeated.

"Well I guess they can understand what we are saying after all," Henrick murmured, impressed. He raised an eyebrow at Radianne. "Good work."

She smiled.

The larger creature stood and its children followed suit. They formed a circle around Radianne and Blink and began to dance, singing the word "Soppernog" over and over again in a unified chant.

Though a little uncomfortable, Radianne stood still and tried to appease them for some time, but soon grew weary and wanted to move on. There really was no time to waste. She still was uncertain of how Blink would respond to the stress of the day's events.

"Ok, let's go," she whispered to Henrick. "Time to escape."

She stepped out of the circle, cradling Blink close, and ignored the creatures. She walked away from the group. Henrick followed.

They tried to keep up a steady and fast pace as they departed, hoping the creatures would not trail them.

Radianne turned her head to take a peek. All the creatures were in formation bounding after them, with the large one heading up the back. No such luck.

"Looks like we have company," she whispered.

"Wonderful," Henrick muttered.

"Maybe if we ignore them, they'll eventually leave," Blink offered.

"I don't know Blink," Radianne said with a smile. "You are quite the charmer. Who wouldn't want to be around you?" She patted him as he sat on her shoulder. "Hopefully they won't try to snatch you up again. I also hope you are feeling well."

"It was actually a little exciting," Blink admitted. "I'm feeling fine."

As they progressed through the jungle, the odd parade of creatures continued pursuing them. Their plumes flew in the air as they bounced and Radianne thought they made quite the sight.

"We should call them Floppersnogs," she decided, and voiced her thoughts out loud. "That must be what they are or what they call themselves, since they keep saying that word."

"We should call them annoying," Henrick countered, with a sigh. "I hope they leave soon."

They continued to walk. There were no fruit or nut trees in sight, and it had been a long time since they'd eaten. Radianne's stomach was growling. They stopped for water at a jungle creek, but the lack of food was making them weary.

As Radianne and Henrick refreshed themselves with a splatter of cool water on their faces, Radianne studied the Floppersnogs again. The furry creatures sat quietly under a nearby tree, staring at Blink who sat at a safe distance away from the water.

"They are harmless enough, I think," she said to Henrick.

And, she thought, later in the day, they proved themselves to be very useful too. At one point, the larger creature bounded up to a brightly colored tree and vigorously shook its branches. Down came a colorful array of fruit. The whole group enjoyed the delicious bounty before moving on.

Radianne wondered how long the creatures would follow them. It was almost nightfall. She didn't mind the creatures so much after spending time with them, but thought it was strange the animals still trailed.

"Most likely they will not leave the jungle." Henrick yawned. "But for now, I think it's time for us to set up camp."

A clearing soon came into sight and the group chose a location near a couple of large trees in the center, after scanning the dark jungle encircling the area for any signs of danger.

As the sun set, all settled down for the night. The mother Floppersnog curled up into a ball, and the ten little ones nestled in close to her fur.

The sight brought to Radianne's mind the picture of her own mother again, and her father. She thought, regretfully, of how she had often taken her whole family for granted. She wondered what they were doing and if they were worried. As she frequently did of late, she brushed away the thoughts and the feelings of sadness that came along with them. She leaned against a tree and invited Blink to curl up in her lap.

Stroking him gently for a few moments, she also covertly watched Henrick, as she usually did, sitting nearby. She felt completely at ease for the first time since they'd met. It was an odd feeling.

"Radianne?"

She drew her attention back to the star in her arms.

"Yes Blink?"

"Would you place me up in those branches above your head? It will help me feel closer to home tonight."

"Of course." She did as her friend asked, tucking him in the overhead boughs securely. His glow was still going strong.

"Goodnight, my sweet friend," she whispered.

"Goodnight, Radianne."

The stars above seemed brighter in that moment, as if they knew

Blink watched from below.

Radianne stared at the sky for awhile. The quiet evenings made it difficult to do much else. The vast beauty of Blink's home was so alluring.

As the evening breeze drifted in, cold tendrils of air flowed over her skin and made her shiver. Wrapping her arms around herself, she turned her eyes to Henrick, who sat shrouded in the shadows, his face slightly illuminated by the moonlight.

Shyly, she stood up and walked over to him. "Do you mind if I join you?" she asked, her heart beating a little faster. She did not enjoy the feeling, but she didn't completely hate it either.

"Not at all."

Radianne sat down. The Floppersnogs breathed softly and made little purring sounds. Strange chirps and insect calls from the cover of the mysterious jungle brush filled the air, but somehow, the noises were oddly comforting. The bright glow of the star overhead was perhaps the most comforting sight of all. It was all so dreamy... so... what was the word she was looking for? Romantic.

Without taking time to think about it, she lowered her head to Henrick's shoulder, reflecting again on how far she had come, and where she was going. Thinking about such things seemed to becoming a habit.

Henrick reached for her hand. His fingers caressed her skin, sending little shivers of delight up and down her arm. And when those fingers finally found hers and laced them in his own, she was already drifting off to sleep.

-14-
Into The Desert

The journey through the jungle of Vancor lasted several long and grueling days. The group survived near starvation, being chased by a pack of lionesses – which were, thankfully, scared away by the bold and boisterous mother Floppersnog – sinking mud pits, and biting attacks from various nasty jungle insects.

Radianne had to hold back a squeal of delight when they left behind the jungle and entered Land of the Ongoing Desert territory. Though her surroundings appeared to be nothing but a seemingly endless sea of sand, she looked forward to the new leg of the journey. Looking from Blink to Henrick with happiness, Radianne smiled as they walked into the sunlight, thrilled that they were that much closer to returning Blink to his mother.

The unpleasant moments of the jungle faded as they took their first steps out onto the sea of golden sand.

The Floppersnogs were still part of the group. The furballs hadn't retreated back to the jungle, and Radianne was secretly glad. She had grown quite fond of the lovable creatures over those last couple of days. The Floppersnogs were also proving to be very smart, and before long, had started to pick up a good deal of the trio's language.

"We are in the desert," Radianne pointed out to the mother.

"Des-ert." The large Floppersnog repeated the words slowly and looked at Radianne expectantly.

She clapped her hands in approval. "Very good!" she exclaimed. She gave the large Floppersnog a pat and turned to Henrick.

"So impressive! They've learned so much since we first met them in the jungle. Which, if I haven't told you lately, I'm so glad to be out of!"

Though, she knew if she were being completely honest with herself, she thought the experience had changed her for the better. And she couldn't help but remember it was not all awful... like that moment she and Henrick shared by the waterfall...

"I wouldn't get too happy," Henrick mumbled, darting her a warning look. Secretly, he had enjoyed the jungle adventure too, but thought Radianne needed to appreciate being in the moment more instead of always wanting what lay ahead. He thought she also was being naive again as she didn't know what they could be up against.

Radianne knew by then what those looks of his meant. She did her best impression of him. "There will be danger and many more uncomfortable moments to come," she grumbled, furrowing her brow. Then she laughed.

He shook his head.

The desert was seemingly empty, like most deserts appear to be at first glance. Cacti of various sizes grew here and there, and scattered spiky plants of unknown origin were the only signs of life on the rolling hills of sand.

The trip was moving along at such a whirlwind pace, Radianne thought. She and Blink had shared several interesting conversations over the course of the last days in the jungle, and she felt closer to the star than ever before. She thought about his return home and how much she would miss him. He still looked about the same, though she feared with every passing day that she might be one step closer to losing him in a terrible way. But she pushed the thoughts away.

The heat grew intense. The Floppersnogs panted, their long, pink tongues lolling out of their mouths. They all needed water – except for Blink, of course – and the flask was near empty. Radianne was about to comment on this when suddenly, life appeared.

Little reddish-colored mice with extra puffy faces scampered across the sand, darting in and out from tiny sand dens.

"How cute," Radianne said out loud.

Henrick snorted. "Cute, maybe. But those are blood-sucking mice. They'll bite you without a second thought and latch on to your skin, draining you dry."

How horrifying! Radianne shuddered. Maybe they weren't so cute after all.

"We're going to have to pull water from a cactus," Henrick announced. He stopped by a towering plant and the group came to a halt. He showed them another of the many survival techniques he'd learned as a Wanderer, and they all watched with fascination as he used his dagger to cut pieces from the cactus. He showed them how to suck water from its skin. He also said they could try to dig holes in the sand and explore for additional water sources.

"Henrick is so smart," Blink whispered to Radianne. "Though I don't need water, you do. I'm so glad he is on this journey with us."

Radianne felt a little hurt at Blink's words. Henrick was indeed very smart when it came to survival in the wild, but she hoped Blink admired her as well. Though, she admitted, she wasn't sure there was all that much to admire. Would she have been completely lost without Henrick?

After walking on and stopping at different water-spots several times, everyone in the group was hydrated enough to continue on for awhile.

But as the heat beat down on them and they traversed through the desert, Radianne grew a little irritable despite her initial elation at their arrival. It seemed to be a trend of the journey... after the initial excitement of a new place wore off. And now she was taking Blink's comment to heart and struggled with negativity. Maybe she had been foolish to believe that she could complete the journey on her own. Why did her thoughts keep coming around to that, full circle? She hated the mood swings. They had to be because of Henrick.

She hadn't been really annoyed with him in days, since the incident by the waterfall, but she once again found herself focusing on his negative qualities. She remembered he had said the Land of the Ongoing Desert could make people lose their sanity, and wondered if her negative thoughts were the start of it.

Maybe it was the unforgiving heat, but as her mind drifted, she also started to reflect on Henrick's life as a Wanderer and wondered how many other women he had met during his travels. Had he bonded with them as well and then just moved on?

Was it a common thing for him to seek out women in distress? Or had he simply pitied her and thought her foolish for venturing out on her own? Maybe he would be more than happy to get away from her after Blink returned home.

A sullen feeling, similar to the emotions she'd felt when she'd first touched down in The Center, began to creep up, despite the fact that Blink was sitting on her shoulder.

The thought of losing two close, even if new, friends, made her feel terrible and she chided herself for her conflicting and irrational feelings. *Henrick might have a lot of mood swings but you aren't much better, she told herself. This is ludicrous.*

When the man on her mind suddenly questioned her silence and surprising lack of interest in her surroundings, Radianne curtly assured him all was well.

But as they progressed through the hot, sandy, and desolate landscape, her mood continued to sour. And she felt guilty about her feelings because Blink happened to be in especially good spirits. He was talking more and was excited that the land of Shondalina was no longer so far off.

He enthused about what he was going to do when he went home, and spoke of the many stories he'd have to share with the other stars.

"They will be amazed!" he said with delight.

The Floppersnogs chattered amongst themselves in their own language and Radianne sourly wondered why they were still following. Didn't they have anything better to do? Or were they just lonely?

She looked over to Henrick, who also seemed to be in a sort of foul mood again as well. What about him, she wondered again. *Why had he really stopped her that day?* Was it all because of loneliness? Or because he was simply bored?

Nothing better to do, she supposed.

At that point, she realized her thoughts were getting jumbled and possibly irrational, but she couldn't shake them off.

Thankfully, the day passed quickly and the sun soon began to set in the sky. Sunsets usually were glorious gifts of nature in Radianne's eyes, but on this day, she thought the sky looked bruised and battered. She couldn't wait to go to bed.

As usual, Henrick selected the camp for the night. "We should stay there," he suggested tiredly, pointing to an area encircled by several large boulders. "We won't have to worry about the Desert Dogs as much there, with a good fire going."

Radianne didn't even want to ask about the dogs. She watched as he attempted to gather natural resources to make a fire, and when he couldn't find anything, he raised his hands in frustration and scowled.

"This isn't good. We might freeze tonight."

Radianne wrapped her arms tightly around her body. The group gathered around the boulders and watched as the sun went down. The air temperature dropped dangerously low and the Floppersnogs came together in a huddle. The cold weather did not bother Blink. He sat a few feet away.

Radianne shivered. She was tempted to huddle with the Floppersnogs for warmth. She did not want to ask Henrick... he sat on one of the boulders and rubbed his arms. A sad look was on his face.

Radianne wondered if he was feeling the same sense of sadness and inexplicable doom she felt. Or, maybe he was was resenting helping them.

She wished she could be as positive as Blink. Her friend stared up at the sky and she followed his line of vision, noting that the starts seemed to look even more vibrant than ever before against the crisp blackness.

It was a hopeful sign that maybe she would have enjoyed the sight of much more if she hadn't been so cold and lost in the maze of unpleasant and confusing thoughts and feelings. Instead of keeping her eyes on the light, she felt pulled into shadows.

Perhaps this desert would turn out to be a nightmare after all.

Shivering again, she decided she'd had enough of the cold. She was just about to make her way over to cuddle the mother Floppersnog for warmth, when Henrick stood up and came to sit beside her.

"Here," he said softly, opening his arms. "No need to suffer."

Wrapping his arms around her, he drew her into an embrace. Her first instinct was to fight against him and pull away, given her emotions at that moment. But she was so cold, and his arms were so warm, that she gave in.

There was no need to suffer more tonight, she decided. But she did wonder how much she was going to suffer after the journey was over with.

All confusion and negativity soon melted away, as the warmth of Henrick's embrace enveloped her and sent her drifting off in peace.

****

Radianne woke the next morning in a better frame of mind and the day initially began on a good note.

The group used Henrick's water hunting techniques to start things off. Though out of food, everyone seemed to be in good spirits for the time being. The lot of them had pleasant conversation together and as the morning progressed, nothing out of the ordinary happened.

But then, around mid-day, a large and fearsome desert lizard suddenly ran out in front of one of the little Floppersnogs. It stood on its hind legs and flicked out its long red tongue, frightening the young one immensely.

The baby Floppersnog fell over face first into the hot sand and began to cry. The cry soon gave way to loud wails and howls, which enraged mother Floppersnog. She chased after the lizard, shouting "Nog! Nog! Nog!"

Radianne and Henrick tried to stop her, but she refused to listen to them as she was too intent on exacting her revenge.

Henrick said he thought the lizard might be poisonous and told everyone to back away from the creature as it ran around in circles.

Mother Floppersnog would only hear the cries of her child. She believed the lizard should be punished for its crime.

"Nog!" She barreled toward the bumpy, sandy-colored desert creature.

It turned and glared up at her with large black eyes.

Mother Floppersnog stamped her foot and the lizard hissed a warning.

"Leave the lizard alone," Henrick instructed again. "Don't bother it."

Turning to look at him, the mother Floppersnog frowned and shook her head. "Nog lizard!" she barked. She then turned her attention back to the offensive desert creature.

"I'm guessing nog means bad," Radianne whispered, biting her lip as she watched the unhappy scene unfold. "Come away, let's leave," she said to the large Floppersnog, gently tugging on her fur. She picked up the smaller, crying furball and cuddled it close. Its howls soon stopped.

As its cries settled, mother Floppersnog made her way toward her baby. But not before turning and reprimanding the lizard one last time. And as she started to bounce away from it, the lizard ran over and attacked one of her furry feet, biting down hard. Then it scurried away quickly.

Howling in pain, the Floppersnog hopped up and down, clutching at her foot.

Henrick whipped his head around. "She's been attacked!" He ran over to her, taking note of the fact that her foot was already starting to swell from the poison.

Mother Floppersnog sat down in the sand and cried.

"Oh, that looks bad," Henrick said quietly as he further examined the injury.

Radianne joined him and tried to console her injured friend, patting her fur until she started to make a purring sound.

The little ones surrounded their mother and also tried to give comfort. After awhile, when the condition didn't seem to worsen, the group decided to move on.

The young Floppersnogs bounced and squealed alongside their limping mother as the group slowly made their way through the desert. Things seemed to be going decently for a time, but then the unsettled feelings began to creep back in, crackling in the air around them.

It was around this time when tragedy struck.

Radianne and Blink were having a conversation about the stars once again when suddenly, there was an odd flopping, thumping sound.

Turning around, they all found mother Floppersnog lying sprawled out across the sand. Her children instantly surrounded her, bouncing up and down and shrieking in dismay.

"Floppersnogs!" Mother Floppersnog moaned and gasped for air, reaching up with one shaky arm toward her babies.

Radianne's heart sank. Things did not look good. She and Henrick ran over as Blink trailed slowly behind.

"Is there anything we can do?" Radianne felt a lump rising in her throat as she took in the Floppersnog's poor physique.

"It's the poison." Henrick shook his head sadly. "I thought maybe it wouldn't harm her lethally given it didn't take her right away. Unfortunately, I don't know of any antidote."

Mother Floppersnog looked up at her children with large, wet eyes. A tear rolled down her cheek.

"Flobbersnogs bog gobber," she said, gasping for air again. "Ma

Floppersnog log Floppersnogs."

She turned her eyes to Radianne and Henrick. "Tog Floppersnogs."

Radianne nodded with understanding as tears fell from her own eyes. She would take care of them. She touched mother Floppersnog's fur gently in consolation, trying to offer some kind of comfort to her in her final moments.

Death was not something Radianne had much experience with. This new situation was unbearable... hard for her to process. *It wasn't fair!*

She turned once more to Henrick. "Isn't there anything we can do?!" she cried. "Don't you know how to save someone who has been poisoned? You do seem to know how to do everything else," she added a little snidely. Though she knew it was out of line, she couldn't help it.

Henrick flinched at her words. He shook his head sadly.

Mother Floppersnog smiled a small and weak smile as she looked around at her babies. As she closed her eyes for the last time and breathed her final breath, Radianne had to look away. She couldn't bear it.

The young Floppersnog children all began screaming and crying. "Ma Floppersnog! Ma Floppersnog!"

They nestled against her fur in grief. As they said goodbye to their mother, Radianne, Blink, and Henrick all slowly moved away to a nearby hill of sand and sat down, so as to give the young ones their privacy. They did not talk for awhile as they dealt with their feelings about the sad situation in their own ways.

Radianne pressed her palms against her eyes and let the tears come. What an awful turn of events, she thought. How horrible to witness a friend's death!

And then – the mother had asked her and Henrick to take the children. She would take them. But how would she raise the creatures and honor the memory of mother Floppersnog? She knew Henrick wouldn't be around to help her... she was so young herself and knew nothing about raising young ones. The thoughts were hard to bear.

After they grieved for some time, Radianne made a resolve. She would do her best. She would handle the situation as a grown-up would. She sniffed and stood up. "Shouldn't we give her a proper burial and perform a ceremony or something of that nature?"

"A burial in this area is impossible," Henrick said, shaking his head. "The sand is always shifting. But we can say some words to honor her if you'd like."

The trio approached the smaller Floppersnogs, who gazed up at them with large, sad, watery eyes.

"Your mother loved you very much," Henrick said softly. "This shouldn't have happened. We should have been prepared. But I'm afraid the time has come now to say goodbye. Your mother wants you to come with us."

Though she wasn't sure the young Floppersnogs could understand all the words, Radianne was a little annoyed with his bluntness and haste. He certainly wasted no time getting to the point, she thought.

She patted each one of the young Floppersnogs, trying her best to console them, knowing that it was what they needed most in that moment.

She walked over to a blooming cactus and broke off a few of the white flowers, carrying them over to place on mother Floppersnog's body.

"She will rest now," Henrick said, as Radianne lay the flowers on Mother Floppersnog's hands, near her heart.

Gathering round, the group said their final goodbyes. And then, it was over all too quickly.

As they departed, Radianne watched the little Floppersnogs turn to look at their mother one last time, crying and waving goodbye. It was a horribly sad sight. A lump rose in her throat again as she thought once more of her own family. What if that had been her fate, bitten by the lizard? What if she never never had the opportunity to see her own family again?

She cradled Blink close as they walked, carrying him in her arms, telling herself the journey would be worth all this confusion and pain.

Blink's energy comforted her once more, even though he too, seemed despondent.

Everyone was silent for the remainder of the day. As night began to fall, they found another area to rest and Henrick set to work building his usual fire.

The Floppersnogs huddled together and Radianne tried her best to console them. However, the bad feelings had started to return. The day's sadness had been too much for her and now her despair was giving way to anger again.

The unpleasant feelings toward Henrick returned as well. After watching Mother Floppersnog die, she now knew with certainty she would have been long gone if Henrick hadn't been along to help. It shamed her. More disturbingly, she knew she would have already failed Blink. She felt like she'd been a foolish child to think she could finish the quest on her own. She wasn't sure why she kept berating herself over those facts, but she supposed it had something to do with her sense of pride and the fact that she had seemed so sure of herself that morning in Miss Lugia's house.

It was to be was her first real adventure, after all. And she'd so badly wanted to be the hero of the story for once.

But she was not any kind of hero. She was just a naive young girl. She looked over to her star friend who sat in the sand, watching the Floppersnogs with sympathy. He would get home, she knew, but not because of any special thanks to her. It would mostly be because of Henrick.

She knew she shouldn't be thinking on such things at that moment, in a time of deep sorrow and loss, but she couldn't help it.

So she sat and brooded. Then, feeling very sorry for herself and unfit to take care of the Floppersnog children, and uncertain of her place on Blink's journey home, she stood up. The Floppersnogs were asleep and Blink also seemed to be asleep. Only Henrick was awake and she didn't want to spend the evening conversing with him. The air was very cold but she decided she needed to get away from the camp for a few moments.

"I'll be back soon," she said quietly.

Henrick jumped up. "Are you out of your mind? It's freezing and this is the time of night that the Desert Dogs begin venturing out."

"I need to be alone for a little while. I need to think."

"Think here."

"No." Radianne narrowed her eyes at him. He thought he could always control what was going to happen and when. Not this time.

"Fine." He frowned and sat down, turning his back to her. He didn't feel like arguing. "Go ahead and go. But don't ask me to warm your frozen body up when you return."

"I don't need your permission. Or anyone to warm me up," Radianne retorted as she marched away, feeling the brutal onslaught of cold instantly, but not really caring.

The sand looked eerie under the shadows cast by the moonlight. As she walked away from the camp, one of the blood-sucking mice scampered across her path, a few inches away from her feet. She shuddered.

Her feelings were spiraling out of control, she knew. There was something harsh and unforgiving about this desert, something foul in the air. Perhaps it was indeed making her insane. Hadn't Henrick said that could happen? She thought it had been the death of Mother Floppersnog that had spurned the feelings on, but she also wondered if perhaps Henrick had simply finally gotten the best of her.

She never would have thought that a man would be capable of turning her world upside down in such a manner, but he had. She struggled with her feelings of inadequacy and not wanting to like him, and, yet, there were those confusing conflicting feelings of not wanting him to leave her when the journey came to an end. She envied and respected him, sometimes felt feelings that she'd never felt with anyone before, but she also couldn't stand him at times. Or how childish he made her feel.

After the day's tragic events, she struggled over the fact that life could end so quickly; that families could be split apart instantly. Henrick's family, the Floppersnog family – torn in pieces in an instant. Shattered forever.

Was there something wrong with her for wanting to leave her own family in the first place? Why had she been so ungrateful for all that she'd once had? Why couldn't she just enjoy the place she had come from?

She walked on for awhile and was just about to turn back, when a heavy hand clamped over her mouth.

She tried to scream, but to no avail. "It must be Henrick," she thought, kicking her legs violently and managing, for a moment, to break free from her captor.

"I can't believe you would do that to me…" she started to say as she furiously whirled around to face him.

The man staring back at her was most definitely not Henrick. A scream escaped her lips and the rough hand clamped down on her mouth again.

"Be quiet," the stranger growled. "I'm not going to hurt you."

-15-
Where Scorpions Dwell

He was about the same age as Henrick, but the young man had something much more wild and threatening about him.

Even under the glow of the moonlight, Radianne could see that his skin was darkened from the desert sun. Long black hair hung to his waist and he was shirtless. *In the freezing air!* A necklace of what appeared to be animal bones or teeth hung around his neck.

Keeping one hand over her mouth, he began to drag her away. She went back and forth in her mind over whether or not to try kicking him again, but then fear took over. What if she never saw Blink, Henrick, or the Floppersnogs again?! Her family! She stiffened, immobilized.

"I'm not going to hurt you," the man said again, sensing her distress and trying to reassure her.

She wasn't convinced.

They walked over the darkened, ghostly hills until he came to a stop at the entryway of what appeared to be a sand cave in the desert floor. There were steps descending into a dark hole and it was down those steps the man forced Radianne to walk.

They entered a room lit up by the glow of dim and eerie candlelight.

Radianne looked around uneasily at the sparse surroundings. There was a rickety-looking bed, a few shelves, a cabinet, and a wood stool. The man ordered her to sit on the stool and when she did so, he stared at her with piercing blue eyes as he quickly tied her up with a rope.

His wildness was intimidating. Fear surged through her but she tried not to let it show. What did he want with her, she wondered. Who was he? She wished she had her own dagger right then. She had grown too reliant on Henrick. If she escaped, she vowed she would make sure she could defend herself from that point on.

The man pulled up another stool, moved it in close to her, and smiled. "Time for a proper introduction," he said. "Hello."

Radianne frowned at him. She could not believe he actually expected her to talk to him when he'd taken her hostage.

"My name is Thomas Volkenor. But you can also call me the Scorpion Man."

Radianne scowled more deeply. Great, she thought. A man named after stinging insects. The traumas of the day had been completely draining as it was and she wondered if things could get any worse.

"I have not seen anyone like myself in a very long time." The man named Thomas moved closer, narrowing his eyes. "Tell me, lovely one, why are you walking in the desert all by yourself? You can't possibly be a Wanderer. Much too soft-looking for that."

Indignant, Radianne raised her chin. She may not be the bravest Eugladian around, and her self-confidence had certainly taken a beating lately, as was evident in her reasoning for taking the ill-fated night walk. However, she didn't like his assumptions. As if he were implying only men could be Wanderers.

Suddenly her wounded sense of pride came back full force, when only moments before she'd been berating her shortcomings out there in the cold night air. She didn't like the fact that this stranger had taken her into this unpleasant hole in the ground. She would not give him the satisfaction of conversation.

"How old are you anyway?"

He kept pressing her to talk, but she wouldn't give in.

When he received no response, he began to laugh.

"I see. Well fine. You don't have to say a word. But I will. I haven't talked to anyone in awhile, so this is a great opportunity and happy occasion for me."

As Radianne sat on the stool, she reluctantly listened as the stranger began to talk about himself and how he had left Eustasia at the age of fifteen, where he and his family had lived like nomads. They'd moved there from Eugladia years prior, when he was eleven years old. Why he was telling her his complete life story, she had no idea. She thought he seemed a little unsteady in the head...

He explained the reasons he had become a Wanderer and how he had been "biding his time."

"You see," he said, leaning forward. "When I was fifteen, the Snorgs captured my family. They killed my parents and kept me as a prisoner in their lair, tormenting me. They also tried to brainwash me with some sort of magic potion and turn me dark, like the others they hold hostage." He lowered his voice. "There were *so* many others. Foxes, monkeys. Once, I even caught a glimpse of a giant ladybug! But I wouldn't give in. I spit the foul fluid out. I got away. When I did, I didn't stop running."

Radianne sucked in a breath at his mention of the ladybug. They still lived! Or at least, one had still been living. Her heart sank as she realized that quite a number of years had passed since Thomas's encounter. Miss Lugia would want to know. Radianne blew out the breath, trying to take in all the information and make sense of his rambling. She couldn't help but notice that his story seemed so similar to Henrick's.

"I ran until I came to this cave," Thomas continued, not the least put off that she wasn't responding to his tale. "I have lived here ever since. That was six years ago. I've lived alone. But the scorpions, well, for some strange reason, they took a liking to me. They don't sting me. They follow me around. And I have a sort of control over them."

So that's why he called himself the scorpion man, Radianne thought. She bit her lip, on the verge of saying something, but thinking better of it. As she battled internally over whether or not to speak to him, Thomas pointed to the floor and laughed.

"There are a few of my friends now," he chuckled.

Radianne looked at the ugly, lethal-appearing insects that had gathered in a horde at Thomas's feet. They were nasty little things. They suddenly turned as if they were looking up directly at her, tails poised as if they were going to strike. She screamed.

"No!" Thomas said sharply. "Don't do that! That will definitely make them eager to attack. You have to be calm, and they will be calm also."

He slowly lowered one arm and patiently allowed the scorpions to crawl up to his shoulders, where they perched like birds on a tree limb. Watching.

Radianne shuddered at the awfulness of what she was seeing. How he could stand it, she didn't know. "How do you let them do that to you?"

"Aha! So you do speak." Thomas smiled at her. "To be honest, I didn't, and still don't, really like them very much. But they follow me wherever I go and they don't sting me. So why should I be cruel to them? Why should I kill them? Why not live in harmony?"

The creatures slowly retreated back down his body and scampered to a dark corner of the room. Radianne shuddered again.

"So, back to our conversation," Thomas said, narrowing his eyes. "I brought you here because I saw you wandering around out in the shadows. I was curious to know why a young woman would be all alone in this dangerous wasteland by herself. I thought 'either she's crazy or some foul misdeeds are about.' So tell me... why are you out here?"

Despite her resolve to remain mute, and despite the fact that the man had actually taken her hostage and had the nerve to tie her up, Radianne reluctantly found herself answering him. She supposed aside from the scorpions, Thomas didn't seem as threatening as she'd initially thought. Perhaps it was because his story seemed so similar to Henrick's and she was discovering she had a soft spot for anyone struck by tragedy.

"I'm not alone. My friends are nearby," she said quietly.

Thomas raised an eyebrow. "Why aren't you with them?"

"I wanted to go for an evening stroll."

"Going for a stroll out in this frigid air and forsaken desert?" he chuckled. "You are one strange girl."

"I'm not the only one who's strange," Radianne retorted. "And you aren't even properly clothed for the elements." Frowning, she struggled against the rope that held her.

He laughed again. "I'm used to it. But I can give you that."

"Why am I tied up? What are you planning to do to me?" Radianne demanded. Her thoughts began to race. Though he no longer seemed too threatening, she imagined he must be lonely. Maybe the desert had caused him to slowly lose his mind. Her heart began to pound as she went through all the unpleasant scenarios her captor could have waiting in store for her. Perhaps she'd been wrong to talk to him at all. *She had to stop talking to strange men...*

"I tied you up because I haven't seen anyone like myself in a long time, and I was curious. Plus, you could be working for *them*." Thomas shifted uncomfortably.

Radianne took note. He seemed a tad worried, much to her surprise. "Them? Who are you talking about? The Snorgs? As for not seeing anyone, well, one of my friends passed through here several years ago. And he didn't mention anything about seeing you."

"I keep a low profile. Don't worry about them at the moment."

Radianne could see how it would be easy for Thomas to keep a low profile. He did seem like he blended in well with his surroundings. A truly wild man, this sort of Wanderer.

And unfortunately, like Henrick, she suddenly noted there was a definite attractiveness to him. She silently berated herself for taking note of how good-looking her captor was. First Henrick, now Thomas. Who would have thought Wanderers could be so attractive? And why was she thinking such things about a man who had her tied up?! She had to escape!

The scorpions began to circle around Thomas again. Radianne stuck out her tongue in disgust as she watched them gather, hating the way they crept around. She had a strong urge to squash them.

"Can you please untie me now?" she asked, instead.

Thomas nodded. "I suppose. Just don't hit me," he warned with a wink, as he leaned forward to free her.

"Where did you get that?" she asked, pointing to his necklace as he untied her bindings.

"On my way through Vancor. A jungle cat attacked me so I attacked back."

Radianne widened her eyes at his words. He changed the subject.

"So, now will you tell me what exactly are you and 'your friends' doing out here in the desert? These parts are not for the faint of heart."

Radianne thought he asked a lot of questions but she explained the whole story to him, surprised again at how easily she was trusting strangers. Perhaps she was foolish, she thought. Perhaps she needed to keep her mouth closed. But, then, she told herself again, Thomas seemed to be harmless enough, despite taking her hostage. And his story was impressive. He seemed impressed with hers as well.

She liked the feeling. Henrick didn't seem too impressed with her most of the time.

"Eugladia is so far away," Thomas said when she finished speaking. "I remember living there as a child, before my parents became obsessed with moving around." He stood and stretched.

"I'm sorry about the loss of your family," Radianne said quietly.

Thomas scowled. "Yes. Well I have not forgotten," he said angrily, his voice growing grim. "One day I will have my revenge."

He sounded exactly like Henrick. Radianne wondered if perhaps the two should meet. "What are you waiting for?" she asked. "Why don't you leave this desert?"

"I don't have any pressing place to be for the time being," Thomas shrugged. "But once I figure out precisely how to do it, I will exact my revenge on the Snorgs for ruining my life. There are just too many of them right now."

Radianne stood up. She hoped he would have justice one day. But at the moment, she she knew she had to get back to camp. Blink and the Floppersnogs needed her. At least she could comfort them in their times of distress. She was good at that. "I hope you do," she said. "I really should be going. I'm sure my friends are starting to worry about me now."

Thomas glanced toward the rocky stairs leading up into the desert and his face fell. It had been so long since he'd talked to anyone and he was sad to see her go.

"Well, you can leave now, if you'd like." He gestured toward the exit and bowed. "I'm sorry I gave you a scare and brought you here. I'm really quite the gentleman, despite my animalistic look."

Radianne eyed her captor thoughtfully. Maybe he could come with her. What would adding another member to their party hurt? By that point, her journey had been full of surprises and this wasn't so different. The adventure was no longer her own, and if truth be told, it hadn't been from the beginning. It was all about Blink's return.

Though she hated to admit it in light of her poor feelings about her own capabilities, she also supposed Thomas would know a thing or two about the desert, which would only prove useful. It would also be nice to listen to someone else other than Henrick.

"Why don't you join me? Meet my friends and travel with us? Perhaps after our present quest is over, we can all come up with a battle plan for the Snorgs." It was the first time Radianne had such a thought but she kind of liked the idea. She was tired of feeling helpless.

Thomas laughed. "I'm not even sure how to act around others these days," he said, pointing to the rope he'd tied her up with. "Obviously. But you're very kind to offer."

The massive group of scorpions came out from the shadows and surrounded him then, as if attempting to thwart him from even thinking of leaving.

Radianne frowned and shuddered. Never mind them, she thought. "I'm sure you'd remember how. All you'd have to do is act as you did tonight. Minus kidnapping and the rope, of course."

Thomas looked at the creatures gathered around his feet. "What about them? They've been with me for quite some time now…"

Radianne shuddered again. She definitely didn't want those things coming along for the journey and could not understand his attachment. Besides, she didn't want anymore injuries from strange creatures.

"You said you can command them. You could tell them to stay put. I'm sure they will be perfectly fine without you…"

Thomas stared at the scorpions with a slightly sorrowful look on his face. "You're probably right," he said. "Perhaps our time together has come to an end. Though I do know that if I leave, I will most certainly meet up with them again one day. We have a most peculiar connection."

He looked at Radianne, smiling at her expression of disgust. "I think I'll take you up on your offer," he said. "It's time to have a new adventure and, more importantly, to face reality again."

She watched as Thomas crouched low to the ground and spoke in a quiet tone to the stinging insects. "I must move on for now," he said as the scorpions fixated on him. "You must stay behind. Be on guard. You know from what. But I also know we will meet again one day. Our time together is not complete yet. Goodbye, my loyal companions."

Radianne thought his words to the scorpions were strange, especially the bit about being on guard, but she brushed them off. He'd had no one to talk to all those years and she supposed the scorpions had truly been his only friends.

With one final look around the cave, Thomas nodded. Then he and Radianne ascended the stairs and headed out into the cold desert night.

-16-
Desert Dogs

"I can't believe I'm leaving," Thomas said to Radianne as they walked in the darkness. He smiled at her in the shadows. "But perhaps it was meant to be. And I'm very lucky that it's a beautiful woman who's taking me away."

Heat rushed to Radianne's cheeks at his words. He was turning out to be quite the charmer, this one. Thankfully, it was too dark for him to notice. She thought it was nice to hear compliments – Henrick didn't give them to her – and strangely enough, meeting Thomas had helped brighten her mood and refresh her confidence. Despite the grief she was still feeling over mother Floppersnog, and despite the despair clawing at her again since she'd entered the desert, being taken captive had in some bizarre way sort of improved the situation. It had distracted her and helped her develop a new outlook on things. Maybe she would find her path after Blink found his way home after all, she thought. And she was certainly going to do her part to get him there.

Henrick jumped up as he saw the two approaching. With narrowed eyes and fists clenched at his sides, he first grimaced at Thomas, then at Radianne.

"Where have you been?" he demanded. "You've been gone for hours. And who is this?" He jerked his head at Thomas angrily.

"You're not my father. And I wouldn't say it has been hours…" Radianne chose not to answer his question about her whereabouts at the moment. Instead, she turned to Thomas. "Thomas, meet Henrick. Henrick, Thomas."

Thomas extended a hand. "Nice to meet you." When Henrick didn't return the gesture, he pulled his hand back to his side, looking a little uncomfortable.

"Blink and I have been waiting," Henrick said with a scowl, glancing once more at Radianne.

Radianne thought he was being rude. But she did take note that Blink had woken up and stared over at her with widened eyes. She didn't want to alarm him.

So she told them a slightly different version of the story – saying she simply came across Thomas's path as she was walking.

No need to make a fuss with the other details, she decided. At least not at that moment, anyway. She then introduced Thomas to the Floppersnogs, who also woke up, and they all sat together by the fire. Though still somber with the dramatic passing of their mother, the Floppersnogs eyed Thomas with curiosity.

Henrick continued to glare at the newcomer. "So where is it you come from, exactly?"

As Thomas told Henrick his story, Radianne noted Henrick did not show any sympathy, nor did he seem too impressed. Instead, he said nothing and continued to scowl.

She had thought for sure he and Thomas would get along right away, since their backgrounds were so similar. But Henrick was apparently not thrilled by the fact that a total stranger had just joined their quest. She could also sense a bit of something else churning under the surface… was it jealousy? Could that be it?

Good, she thought. Perhaps he needed a bit of shaking up.

Blink, though appearing a little tired, seemed very taken with their new visitor and listened intently as Thomas talked about his adventures in the desert.

As the night grew old, Radianne realized how exhausted she was. The changing emotions over the last few days had done her in. She said goodnight to everyone and crawled over to the Floppersnogs who still needed her comfort. As they nuzzled up against her with their warm bodies, Radianne drifted off to sleep to the sound of Blink laughing at something Thomas had said. She was vaguely aware of Henrick sitting aloof, back in the shadows of the flickering fire. Watching her.

****

Henrick did not talk most of the morning. Instead, he darted irritated looks every now and again at Thomas, who had managed to hold captive the attention of every member of the group since his arrival.

Radianne wasn't surprised. She continued to find their new guest very intriguing as well. He entertained them all with stories of his travels in the jungle and the desert, speaking of hidden places and magic potions, sharing thoughts about how to get back at the Snorgs before they caused even more destruction.

His chatter was a good distraction from the unsettled feelings Radianne continued to experience, especially when it came to Henrick.

She glanced over at Henrick then, wondering with annoyance why he wasn't adding input to the conversation. She expected him to contribute to the discussion, as serious as he was about exacting revenge on the Snorgs. But he just walked along silently, his mouth seeming to be permanently set in a very unattractive grimace.

The Floppersnogs continued in their silence as they walked. Still having a difficult time dealing with the death of their mother, they would periodically hop over to Radianne and nudge her legs, asking for a comforting touch. She patted them gently, sometimes stroking their fur, as Blink sat on her shoulder and chatted away to Thomas.

After awhile, her stomach reminded her that it had been quite some time since they'd eaten.

"We really should stop and try to find something to eat," she said to no one in particular.

Henrick turned and came to a stop. "I told you before," he retorted. "There's hardly anything to eat in this desert. You will just have to wait a little longer."

As soon as he said the words, Thomas coughed.

Radianne smiled. Time to show Henrick he didn't know everything. "Well Thomas knows how to find food, as he's lived here for years," she said. "How do you think he's managed to survive on his own all this time?"

Henrick glared at Thomas and snorted. "I have no idea. OK, desert boy. Talk."

Radianne frowned at him. She couldn't believe how rudely he was acting! But Thomas handled the situation well.

He valiantly ignored Henrick's attempt at insulting him and addressed the rest of the group. "Mostly desert rabbit and cactus fruit," he offered.

Henrick laughed. "Cactus? That's absurd."

Radianne turned her back on him and her full attention to Thomas.

"If you can show us how to harvest this unique sustenance, tonight we can have a feast," she said cheerfully. "I think it sounds lovely."

Thomas nodded. "Of course."

Henrick rolled his eyes.

The group continued to walk along, stopping every now and then to try to gather water. Thomas took out a knife and cut away at chunks of cactus as they went, placing them into a large pouch he produced from a pocket in his pants.

"So Thomas and I were thinking," Radianne said to Henrick, in an attempt to pull him into the conversation despite his sour attitude. "Maybe after we help Blink home, all of us together can figure out how to stop the Snorgs. We already have the start of an army right here. I'm sure there are others who would be happy to join the fight with us."

Henrick rolled his eyes. "As if you are going to be part of any army," he sneered. "You're going home. This isn't your fight anyway. Back to Eugladia and your perfect little life there. We will need a great amount of help. I will figure it out myself."

Tears filled Radianne's eyes and she quickly turned her head so he couldn't see. His words pierced her heart. It was the first time he'd spoken to her that harshly. She'd only been trying to help… at least she knew where he stood. Once Blink was gone, Henrick would be out of her life for good too.

She smarted from his comment about it not being her fight… she lived in a world where the Snorgs were wreaking havoc, so it most certainly was her fight too. But she was unable to form the words to tell him exactly what she thought.

As if sensing his friend's hurt feelings, Blink patted Radianne's neck from his perch on her shoulders. The electric current moved through to comfort her, as it always did.

What she wasn't expecting just then was Thomas's sympathy. The impact of Henrick's words on her had not gone unnoticed, and he leaned in close to her ear.

"It would be an honor to have you fighting alongside me in my army," he whispered. "I think you'd do a fine job. You're a brave soul." He gave her shoulder a gentle squeeze.

Radianne forced a small smile at his kindness, though his words did little to ease her wounded heart. She hadn't known a man could hurt a woman so much until she'd met Henrick. She thought maybe the time had come for her to harden herself against him completely, as she'd done when she'd first met him.

As the day progressed, the Floppersnogs broke their silence and began to talk quietly to one another. Perhaps they were starting to make peace with the death of their mother, Radianne mused. Though everyone was sad with the passing of Mother Floppersnog, they all knew they had to keep pressing on.

The situation was still so fresh and sad and she didn't even know how she'd take care of all of them once she was back in Eugladia, but she was glad they were there and she pitied the little creatures for their great loss.

As the hours went by, she couldn't help but notice that Blink seemed a little weaker than he had been in previous days. With alarm, she observed her friend was a tad more stone-like and pale in appearance and he also began to weigh a little more heavily on her shoulder.

He was still in good spirits. As the desert despair began to claw at Radianne again, however, she wondered how much longer her friend would remain in good health. She didn't say a word to Blink about it, because she didn't want to alarm him, but she wondered if Henrick even noticed. Or if he was too busy worrying about Thomas taking charge of things.

At some point during late afternoon, Thomas and Henrick both announced, simultaneously, that they knew of places to stay for the night.

Henrick said he wanted to camp by a cluster of giant cacti, but Thomas said that the shelter of an empty sand cave would be a much better choice.

As the two of them argued, Radianne mused about how little they both considered her opinion. No one asked what she thought or where she wanted to go. Perhaps she shouldn't have invited Thomas after all. She was starting to see that Wanderers always thought their ways were the best and that they knew everything, caring little for the opinion of others.

"We are staying the night at my location," Henrick stated with finality.

Thomas opened his mouth to say something, but seemed to think better of it, and closed it.

Henrick led the group to a sandy sort of ditch surrounded on all sides with clusters of giant cactus plants. "You see," he said, making a wide, sweeping gesture with one hand, "this place is well protected. It will be perfect."

As Thomas started the fire and scraped the spines off the cactus pieces in preparation for dinner, Radianne thought of her best friend back home. She desperately wanted to talk to Piri. This "man" thing was getting to be too much. The egos were ridiculous.

Thomas cooked the cactus and kindly offered her the first piece. She chewed on it thoughtfully. The taste wasn't bad, but it was bland.

"It's different," she said. "But not awful. At least it's something."

Thomas laughed. "It needs salt. Unfortunately, I don't have any with me. I've had to eat it cacti for years. You get used to it after while."

Blink sat quietly beside Radianne. The Floppersnogs also ate, but Henrick sat with a disgusted look on his face and watched Thomas serve the cactus.

"Probably poisonous," he said out loud. "I'll wait for something more palatable to come along." Thomas set his mouth in a slight grimace but said nothing in response.

As night fell, strange howls echoed through the darkness. The sounds sent tingles up and down Radianne's spine as the group sat at full attention and listened.

"Desert Dogs," Henrick muttered.

Radianne looked around for any sign of the mysterious creatures. The howls sliced through the night again and the Floppersnogs scampered to her side and began to whimper. She cradled one of the tinier ones in her arms while placing another hand reassuringly on Blink.

"It sounds frightening, Radianne," he whispered.

"It will be OK."

"No one move!" Thomas commanded, staring at something outside the circle of cacti.

Radianne followed his line of vision to the top of the sandy ditch. Several horrid creatures stared down at them, baring their teeth and flashing evil, yellow eyes. She had never seen such creatures before. They were enormous, with wicked-looking pointed ears. *The Desert Dogs.*

As large as Eugladian Grizzly bears, their black tongues lolled out of their mouths and coppery fur stood straight up on their backs like spikes. The strange canines focused their gazes on the young Floppersnogs and Henrick, licking their bared jaws hungrily.

"Ma, Ma," the Floppersnogs said softly as they slowly backed away from Radianne and the sight before them with fear. They huddled together in a darker corner of the camp.

Henrick picked up a rock near to where he sat.

"No, don't throw that," Thomas warned. "These are not your ordinary Desert Dogs, in case you haven't noticed how much larger they are than usual. These, I'm afraid, have been altered…"

No sooner had he said the words than Henrick let the rock sail through the air. It hit one of the beasts squarely on the nose, sending the creature into a violent rage.

There was no time for anyone to question Thomas about what he'd meant when he said the dogs had been altered. Though they'd seemed to be wary of the fire at first, Henrick's action had enraged the creatures. The beasts snapped their jaws viciously at the air and growled, glaring at the Floppersnogs and Henrick with bloodlust in their eyes.

Then, the monstrous dogs leaped into the air in a chorus of howls and sprang past the fire, heading toward Radianne, Blink, and the Floppersnogs. The largest and most fearsome of the pack lunged toward Henrick.

He stood up and began hurling more stones.

Thomas ran over and jumped on top of the dog targeting Henrick. It bucked and growled, twisting its body this way and that in an attempt to throw him off.

Tossing him into the air, it swiped at him with one giant paw and its knife-like claws tore through his flesh. As Thomas tumbled sideways and clutched at his side, doubled over in pain, the creature flicked its murderous gaze back to Henrick, who had stopped throwing stones to watch Thomas's battle with great – and stunned – interest. He appeared to be frozen in place.

During all the commotion, Radianne grabbed Blink and ran under a cluster of giant cactus that were bent together to form a sort of cave. The Floppersnogs were still frozen to the spot where they'd run off to. Radianne had no choice at the time but to run as well as it would have been impossible to gather them all up at once. Guiltily, she wondered how she could sneak back and pull them all out of the line of danger. She had to go back for them. *She had to.*

But she didn't have the chance.

At that precise moment, taken by surprise by the onslaught of the enormous Desert Dog, Henrick stumbled backwards and hit his head – hard – on a large desert sandstone boulder.

The fall rendered him unconscious. Radianne watched in complete and utter horror as the other Desert Dogs rushed forward and plucked up the bundle of Floppersnogs in their jaws, carrying them away as if they were a pack of pups.

The little bright furballs cried out in terror as they were carted off into the inky darkness. The sound of their cries hit Radianne squarely in the chest, and with a sinking heart, she crawled out from her cactus cave.

She looked around wildly. With wide eyes, she took in the sight of Thomas sprawled out awkwardly on the sand. He lay panting on his back as blood poured from a nasty gash running down his torso.

She knew he needed help, but more pressing was Henrick. She had to focus on Henrick for a moment.

Her eyes moved to where he lay unconscious. Her heart skipped a beat. She froze. The last remaining Desert Dog, the largest of the pack, was heading straight for his throat. In the moonlight, Radianne could see the sparkle from the saliva dripping down its lethal-looking fangs.

Thinking quickly, she set Blink a safe distance away and yanked at the large prickly arm of a nearby cactus, ignoring the pain from the spikes that seared through her hands as she ripped the limb apart. Blood trickled down her fingers but she didn't care.

Her heart pounded furiously as she watched the Desert Dog close in on Henrick. She knew what she had to do. She hadn't been able to save the Floppersnogs, but she had to save him!

Holding the cactus arm high above her head, she lunged ahead and swung the desert plant directly into the beast's head. Her weapon struck the creature directly between the eyes. With a shriek, it reared up on its hind legs, momentarily blinded. Then, in one violent whir, it raced toward her and pushed her back, knocking her down.

The air rushed out of her lungs. She watched helplessly as the monster descended on her with its cruel yellow gaze. Bracing herself for the pain and death she was sure would come, she closed her eyes and thought of home and all she'd left behind. All the things she'd taken for granted... her family, her friends. Now she would never see them again. Blink would never return to his rightful place... her poor star friend would never again shine his beautiful light on the world.

As the tears began to trickle down and she felt the foul hot breath of the monster on her cheeks, she silently thanked The Creator for the life He had given her and apologized for not showing more gratitude.

Then, to her complete surprise and amazement, the Desert Dog turned away. She heard a groan and the sound of something heavy dragging.

Cautiously, she sat up. She was grateful the creature hadn't snapped her in two, but she was also confused as to why it didn't. Almost instantly, she had her answer. She watched in horror and disbelief as the beast ran off into the night. It dragged Henrick with it through the sand.

Jumping up, she began to run after the desert monster, but remembered Blink and Thomas. Her heart tore in two. She would have to be rational, she decided.

She knew she first had to tend to Blink and Thomas and then they would find Henrick and the Floppersnogs. Hopefully they would reach them in time, wherever the beasts had taken them.

Walking back to where Henrick had fallen, she noticed something shiny glinting in the moonlight. It was his dagger. She picked up the weapon gingerly, trailing a finger along its smooth surface. If only she would have had her own weapon a few moments before – something much deadlier than a silly desert plant. If only. Never again would she be so unprepared.

Sighing, she tucked the dagger away out of sight into a pocket in her tunic, next to the rolled up sack Miss Lugia had given her.

Blink timidly walked out from behind the cactus and stumbled toward her. She could tell he was struggling. The horror of the attack had seemed to weaken his state. She ran to him and plucked him up, cradling him against her chest. Her tears fell freely as she took in his sorry state – the stone-like in appearance was starting to show more now than ever before – perhaps the terrible event had caused it. His glow had begun to dim.

What to do? What to do?

The journey had definitely taken an ugly turn, she thought. She looked helplessly at Thomas, who still lay bleeding in the sand. Her heart ached for the Floppersnogs, who could very well have been carried off to their deaths. Then there was a hollow, helpless feeling when she thought of what fate might await Henrick. Despite all the mixed emotions she'd been struggling with, and despite the despair the strange desert had tried to suck her into, she knew she truly cared for him.

"I was so scared for you Radianne!" Blink cried, weakly. "I thought that monster would make an end of you... I'm sorry I couldn't help. And then Henrick..." he trailed off and began to cry his glittering star tears. Radianne patted him gently.

"All is not lost Blink," she whispered to her friend as her own eyes welled up again. "We will think of something." She feigned confidence. She was beginning to doubt herself even more just then. Blink would not last much longer, his body was transforming before her very eyes. It had happened so suddenly, but it was a sign their time was running short.

The way his light had pulsated back in Eustasia had been a warning, and that had been so many days ago. Now they would have to find Henrick and the Floppersnogs too. With such limited time. She could never leave them behind. And Blink wouldn't want her to. She had to save them all. It was a disaster.

At the moment, she knew she had to focus her attention on Thomas. One thing at a time. Back to the present. Rushing to his side, she ripped off a section of her tunic and quickly bound his wound. She sat in the sand and shook him gently, waiting for him to come to his senses.

When he opened his eyes, the first thing Thomas did was apologize. "I'm sorry Radianne," he said. "This is all my fault."

She stood up and dried her eyes with back of her hand. "How could this situation be your fault?" she asked. "Those creatures just came out of nowhere."

"There are some things you have no knowledge of," Thomas said quietly. "And those were not ordinary Desert Dogs…" his words trailed off.

"What are you talking about?" Radianne raised an eyebrow. "You're not making much sense."

Thomas sat up and flinched. "I will explain on the way there."

"The way there?"

Thomas struggled to his feet. He sighed. "Radianne, your friends are in terrible danger," he said. "There's no time to waste. There is also something you should know. But we must leave now."

-17-
Sand Trap

As Thomas led her through the dark and cool desert night, Radianne shivered. Blink sat on her shoulder, his fading energy still giving her a little spark of hope as they pressed on.

"I have not been completely honest with you Radianne," Thomas said quietly.

She turned to look at the Wanderer in the moonlight. His furrowed brow told her she probably would not like what he was about to say.

"This desert is vast and deeper than you know. Underground..." Thomas began. "Though the main lair of the Snorgs is in The Center of Eustasia, over the years they have formed an intricate underground system of tunnels and caverns throughout our world. They have been working on this for many, many years, and by now they may even have a tunnel system running under Eugladia. I'm most likely the only one outside their circle who knows."

He paused and then took a deep breath. "One of the systems sits under this desert. Though the Snorgs rarely surface here, as they don't find the weather to be very agreeable to their health, one of their holding and training caverns is located under this very wasteland of sand."

Radianne was trying to take it all in, but some of what he was saying didn't make much sense to her. Tunnels under Eugladia? Holding and training caverns? She opened her mouth to speak, but Thomas began talking again.

"After I was captured, the Snorgs brought me on a long underground journey from Eustasia to this cavern. It's just one of the many places where Snorg slaves are kept and brainwashed. Once the slaves have been turned dark, they are put through specialized training programs, based on what talents they can bring to the Snorg cause. This is how the Snorgs continue to build their army. One day soon, the ever-growing dark army will be unleashed into our world. This army is more dangerous than any of us can imagine."

He paused again.

"When I was held captive, the Snorgs tried several different tactics to turn me, but to no avail. One of the tactics involved manipulation by a seemingly sweet girl who had taken up with the Snorgs – no doubt she had been kidnapped and brainwashed as well. She was about eleven or twelve and tried to convince me that I had no choice but to join up with the fiends, that theirs would be a cause I would be proud to be a part of one day – that they really meant to bring good and balance to the world. Of course, I knew the truth in my heart, and when I looked into her vacant eyes, I knew that the empty words were nothing but lies and trickery. I'd often hear the girl crying in a cage set near mine, sobbing in the darkness, telling me they would kill her if I didn't join them. There were moments she'd smile at me in the shadows, her face beautiful and seemingly innocent, telling me all would be well when the Snorgs came to rule the world. She was not well in the head. They had changed her. And she tried to lure me in to her beliefs, a tool they used.

But it didn't work.

"The Snorgs tried other tactics too, many others. When those also failed, they realized they had no choice but to keep me tightly guarded until they could figure something out. If all else failed, I was to be brought back to The Center and fed to their pet in the black lake. So, this is where the scorpions come in."

Radianne's eyes were wide as she tried to understand all he was saying.

"Are you still with me?"

She nodded.

"Good." He continued. "The scorpions were placed around my cell, ordered to guard me at all times and sting in unison the instant I tried to escape. But for some odd reason, the creatures took a liking to me. Perhaps I reminded them of the wild life they'd led before they had been taken captive by the Snorgs. Sometimes at night, the scorpions would creep into my cage and sit on my arms and legs, curious and watching. I was too scared to move, so I let them be. We formed a friendship. Over time, I was able to command them to do my will. Their affection and connection with me overpowered anything the Snorgs had done to them. The girl never seemed to notice. One day when she was sleeping and the Snorgs that patrolled were not in sight, I dug out of my prison and managed to escape. The scorpions followed and we fled to a very remote part of the desert, far away from here, where I stayed for some time until I was sure no one was following. No one did. I then came back and took up residence in the cave where you met me. I was always on guard, but I chose not to leave the desert. I wanted to remain close to the lair so when the day came and I had my own army formed, it would be one of the first places I'd attack. I'd try to free all the victims inside."

Thomas stopped talking for a few minutes so Radianne could

gather her racing thoughts.

To think that Snorgs could possibly be under their feet at that very instant, she mused. That would explain the bad moods since entering the desert. She wondered, sadly, how many other victims there were. She wondered what had become of the girl.

One thing really confused her.

"Why wouldn't they have come after you?" she asked Thomas. "That doesn't make much sense."

He shook his head. "I've often wondered that myself. The only logical explanation I can think of is that the handful of Snorgs who run the cavern figured I fled the area long ago with the scorpions. And as they are not fond of the desert, like I said before, they probably didn't feel like coming after me. They are not always very bright and are often very lazy. However…" he suddenly trailed off, and looked away, with a guilty expression on his face.

"What is it?"

"I now know that it's my fault Henrick and the Floppersnogs were taken," he added, quietly.

"How is that your fault?" Radianne raised an eyebrow. "You didn't hand them over."

Thomas shook his head. "Maybe not directly, but it is my fault. I didn't know this at the time, but I'm pretty certain that after I said goodbye to the scorpions and left with you, they went back to the holding cavern. When they were with me the spell over them was immobilized for whatever reason, but after I left, they no doubt felt a magnetic pull back to the Snorgs. I am afraid that with their arrival there they somehow revealed I was in the area again, and the Desert Dogs were unleashed to hunt me down."

Radianne frowned. "Well, if that's the case, why didn't the creatures take you hostage then, instead of Henrick and the Floppersnogs?"

"The only conclusion I have is that when the Desert Dogs saw there were others in my company, they realized it would be better to take fresh captives who might be more easily brainwashed. Perhaps they thought this would please the Snorgs more," Thomas shook his head. "They couldn't take all of us, so they singled out Henrick and the Floppersnogs. Henrick would make a good addition to the army and the Floppersnogs would too, as they are so cute that no one would suspect them of maliciousness. However, I'm sure the dogs will come back looking for us, or will be ordered to."

Radianne was quiet for a few moments. Thomas couldn't have known what would happen when he'd left his cave. It was an unfortunate incident. She told him as much as they continued to walk, but grew solemn at the thought of the task that lay ahead.

Into *their* lair. She knew she was heading toward a very black place. She would have to summon all the courage she had within herself to face the monsters in the darkness.

With Blink fading as he was, time was also of the essence. He had been a source of light and hope for her all along, but now that his light was fading – his life was fading – she found herself growing despondent again. She hoped Blink's waning light and her goal of saving him would be strong enough to pull her through, but at that moment, she wasn't so sure.

She knew she had a duty to Henrick and the Floppersnogs as well, and Blink would not want to leave them to be tortured. She could not bear to leave them to be tortured. If only she and Thomas could act quickly to get everything done in time.

"How much further then? Until we get to this secret Snorg lair?"

Thomas pointed to a large dune just ahead, where a hole had been dug out in the mound. "It looks like the Desert Dogs tunneled in over there," he said. "There are many places to tunnel in, but it might be easiest to just follow their trail."

Radianne shuddered to think of how close she and her friends had been to the evil Snorgs, all that time, without even knowing it. The fiends were literally right under their feet. She was surprised she and her friends hadn't been discovered long before and was thankful the Snorgs didn't fare well in the desert.

"How are you Blink?" she whispered. "Are you up for the task ahead? I'm sorry it has come to this."

Blink patted her shoulder weakly, sending a little tingle of hope down her spine. "We must do what has to be done. The Creator would not bring us this far for me, or any of us, to perish now. We have to save our friends, and then we can focus on my predicament."

Tears sprang to Radianne's eyes at his selflessness. The star was certainly teaching her a lot about sacrifice. Her hand touched him reassuringly.

She hoped he would survive the ordeal ahead. She hoped they all would.

They'd arrived. She and Thomas stood at the threshold of the dark opening in the dune.

"Are you ready for this?" he whispered.

Her heart thudded in her chest. She reached into the hidden pocket in her tunic, her fingers trailing along the cool, smooth blade of the dagger. She set her mouth in a grim line.

"Let's go get them."

-18-
Into The Darkness

It seemed as if the darkness would carry on forever. The sandy and foul-smelling tunnel led them this way and that, ever deeper into the dark and mysterious desert underground. Blink still gave off enough light to help them find their way, and for that, Radianne was once again grateful. Without his glow, they would have been forced to feel their way along the sides of the stinking tunnel. It smelled of death and rotten meat and the strong odor of dirty Desert Dog.

Radianne's heart beat faster as they progressed deeper into the realm of the unknown. She and her companions stayed silent as they tried to keep their presence undetected. Thomas turned and took her hand for a moment. He gave it a reassuring squeeze.

After what seemed like an eternity, a dull light appeared overhead. At the end of the tunnel, Thomas held up a hand as he slowly poked his head around the exit, scanning the area for threats.

"We're in a long corridor," he whispered. "There doesn't seem to be anything lurking about at the moment. Let's go."

They stepped out from the tunnel and into the dark corridor. The walls of the earthen, sandy hallway were narrow and the path ahead was dimly lit by the flickering flames of candles placed in wall sconces. The light caused their shadows to look gigantic as they walked.

"There are many corridors such as this, most leading to the main holding and training cavern. I'm sure we will be there in no time at all," Thomas whispered. "The question is, what will we do when we get there?"

Adrenaline coursed through Radianne's body as they moved forward. She knew there was no question of what she would do – she would use that dagger if she had to in order to free her friends.

"The light will always prevail," Blink whispered in the shadows. "The light will always find a way."

Radianne smiled at her friend's encouraging words. She knew in her heart he was right... he had to be.

The trio turned round a bend at the end of the corridor and walked down another long hallway until they came to a door.

Thomas grimaced. "This will open into the cavern," he said. "I'm going to open it quietly. Maybe I'll be able to see something to give us enough warning... so we know what we're getting ourselves into."

Radianne and Blink watched silently as Thomas very slowly opened the door a crack. It barely made a sound. He poked his head in and looked around.

"I can't see much, but it seems pretty quiet in there," he whispered. "The Snorgs may be in another chamber at the moment. I'm not sure if Henrick and the Floppersnogs have been placed in cells yet, but we can find a place to hide inside until we can get a better feel for things."

Pulling his head in, he faced Radianne and Blink. "Are you both ready for this?"

They nodded.

Opening the door a little wider, Thomas motioned for them to follow. Stepping cautiously into the shadowy cavern, their eyes searched everywhere at once, scanning for signs of life or danger. It was a giant, airy space that also looked like an arena of sorts. A strange black pond sat in the middle of it.

Large boulders encircled the perimeter of the sandy arena, and stone stairways were placed at its four corners. These led up to heavy wood platforms reinforced underneath by tree trunks.

Though it was difficult to see in the dim lighting, Radianne could make out what appeared to be cages or cells sitting on the platforms.

On the far end of the room, sitting high up on another stone staircase, was a foreboding-looking ebony throne.

Radianne wondered who it belonged to.

Thomas seemed to be scrutinizing the strange chair as well. "That wasn't here before," he whispered. "I wonder what it's all about."

There didn't seem to be any movement in the cavern at the moment, so the group cautiously continued forward.

"If we get up above, we might be able to see if Henrick and the Floppersnogs have been imprisoned," Thomas said. He crept up the nearest crumbly stone stairway and Radianne followed.

When they arrived at the top and stepped out onto the platform, they took note of a series of cages on one end. Across the way, on the other side of the arena, sat another cluster of cages. Some of the cells were empty, but some held prisoners.

None of them were Henrick and the Floppersnogs.

"Remember, we arrived here not long after the Desert Dogs," Thomas whispered, trying to reassure Radianne and Blink. "I'm sure our friends will be coming along shortly. Let's find a hiding place and wait things out."

They walked along the platform until they came to the end with a cluster of empty cages. None of the prisoners in the occupied cages made a sound, they seemed to be asleep or in a daze.

The space behind the empty cages was dark and shadowy, a perfect place for hiding for the time being. As long as no one came too close, the trio would likely get by undetected.

They stepped behind one of the cages then, and leaned up against the cavern wall for support. Blink hid under Radianne's hair so his glow would not reveal their presence.

Radianne and Thomas could see through the empty bars of the cage to sections of the arena below, and across the way to several of the other cells.

The two said nothing as they waited for what would come next, but Radianne's thoughts were racing. She'd spotted a Gentle Giant imprisoned across the way. The creature appeared to be asleep at the moment, but Radianne's heart fell as she wondered what torments it had already endured. In another cage sat a fox, and in another, a monkey that looked as if it had come from the Jungle of Vancor.

Radianne wanted to free them but knew it wasn't the time. She stood with Thomas for what felt like ages. It seemed as if days had passed, though in reality, it had only been about an hour.

A door on the opposite side of the cavern was suddenly flung open. In marched three Snorgs, pushing and shoving the newest training camp arrivals. Behind the Snorgs trailed several Desert Dogs – the same pack that had snatched up Henrick and the Floppersnogs.

Henrick was at the head of the group, shoved by two large and nasty-looking Snorgs. One of them prodded him on with a long, jagged stick, as if he were a horse. His hands were tied behind his back and his clothes were torn. Behind him, the Floppersnogs huddled together like one big marching colorful furball. They too were being prodded along by a nasty stick-wielding Snorg.

"Such luck, such luck!" the Snorg monitoring Henrick growled. Its voice echoed throughout the cavern. "Fine prisoners and morphlings you will be."

"Ha!" Henrick sneered back. "We'll see about that, you rotten, stinking pile of trash."

The Snorg raised the stick and struck Henrick sharply across the head. He doubled over in pain, and another Snorg kicked him in the legs, causing him to lose his balance and stumble forward.

"Quiet, you fool!" the Snorg growled. "Or you will pay an even steeper price later."

Radianne covered her mouth with one hand to keep from screaming. She felt so helpless watching the scene unfold... it was awful seeing her friends treated in such a manner. She had to restrain herself from rushing out of hiding right then and there.

Thomas reached for her free hand and gave it a firm squeeze. The touch helped eased her nerves, slightly. She knew she had to stay silent, at least for the moment.

Though it was difficult to see everything that was going on in its entirety, she could make out Henrick and the Floppersnogs as they were marched up the stone stairs on the opposite side of the arena. There was the sound of opening and closing squeaky cell doors and wicked Snorg laughter.

Meanwhile, three of the Desert Dogs circled around the arena. Suddenly, one of them stopped and sniffed the air, then paced again, then stopped to sniff the air again and looked directly at the platform in which she, Thomas, and Blink were hiding. Letting out a low growl and narrowing its eyes, the lumbering creature raced toward the stone steps leading up to the platform.

"Oh no," Radianne whispered to Thomas. "I think we've been

found out!"

"My mistake. I should have thought about them earlier!" Thomas said with frustration. "I didn't think the dogs would be with the Snorgs when they arrived. Whatever happens, remember to stay calm. Don't give in."

Thinking fast, Radianne pulled Blink out from under her hair. She had to protect him. Even if she and the others didn't make it out, there was still hope for him if he could get to Shondalina.

"Whatever happens Blink, you try to get out of here if you can," Radianne told him. "When they catch us, run! Get away from here, figure out how to get to the Winged Ones, figure out how to get home!"

Blink stared up at her with wide eyes. "I'm not leaving you, Radianne."

Tears filled Radianne's eyes as the snuffling sound of the Desert Dog fast approaching grew louder. She gave the star a kiss and set him on the floor. "Don't get caught, go and hide for now," she whispered, waving him on, as he took a few steps away from the cage. She nodded and he headed off into the shadows.

No sooner had Blink scampered off to unknown parts than the ugly snout and bared teeth of one of the Desert Dogs poked through the narrow opening in which Radianne and Thomas were hiding. The beast began to snarl something horrible and soon began barking. The noise alerted the others and he was quickly joined by several members of his pack.

Thomas and Radianne thought about making a run for it, squeezing through the back of the cage and out the other side. But then there was the sound of heavy footsteps approaching, and a rotten smell – even more rotten than the scent of Desert Dogs – filled the air. *The Snorgs.*

Radianne sucked in a breath.

"What is the matter with you dumb beasts?!" one Snorg growled as it clambered up the stone steps.

"I think I see something hiding there in the shadows!" another Snorg bellowed. "Looks like our dumb beasts have found hidden treasure!"

Radianne looked for any sign of Blink. He was nowhere to be found, and this brought some sense of peace to her. At least her friend would not be caught. At least not just then.

A bulbous nose poked into the space between the cage and the wall. Then, two blackened and narrowed eyes.

"Well look what we have here!" the nosy Snorg bellowed. "If you want to live… for a little while anyway, you'd both better come out of there right now!"

As the Snorg spoke, bursts of foul air wafted up from its mouth into Radianne's nose. She gagged.

"Just do as they say, at least for now," Thomas whispered. "We'll figure a way out of this."

With trepidation, Radianne slowly moved out from her hiding spot. She brushed up against the disgusting Snorg in the process. Thomas followed close behind. Though she was feeling quite nervous at the moment, she tried not to let it show. She would not let them intimidate her. Instead, she took advantage of the first opportunity she'd had to size up the Snorgs and got a good hard look at what the horrible creatures were like up close.

They were taller than she expected. The three of them loomed over her head and as she took in their physiques, she couldn't keep the disgust off her face. Dark unruly hair sprouted up every which way from their heads and out from the innermost parts of their curved ears. More of the dark hair covered their arms and legs. Their skin was a sickly shade of yellow-green, covered in bumps. Their brown and ragged clothes were smeared red with what could have been the remains of a recent rank lunch – or, possibly, blood. Worst of all was their smell. Radianne had never smelled anyone or anything so unpleasant before. It was like decaying garbage, and, she thought uneasily, hints of death.

"Like what you see?" one of them growled at her. Reaching out with a beefy, hairy arm, he grabbed her forcefully by the shoulder.

She bit her lip as his curved blackened nails dug into her flesh, but she didn't cry out. She wouldn't give him the satisfaction.

One of the others grabbed Thomas. "Why, look who it is boys!" he snarled. "Long time no see." The other two Snorgs turned to look at Thomas, narrowing their black eyes in recognition and dismay. They frowned, baring sharp and jagged yellow teeth.

"You little rat," the Snorg holding tight to Radianne spat out at him. "You may have escaped once before, but you won't get out of here so easily this time. At least, not alive!"

Thomas and Radianne were silent as the Snorgs forced them down the stone steps and across the sandy arena. The Desert Dogs trailed close behind. As they walked, Radianne turned her head nonchalantly, searching for Blink. There was still no sign of him.

"Yes, take a good look around my lovely," the Snorg whispered into her ear, covering her cheek in spittle as he spoke. "This is going to be your home for quite some time. Hope you enjoy the look of things."

Feeling as if she were going to vomit, Radianne reached up and brushed the slime off her face. She knew he was wrong. They were going to get out of there, one way or another.

Surprisingly enough, the Snorgs led them to cages directly near Henrick and the Floppersnogs. Perhaps they really were quite dumb after all, Radianne thought. If she were a Snorg, she would have wanted to keep the Eugladians far away from one another. Apparently the Snorgs hadn't thought of what several Eugladians placed in close quarters could conspire to do.

She and Thomas tried to keep their faces void of emotion as they approached the cages that contained her friends. Henrick was smart enough to do the same.

The Floppersnogs, however, had a difficult time containing themselves as she and Thomas approached. Radianne could see them excitedly bouncing up and down in their cages.

One of the Snorgs noticed too, and ran over.

"Now then! Settle down you furry vermin, or I'll squash you flat!" he shouted, giving their cage a vigorous shake.

The Floppersnogs squeaked and instantly cowered and quieted.

Radianne's temper flared but she knew that little could be done for them at the moment. She allowed the foul Snorg to lock her in a cage next to Henrick. Thomas was imprisoned in a cage to her left.

"Listen now!" the Snorg who'd manhandled her shouted. "You are all to take part in our training and to become morphlings. You WILL become part of our alliance. You WILL have no choice but to join forces with us – or DIE. Your training WILL begin tomorrow."

The creature paused, looking at each new prisoner with hatred in his eyes. "Tonight, you will meet one of our revered leaders, who will be along shortly. Until then, shut your mouths and don't make any noise! And no funny business," he added, giving Thomas a pointed look. "Your traitorous scorpion friends have been properly disposed of, so don't expect any help from them! And there are guards standing by in the shadows."

With that, the Snorg grunted something at the others about dinner, and they all marched off, the Desert Dogs following suit.

Radianne glanced over at Thomas. His face had fallen at the Snorg's words about his insect friends. She knew he would blame himself for their deaths and felt sad for him. As sad as his loss was, however, there were also more pressing matters at hand and there was no time to dwell on such things.

As soon as she was sure the Snorgs were safely out of sight and earshot, she quickly turned toward Henrick's cage. Though the light was dim, she could see him well enough.

"Henrick!" she called out in a loud whisper. "Are you OK?!"

Looking a little bruised and battered in the shadowy light, Henrick stepped forward and leaned up against the bars of the cage, wearily.

"I'm OK," he replied. "But what are you two doing here? This is very dangerous, you shouldn't have come! And where's Blink?!"

Radianne scanned the area once more for any sign of the star. There was none.

"I'm pretty sure he's somewhere around here," she whispered. She lowered her eyes and her face fell. "He said he wasn't going to leave me, though I am afraid I honestly don't know how much time he has left."

She felt so helpless locked up in the cage and couldn't bear to think of failing Blink after how far they had come.

Henrick slumped against the bars and sighed. "So his power is fading then. I'm sorry I failed again, Radianne," he muttered. "Those beasts overpowered me, and for the second time in my life, I felt completely helpless. I can't believe it. You probably should have left with him – " he jerked his head toward Thomas, though he frowned as he did so, "when you had the chance."

"Right. Like she would have left you and those furballs to your deaths," Thomas said as he rolled his eyes, joining the conversation.

"Stop feeling sorry for yourself man! This is what they want. Despair and negative thinking. It's time to put our heads together and positively think our way out of this."

His words struck a nerve with Henrick, who tensed again and thrust a finger through the bars, jabbing it in Thomas's direction.

"A lot of this is actually your fault the more that I do think about it," he snarled back. "We'd been doing perfectly fine before you came along and decided to join us…"

Thomas laughed. "My fault? Perhaps, to an extent. But it's not my fault you couldn't handle that Desert Dog back there and got yourself knocked out in the process. It's your fault you have such a poor and negative attitude all the time. You're not the only one who has suffered great loss, you know. But it is no time to whine about your lacking fighting skills or your unpleasant personality."

Radianne sucked in a breath. She could tell the argument was going to escalate, and possibly attract unwanted attention. She thought the very idea that the two of them were choosing to argue at such a dire moment was quite ridiculous.

"Both of you, stop!" she whispered sharply. "Things just happened. It's no one's fault. It's not about who is tougher or weaker… it's just the way things are." She sighed. "This desert, this place, anywhere where Snorgs can be found close by… I'm realizing they really do have a way of making people angry, making people despair and lose hope. It's been happing to me too. We can't let that happen, Henrick. Thomas is right, it is what they want. We can't give in. We have Blink – and our world and the rest of our lives – to think about."

Her eyes locked with Henrick's as she said the last words, and then they both looked away quickly. The three Eugladian natives stood silently in their cages for a few moments, trying to calm themselves.

"We have to be rational and really think about what our next course of action should be," Radianne said some time later. "My hope right now is that Blink will come to our aid, because I feel he is still here. Even though I told him to leave. And if not – " her voice broke with emotion, as she thought of her friend and the faith she held that he would make it alive through whatever was to come – "if not, we still have to have another plan. We need to put our heads together and think about how to get out of this and how to outsmart the Snorgs. For now, let's just sit a few moments more and gather our thoughts. It's been quite the night."

The two men agreed and all three of them slunk to shadowy corners of their individual cages.

Radianne sat with her head in her hands, praying to The Creator for the strength to get through whatever obstacles she was to face in the coming days.

Blink had inspired her all along, and now that he was gone, that terrible dark feeling started to claw its way deeper into her spirit. However, she knew that at that moment, more than ever, she had to be strong, think about all that was good, and fight against the enemy.

What a whirlwind of a journey this had been so far, she thought. Now there she was, in one of the darkest places she'd ever been, without any idea how to move forward. She truly hoped Blink was still around, somewhere in the shadows. Though she knew she had to find strength within herself, she also hoped his light would still be there to guide her. She needed him as much as he needed her.

Feeling very tired, she closed her eyes.

Some time later, she snapped awake to the sound of a heavy door squeaking open. Then there was the unmistakable sound of Snorg voices. Jumping up, she clenched her fists and made her way to the front of her cage, her heart pounding wildly. She remembered the beasts had said earlier that one of their leaders would be along to visit with the prisoners… well, this was the time, she thought. And she was not about to be intimidated. She would face this leader boldly and head on.

Henrick and Thomas also stood alert at the front of their cages. The three captives quickly glanced at one another, listening intently as the

Snorgs made their way up the stone steps and onto the platform.

There was clearly someone else with them this time.

"Well I must say that I'm delighted to see who we've added to our alliance," the new voice said.

Strange, Radianne thought. She couldn't yet see who it was, but the speaker sounded oddly feminine.

"You will be very happy, we think," one of the Snorgs growled.

"I'm sure I will," the voice spoke again.

It was a female speaker, Radianne was quite sure of it. Perhaps a lady Snorg. She supposed it would only make sense that the Snorgs had wives and other females among them. She shuddered at the thought of little Snorg babies running around. She prepared herself to meet the female Snorg and wondered if the female version would be just as smelly and unpleasant as its male counterpart.

As the Snorgs and their leader approached, Thomas sucked in a breath.

"It's her!" he exclaimed. "But it can't be!"

"Huh? Who?" Radianne questioned.

But before he could answer, she saw who he had been staring at and her mouth dropped open. A young woman, close to Radianne in age, came to a stop a few feet in front of her cage.

She appeared to be Eugladian and was actually quite pretty. Her garb was similar in appearance to the Snorgs, except what she wore was much tidier and more becoming as it consisted of form fitting black pants and an equally flattering black sleeveless tunic top with a hood, which as draped over her head. She wore dark boots laced up to her knees. Long blonde hair fell out from the hood and cascaded past her shoulders, and though it was difficult to tell in the shadows, her eyes appeared to be a sort of steely gray mixed with blue.

"Shocked, are we?" the young woman said with a smile as she took in Radianne's surprised expression. She cast an equally amused glance over at Thomas, and then back at Radianne.

"I think these two will do quite nicely," the woman said to the Snorgs. "As for the third..." She stepped away from Radianne's cage and walked slowly toward Henrick.

As she approached his cage, her smile faded. Her eyes clouded over and her face grew very serious. When she came to a stop in front of the cage, she cocked her head to one side and laced her fingers together behind her back.

"He might be difficult," she whispered.

Radianne turned to look at Henrick. Even in the shadows, she could see that all color had drained from his face.

"It can't be," he said softly.

The young woman smiled coldly and pulled back the hood of her tunic. "Hello, brother."

-19-
Abandoned

The long lost brother and sister stared silently at each other. It seemed as if an eternity had passed before before either of them spoke again.

It was Henrick who broke the silence.

"Elin," he whispered. "How is this possible? You and mother... I thought..."

The young woman laughed, a cold, shrill laugh. Then her eyes grew stony.

"You thought. You thought what?" she snarled. "I was dead, perhaps? Well, I didn't die. Mother grew sick and died."

Her eyes clouded over momentarily with emotion as she said the words, but then they grew icy again. "You left us there... at the mercy of the wild beast in Black Lake. The one who devoured father. However..." she trailed off and gestured with one hand to a few of the Snorgs standing nearby. "It was they who saved us. The Snorgs saved us from the beast. In time, I learned that the beast was being tamed and used for a higher purpose. At first I didn't understand, I hated the creature, but now I *know*. I understand all of it. *Except...*" She took a step forward again and pressed her forehead up close to her brother's cage. Letting out a deep sigh, she shook her head slowly against the bars. "I don't understand how you could live with yourself. For fleeing like you did. Abandoning us. A coward, you are."

Radianne flinched. She watched the discussion unfold with a racing heart and felt anger boil up at Elin's thoughtless words to Henrick. She noticed his look of sadness. She hoped it was obvious to him that the Snorgs had brainwashed this girl – his sister – and distorted her sense of reality. She obviously didn't know what she was saying.

Thankfully, despite his poor sense of self esteem at the moment, and though Radianne suspected the coward part stung a little, Henrick also seemed to be well aware of this fact. Which was part of the reason for his expression of sadness.

"You don't know what you are saying," he replied to his sister. "What have they done to you? I know you aren't in your right mind to be saying such things."

"What have they done? I am more than in my right mind. You see, I've been enlightened. They have helped me see the truth. And in time, you will see the truth too. Even though I fear it may take awhile." Elin paused and smirked for a moment before continuing. "These other two will be especially easy to convince though."

Turning, she walked toward Radianne and Thomas, to where she could get a good look at them simultaneously.

"You both really will do quite nicely. You will learn well."

Radianne had heard enough.

"What makes you so sure?" she demanded. "I will never join you. I think you are overconfident in your delusions."

"Yes, I agree with that statement," Thomas added. "If I recall, your brainwashing didn't work on me in the past. And back then, you were an innocent, a confused little girl."

He shook his head. "It would have been much easier to listen to you then. But now, now I must say that you are a black-hearted traitor to your kind – no doubt now a murderous fiend like the Snorgs as well. I wonder how many souls you've destroyed."

Elin stepped forward, keeping a calm demeanor, no sign of rage showing on her face. She reached into the bars of Thomas's cage and trailed one finger along his cheek.

"I have my ways," she whispered.

"So I see you are more of a black-hearted vixen now," he muttered.

With a snap, Elin pulled her hand back and scowled. Then she turned again on her heel and yawned.

"This meeting has proven to be too much for me tonight," she said, casting a pointed look at Henrick.

"But tomorrow, when I am refreshed, we will begin. We will start with those furry creatures over there…" She nodded toward the Floppersnogs. "They will be very simple to work with, I'm sure. And you three will follow later."

"In the meantime," she said to the Snorgs, who were still standing nearby, "make sure the prisoners have food and drink. You know what to do."

She then turned to Henrick again.

"It is good to see you again, brother, despite the unpleasant reminders of the past. Especially the painful reminder of your cowardice. Hopefully our time together will heal the bond that was ripped apart all those years ago. Hopefully you can prove yourself useful these days."

Before Henrick could comment, Elin nodded to the Snorgs, and away they all went, leaving the three prisoners standing once more in the shadows.

"Before they come back, let me give the both of you some vital advice," Thomas said, when he was certain Elin and the Snorgs were gone. "Do not, absolutely, DO NOT eat or drink anything they give you. Except the water. That may still be safe. Maybe."

"And why are you telling us this?" Radianne asked.

"The food is just one of the many ways they prepare you for the training," Thomas replied. "Some sort of concoctions that make reality turn, perception becomes flawed, memories fade. I made the mistake once and I will not do so again. The effect wore off in a day or so, but I was lucky. For some, the damage takes hold permanently and distorts everything they once knew to be true."

Radianne shuddered. She looked over to Henrick, who was quiet. He was, no doubt, brooding over the shocking encounter with his villainous sister. The sister he'd thought he'd lost years before.

"How are you ?" she asked him.

He shook his head and spoke slowly. "I honestly find this all hard to believe. My sister alive… now turned to the dark side."

"We are in a place where truth gets distorted and hearts grow cold. Where goodness is sucked away, forgotten," Thomas said in the shadows. "As I've been saying, we have to fight against it. Your sister apparently couldn't, as sad as that is. But I do believe we are all strong enough – especially armed with my knowledge and previous experiences here."

Henrick shot a dirty look in his direction. "You don't know much about my sister," he spat out. "There still may be hope for her yet. You don't know her. Once, she was good and she was kind…"

Thomas interjected. "And that, my friend, was a long, long time ago. The little teary eyed girl I met years ago has long since vanished, I'm afraid." He shrugged. "But one can hope."

Before the tense conversation could escalate further, Radianne quickly changed the subject. "They said the Floppersnogs will be the first," she said to Thomas. "What does that mean?"

He sighed. "I'm assuming that tomorrow, after the Floppersnogs eat or drink something tonight that messes with their minds, they will be gathered up and forced to look into the pool sitting in the center of this cavern. What they see there will further distort their perception of reality, and then they will be taken away to one of the outer rooms for the real training. What they will endure, I don't know for sure, but I'm afraid it will involve a good deal of torment and more distortion of precious memories."

Tears welled up in Radianne's eyes and anger in her heart. Something had to be done! The Floppersnogs were so innocent and trusting. She looked over at the little furballs just then, cowered in a bunch together in their cage, looking around the dimly lit room with wide eyes. She had promised she would take care of them...

But what to do? The Floppersnogs did not have a solid grasp of Eugladian language, so it would be difficult to warn them of the danger to come.

"We have to find a way to get them, ourselves, Blink, and my sister out of here," Henrick said. "That's all there is to it. And soon. No time to waste."

"Getting your sister out will likely be impossible," Thomas said slowly. "She won't want to go, and we'd have to kidnap her. No time for that. We may be able to save ourselves somehow. And we have to find Blink."

Before Henrick could argue with him, the group was interrupted again. A small but brilliant hero was headed their way.

"Oh Blink! My dear Blink!" Radianne called out softly. "You're safe!"

Blink ran down the platform toward Radianne's cage. "I hid in the shadows," the star said with pride as he came to a stop in front of her.

He looked around at the others and beamed. "And there aren't any guards out in the shadows at present. I think those creatures were telling lies."

"So you heard everything?" Radianne asked.

"Most of it," Blink said.

He turned to Henrick. "I'm sorry about your sister. It's very good news she is alive though. Remember Henrick, never lose hope."

Henrick smiled softly at the star. "And it is equally good news to see that you are still here with us, my friend."

Blink looked quite worn out, and more alarmingly stone-like than before, factors which worried the others. But they said nothing to him about his current state as they knew commenting on it would not fix anything and may even cause worry on his end. They focused instead on what needed to be done.

"Now, how to get all of you out of here?" the star asked.

"You have to find the silver key with the red stone," Thomas told him, trying to describe to Blink what a key looked like and how it was used. "It's the only key that will open the cages. And I have a feeling it's somewhere very close to Elin, as she seems to be running things in this base at the moment."

"I will do my best to find this treasure," Blink said. He nodded to his friends. "I'll be on my way now. See you soon."

"Be careful Blink!" Radianne called after him worriedly. "Stay in the shadows."

****

Some time later the Snorgs carried in an array of fruit and earthen goblets filled with sweet-smelling liquid and presented them to the captives. The evil beasts said nothing as they passed the items through the bars. The plan was to let the prisoners become tempted by the twisted sustenance and its enticing aromas.

The Snorgs left as quietly as they'd come. They knew they didn't need to stay for the food to do its work.

Radianne found herself alarmingly drawn to the food and drink presented to her. She raised the goblet to her lips, her desire to taste its contents overpowering.

But she remembered what Thomas said.

Dumping the liquid in the goblet on the floor, she watched as a cloud of smoke rose from the puddle. She shuddered. She had to convince the Floppersnogs not to eat or drink.

Turning toward their cage, she tried using words and hand gestures to distract them. Henrick, who was closer to them, did the same.

Some of the Floppersnogs seemed to understand, but about five of them did not quite get it. Without hesitation, they dove happily and eagerly into the fruit and drink that lay before them.

The Floppersnogs who seemed to understand took a few steps away from their siblings, covered their eyes and trembled, fearing the inevitable. When they peeked between their fingers and saw that nothing seemed to have happened, they looked up at Radianne and Henrick with confusion.

Radianne shook her head and placed her hands around her neck, making a choking sound.

The Floppersnogs who'd consumed the poisoned food and drink seemed to be fine at the moment, but Thomas said the foul magic could take some time to work. The others who did not partake moved to another corner of the cage and sat, huddling together.

All the captives waited in the darkness.

Time ticked on by.

Radianne was so hungry and thirsty. She was growing weary and wanted to rest. But there would be no sleeping tonight. Instead, she closed her hand around the dagger in her tunic. She knew she would fight to the death for her freedom, for the freedom of her friends and for Blink's safe passage to the sky. The Snorgs and Elin – sister of Henrick or not – would not take her down without a challenge.

Suddenly, one of the Floppersnogs let out an ear-splitting howl. Radianne turned. Though the light was dim, she could make out a little blue furball foaming angrily at the mouth.

-20-
Escape

One by one, the Floppersnogs who'd so eagerly consumed the foul food and drink were beginning to transform. One or two of them shivered and cried, while the rest began to snarl angrily at their non-poisoned siblings, who trembled in a huddle.

Radianne's heart sank as she watched the disturbing scene unfold. "Will they attack?" she asked Thomas.

"I'm not sure," he said. "Probably not at the moment. Right now, they are of course not in their right minds and are confused, it's all just starting to morph."

Radianne found it difficult to believe that something as simple as the food or drink provided could have done this to the creatures, but then again, she didn't know what had been in the concoctions. Whatever dark potion had been mixed, coupled with the sadness and dreariness of the place, could indeed be enough to make one confused and unwell in the head. She guiltily prayed to The Creator that somehow her little furry friends would be saved in the end. They were her responsibility, after all.

After her prayer, she sat back and observed the situation while trying to formulate a plan with Thomas and Henrick for if and when Blink returned with the key to their freedom.

Eventually, the confused Floppersnogs settled down somewhat. They stood at an opposite side of the cage and had fits of shaking every now and then, but thankfully, not one of them attacked.

In the very early hours of the morning, Blink returned. The group was relieved to see him return in one piece and with the key in tow. They praised his courage and thanked him as he whispered the story of how he'd snatched the key from Elin's chamber as she slept. For the next several minutes, they worked silently to free themselves from their prisons.

The star slid the red-stoned key through the bars of Radianne's cage first and she picked it up, turned it easily into the lock, and let herself out.

Since Thomas was closest to her, she let him out next, and then moved on to Henrick.

As heart-breaking as it was, the group decided the Floppersnogs would have to be left behind for the time being. It would be dangerous to attempt to let them out, when there was no telling what the confused and warped ones would do. They could possibly give the escape away.

With an extreme sense of guilt, Radianne quietly made her way to the end of the cage where the untainted Floppersnogs huddled and she stroked them gently through the bars.

"I'm so sorry, my dear little friends. We must leave you behind for now," she whispered. "But we will return for you as soon as possible, you will not be forgotten. I will keep my vow." With tears she said the words, remembering the promise she and Henrick had made to mother Floppersnog. It was a horrible turn of events to have to leave them behind, but there weren't any other options just then. She only hoped that when she returned for them, the Floppersnogs would not be too far gone.

The creatures looked up at her with large, sad eyes. Henrick appeared by her side and also offered a few words of consolation, hoping they would understand. When one of them nodded slowly, Radianne and Henrick knew the language barrier had been crossed. The two raised fingers to their lips and backed away from the cage.

Radianne plucked up Blink and set him on her shoulder for safekeeping. They all quickly made their way across the platform and down the steps, into the dusty and eerily quiet arena. Since it was already well into the first hours of the morning, Thomas said the Snorgs and Elin would be along shortly with a breakfast – poisoned – to get the day started off on the right foot. At any moment, one of the four doors of the arena would fling open and all hope of escape would be lost. The group continued to tread quietly, but quickly, across the arena toward the door that Radianne and Thomas had initially come through.

They arrived without incident. But as Henrick went to push it open, they found it would not budge.

"I've forgotten they lock from the inside," Thomas murmured. "What to do, what to do…" He looked around the arena, as if trying to remember something important.

"Aha! There it is," he said, pointing to an odd metal lever sticking out of the dirt wall on one side of the room. It nearly blended in with its surroundings and if one wasn't looking for it, one wouldn't have noticed. "The door opener, of course. Wait here."

The rest of the group watched as he noiselessly raced across the arena floor, kicking up dust in his wake. When he reached the wall, he gently pushed on the lever and the escape door made a sharp clicking sound as it unlocked. Just as he turned to return to his friends, a door on the opposite side of the arena squeaked open.

Elin and one of the Snorgs appeared.

"Run!" Thomas shouted to the others, as he made a mad dash toward the escape.

The Snorg also rushed forward. Elin stood in place, her features frozen and devoid of emotion. She let out a shrill whistle and almost immediately, two of the hulking Desert Dogs appeared. They too raced toward the escapees.

Thomas by that point had somehow managed to move halfway down the escape route, into the long corridor, with the rest of the group.

The dogs fell on him and then Henrick, causing a great struggle. Meanwhile, the Snorg approached Radianne. The foul fiend leered at her, his crooked teeth stretched into a sickening grin as he came forward with outstretched arms that were eager to snatch her up.

But she was ready.

The blade of the dagger flashed dangerously in the dim light of the tunnel. Without hesitation, she ducked out of the Snorg's reach. They did a little dance for a few moments as the Snorg continued to lunge for her and she darted quickly out of his way. At an unsuspecting moment, she brought the weapon down – hard – stabbing his foot. Just as swiftly, she pulled the blade out, plunged it into his chest, pulled it out again and turned quickly on her heel. As she did so, she noted with with satisfaction that the Snorg howled in pain and fell backwards, hitting his bulbous head on the floor.

During her battle, Blink had fallen to the floor and scampered off to one side looking worriedly at Radianne and his other companions. He felt as if he should do something, but he didn't know what. In his weakening state, he knew that his bites would be futile and the nasty creatures would probably stomp him to stardust.

Radianne seemed to be handling her situation nicely, but Thomas and Henrick were not faring well with theirs. As they struggled to keep the fangs of the beasts from sinking into their necks, Blink remembered something he'd overheard when he'd stolen the key from the table in Elin's chamber. She had been trying to sleep and one of the Desert Dogs that acted as a guard to her quarters kept whining and pacing the room.

"My aching head!" she'd yelled. *"Smurgoff!!"*

As she'd shouted the words, the Desert Dog quieted and lowered itself to the floor, soon falling fast asleep. Maybe that command would work again, Blink thought.

He yelled the strange word just then. Instantly, the Desert Dogs pulled back and sat upright on their haunches. They then lowered themselves to the floor. Henrick and Thomas watched in amazement as the beasts pulled away and were shocked when the Desert Dogs began to close their eyes.

The two men quickly jumped up.

"A word to remember," Henrick said, as they breathlessly joined Radianne, who'd just finished defeating the Snorg. "Excellent work, Blink!"

There was no time to rest, however.

Radianne plucked up Blink once again and they all began to race down the hallway. The sound of Snorgs and Desert Dogs approaching forced them to move faster than they'd ever moved before. The snarls and enraged shouts echoing in the tunnel shook the walls and the impact of the thundering chase caused sand on the sides of the tunnel to cascade down like small avalanches. The villains would show no mercy this time. Escaping was critical.

It seemed like an eternity before the entrance to the tunnel that would lead them above ground appeared, and when it did, Radianne and her friends hurled themselves in. They struggled to scramble upward as fast as they could, toward the desert, toward freedom.

Radianne's thoughts were racing. Thomas said the Snorgs didn't care for the desert, but would that stop Elin and the Desert Dogs? She doubted it and knew there would be a much bigger battle ahead.

They tumbled out of the underground tunnel and onto the sandy desert floor just as the sun was rising on the horizon.

The sky greeted them in a breathtaking array of soothing, vibrant color and, for a moment, they all gave a sigh of relief. But just for a moment. For they knew there was still no time to waste.

Bodies covered in sweat and throats parched from the lack of water, they struggled to stand and when they did so, they ran. Where they were running to, they had no idea, for the delay in the Snorg's domain had confused the way to Shondalina. Thomas had never been to the land of the winged horses before and could not provide help with direction.

They continued to run until they could not run any longer and they came to a stop in the middle of nowhere in the vast desert. They panted and scanned the area for any sign of Elin, Snorgs, and Desert Dogs, but there were none. Unanimously, they agreed to take a bit of a breather for a few moments as they planned their next course of action.

Radianne tore a piece of her tunic off and examined the dagger. It was stained with blood and the sight unnerved her a little. She'd never done anything so violent in her life. But in that moment, she felt a little braver than she had been before. Just a little.

Cleaning the blade with the cloth, she held it out to Henrick. "I believe this is yours," she said with a slight smile. "Thanks for letting me borrow it."

For the first time in a long time, Henrick also cracked a smile.

"Why don't you keep that one," he said softly. "You've earned the right to it. I'm sure I can get another sometime soon."

"Good work with the blade Radianne," Thomas said appreciatively. "Told you you were army-ready."

Radianne blushed at his words. She tucked the dagger back into her tunic and turned her attention to Blink, who had been very quiet as he sat in her hair.

As she pulled him down gently into her arms, she found herself alarmed once more at the state of his appearance. He looked more rock-like than ever before and his eyes and mouth, though still animated, appeared hard as well.

"Thank you so much for all you did for us back there," she whispered to him. "You were so courageous and selfless. We are indebted to you."

Henrick and Thomas crowded around, also offering their thanks to Blink for his bravery and quick wit using the magic word that had immobilized the Desert Dogs and saved them.

"How are you feeling, my friend?" Radianne asked.

"I feel very drained," he said weakly. "I don't think I'm going to last much longer."

Radianne's heart sank as she exchanged nervous glances with Henrick and Thomas. Despite the fact that they'd just escaped, she felt the despair coming on again. She felt she had abandoned him in a sense because she hadn't pressed forward with the journey. *But hadn't it been right to go after Henrick and the Floppersnogs?*

She was so certain it had been the right thing to do... it had to be. Her heart told her she had to take care of all of them. Yet, combined with the guilt of leaving the Floppersnogs behind, the emotions weighed heavy on her in the light of day.

She wasn't the only one struggling.

As Henrick dealt with shame of being defeated by the Desert Dog and throwing everyone off course in the first place, he stared at the way from which they'd fled.

He thought of his sister. And how he'd left her behind. Again.

****

For whatever reason, Elin, the Snorgs, and the Desert Dogs seemed to have given up the chase. At least for the time being. It was odd, the escapees all agreed, that they hadn't been pursued. Thomas said he was certain their pursuers would appear at an unexpected moment. It was nearly evening and there was still no sign of an impending attack, but everyone was on guard.

The group came across a little encampment of catci and took up a rest until they could gather their wits and decide which way would lead them to Shondalina. As Radianne tended to Blink, Thomas lay back with his head on the sand.

Henrick removed himself from the group, outside the circle of cacti.

He thought of his sister, and how complicated the situation was. He knew in time, after Blink was safely returned to the sky – if that were even to happen, he mused – he would return and rescue her.

He had to make Elin see how cruelly she'd been brainwashed and how wrong she had been to falsely accuse him the way she had. Though, perhaps, she was right to some degree…

His thoughts turned to Radianne and Thomas. It was humiliating that he'd been taken down by one of the Desert Dogs in the first place. To add to his embarrassment, Thomas had seemingly saved the day in the end, when he'd found the magic lever that led to their escape.

Though, he supposed, it was actually Blink who had saved them all. He'd done all the hard work, getting the keys to set them free. The little star was amazing.

Henrick felt almost as cowardly as the day he'd run away from the Snorgs, leaving his family to their awful fates.

It was his fault they had veered off course.

And then there was that other matter.

Radianne.

His eyes trailed up to the sky and back across the desert. Radianne had been somewhat nasty to him when they'd first met, and there were days where she still acted as if she didn't care for him. He thought her feelings were starting to change. She gave him something to look forward to and to fight for. But when she'd come back to the camp with Thomas, he'd been so jealous... a sort of jealously he'd never experienced before. Admittedly, his feelings for her had grown deep, despite his annoyances with her at times.

The fact that Thomas was there put a dent in things. Perhaps Radianne would not need him any longer. Blink would not need him. He thought he should go back then, to save his sister and the Floppersnogs. *Right then.* No waiting. Because he knew without a doubt he was falling in love with Radianne. It would be another good reason to leave.

Before this mess with his sister, he had been reflecting on what would happen with his relationship with Radianne when Blink was gone. He wasn't used to living an ordinary life, and the thought of doing so scared him. He also didn't think he was ready for all that came with love... he was serious about gathering an army... and he didn't want Radianne to be part of it. The thought of losing her too was too much to handle.

None of it really mattered now, he thought. Radianne would probably want nothing to do with him when all was said and done. Maybe she and Thomas would end up together. She seemed to admire him.

Thomas had certainly come along and changed things...

But back to his sister. And that matter of rescuing the Floppersnogs. He sighed inwardly. What to do?

As he looked out into the sea of sand and fought against the turmoil inside, he almost left right then and there. His eyes drifted back up to the sky and he noted the stars beginning to appear. A strange, warm, and magnetic feeling washed over him. It was as if they were pulling him in, winking their encouragement. As if they were saying, "You are in the right place. Things will work out as they should in time, you'll see."

He knew then that he could not abandon his friends. The right thing was to see this quest through. And, at the end of it all, if Radianne chose Thomas, he would accept it – he would resign himself to it. Love was too dangerous. Life as a Wanderer suited him best anyway.

He'd get back to his sister. And he'd try to forget how he felt about Radianne. Even if he found himself standing up at that moment and moving, inevitably, to where she was.

****

Radianne couldn't help but laugh as Thomas did an impression of yelping Desert Dogs and the oafish Snorgs. Laughing felt nice. She knew he was trying to take her mind off Blink, who lay sleeping in her arms, and the guilt she told him she felt about having to leave the Floppersnogs temporarily behind.

Thomas stopped his impressions to feed the waning flames of the fire just as Henrick returned to the camp. Radianne's heart leaped in her chest as she watched him walk toward them.

"Welcome back," Thomas said, a little too cheerfully.

"Thanks."

Henrick looked at him briefly and then flicked his eyes over to Radianne.

They stared at each other for a moment and a flicker of something passed between the two of them. But then, he looked away, his face devoid of emotion.

Radianne couldn't fault him for that. The events of the last couple days had drained them all. Though she'd been laughing a few minutes before, she sobered as she thought again of the predicaments they were all in.

None of the them slept that night.

On guard and waiting, they watched the fire silently and hoped the dawn of a new day would somehow make things seem brighter.

****

They traversed across the desert floor, not speaking. Time in the endless sea of sand was wearing thin and Radianne wasn't sure how much more she could take.

They'd managed to find water and a little food, but fears of Blink's possible demise, the plight of the Floppersnogs, and the constant checking of their backs for Elin and her entourage were becoming quite stressful and tiresome.

The group pressed on as quickly as they could in the direction Henrick said he thought Shondalina lay. Radianne wished she hadn't been so careless with the map, as she'd lost it some time ago.

Blink commented that he could no longer feel his points, as they had begun to dramatically harden, and his words frightened her. She pulled out the rolled up bag Miss Lugia had given her and made a secure seat for him so she could carry him along without worrying he'd topple off her shoulder. At the moment, his eyes were focused on some far off, unknown place – most likely, home. She knew he was wondering if he really would ever be back among the stars again.

"It won't be much longer now Blink," she told him softly, straining to keep her voice light. "Your mother sure is going to be happy to see you."

The star nodded.

"Another day or so should get us across the border and into Shondalina," Thomas piped up.

"How would you know," Henrick countered. "It could take much longer, depending."

The two men had tolerated each other since their escape from the Snorg training lair, but at that moment, they started arguing about their final destination. The bickering grew louder and Radianne asked them to stop, several times. But they wouldn't listen.

She fumed. For most of the quest, she'd followed Henrick's lead and hadn't really branched out on her own as much as she would have liked. She knew this was partially because she was naive in the ways of the world, however, somehow it had become all about him and what he wanted, when he wanted it. And then there was Thomas, complaining about the way he thought they should go.

She decided right then and there that the time had come to take matters into her own hands. They could stand there arguing all day and night about who was right, but Blink was deathly ill. There was no time to waste standing around clucking like hens. She wouldn't put his life at risk.

Turning on her heel, away from them, she began to walk faster. It took some time for Henrick and Thomas to notice she had left their presence. When they finally did realize she was gone, she was a good deal ahead.

"What are you doing?" Henrick called out, his voice trailing on the wind. "You don't know where you're going."

Apparently, in Radianne's enthusiasm, she had veered off course a little. Pride wounded, she told herself that if she kept walking, she would run into Shondalina. Her path couldn't be too far off course.

"There's no time to stand around while you two argue," she said airily. "We want to keep moving."

Thomas and Henrick ran ahead and caught up with her.

"He's right you know," Thomas panted. "This isn't the way to Shondalina, at least from what I've heard."

"That," Henrick said, pointing west, "is the way to Shondalina. If you still had the map, you'd know this."

"And because I lost the map, that's the only reason I've been letting you lead the way up until now," Radianne retorted sharply. "I've had enough of you two bickering and trying to control things, trying to save the day. Things are going to be on my terms now."

Henrick raised an eyebrow. "So that means you'll get lost and delay Blink even longer?"

Anger boiled up inside Radianne. Her pride told her that she had to prove to these two that she could do something on her own, without their help. However, without saying a word, she did turn a little west, toward the direction Henrick had pointed. But she tried to make it happen naturally, as if she knew what she was doing.

An ever-greater expanse of desert greeted them. The heat was taking its toll and soon they all became quite cranky.

Henrick and Thomas scowled as they walked. Beads of sweat trickled down Radianne's forehead and she grumbled.

Then, suddenly, in a strange and sudden turn of events, the winds began to pick up.

Blink felt something was off. "I can sense it," he said. "An odd event is about to happen."

"I think a sand storm is coming. We must find shelter." Thomas shielded his eyes from the sun, scanning the land and horizon for possible places of safety to retreat to.

"I've never heard of a sand storm," Henrick retorted, starting to argue with Thomas again.

No sooner had he made the statement than an ominous looking funnel cloud appeared in the near distance. It began to violently churn up sand, sucking it up into a whirlwind.

"And there you go," Thomas muttered.

Also at that precise moment, a chorus of eerie howls echoed across the land. Just ahead, a pack of altered Desert Dogs appeared over a sand hill. The Snorgs, desert-adverse as they were, were not with them. But Elin was.

"Just perfect," Thomas sighed. "Wonder what else is going to happen today."

"We will not run," Henrick said. "Let's try to reason with her."

Thomas was about to say something sharp in retort but apparently thought the better of it as Radianne shot him a warning look. The group had no choice. They headed toward the dogs and Elin, fighting against the wind of the funnel cloud coming ever closer. Sharp little pellets of sand began to hit them in their faces and Radianne tried to shield her eyes from the stinging grains.

"Forget trying to negotiate with her, we have to find shelter before this storm makes an end of us all," Thomas warned, but his words were drowned out by the wind.

Just then the sand struck at all angles, first forcing them to their knees, and then flat onto their stomachs. Radianne pressed her hands against her eyes, trying to block out the painful elements, worrying about Blink, worrying about Elin and the Desert Dogs, and wishing she was home.

Home. Where she would be safe with her family... the thoughts comforted her. She held Blink close to her heart, trying to protect him from the sand assault. She had to get *him* home. Getting him home was the important thing. That had been the goal from the beginning and the entire, most important, reason for the journey.

Then something extraordinary happened. The group found themselves being swept up into the belly of the funnel cloud as it quickly passed over them. Once inside the cyclone, there was a calm, and they were simply suspended in mid-air. Outside, the cloud was still churning up sand violently, however.

Elin and the Desert Dogs stood near the whirling funnel. One by one the dogs tried to enter, but to no avail. They were tossed to and fro, their bodies thrown violently up into the air and flung great distances away.

When there were no beasts left standing, Elin stood with fists clenched, her hair whipping wildly in the wind, rage on her face. She was so angry, she didn't even shield her face from the sand's assault.

"Coward!" she yelled, and despite the tremendous noise from the swirling sand outside their safety zone, the group could still hear the echoing coldness of her words. And they knew who the words were intended for.

Then another odd thing happened. The funnel and its occupants began to drift away, slowly. The storm moved as if a living thing, a vehicle carrying its passengers to some unknown destination. There was nothing to do except wait and see where they would be carried off to next.

As they moved across the desert, Radianne watched with wonder as Elin became smaller and smaller – soon she was just a tiny speck standing on the horizon. Though she was relieved to get away from her, Radianne's heart sank a little as she took in Henrick's forlorn face.

Before they completely lost sight of his sister, he sent a message across the desert.

"I will come back for you!"

And then, Elin was gone. And the cloud moved on.

-21-
Between Worlds

There was nothing to do at the moment except wait to see where the cloud would take them. The group hovered in the storm's belly, suspended in thin air, watching the sand beneath their feet roll on like the waves of the ocean. Time seemed to stand still and it was as if they would never get to where they were going.

To Radianne, it seemed that they may very well have been trapped in the spiraling funnel for an eternity.

Then, without warning, the cloud came to an abrupt halt. The wind died down and the sand violently swirled one last time as the group was unceremoniously dropped to the desert floor. The cloud vanished without a trace, as if it had never been at all.

Everyone lay motionless on the desert floor for a few moments, their bodies and minds in a state of shock.

Radianne slowly opened her eyes and checked on her companions. Blink's eyes were wide open, and Thomas struggled to his feet and breathed a sigh of relief.

"Haven't been through a sand storm like that before," he said to no one in particular. "Never caught up in the belly either. Odd."

Henrick remained flat on his back a few feet away from Radianne. His arms were thrown over his face.

Radianne stood up and the sand cascaded from her hair as she rushed to his side.

"Henrick? Are you alright? Talk to me!" She crouched down beside him.

"I can't see," he moaned.

She gently pried Henrick's hands away from his eyes and told him to open them.

"I can't." He winced.

She reached out and gingerly touched one of his eyelids.

"Ouch!" he yelped.

"Sorry!"

Radianne glanced up at Thomas, who had walked over to assess the damage. "Have you ever experienced anything like this?"

Thomas shook his head. "Sand got into his eyes when we were tossed out. It will just have to work its way out. Here, let's get him up." He reached down and began to lift Henrick.

Without his sight, Henrick couldn't exactly protest Thomas's help, though he certainly wanted to. Radianne and Thomas both helped him to his feet and each took one of his arms.

"This is just great," Henrick muttered. "If it's not one thing, then it's another. What did I do to deserve this? When will the ridiculousness end? Now I'll probably be blind forever. This adventure just keeps getting better," he grumbled sarcastically.

"No, you won't go blind," Radianne countered as she leaned closer to him. "Sometimes when it rains, it pours you know. You've just had a run of bad luck at the moment, but it will get better. Have a little faith."

In that moment, she knew that everyone was going to have to have a lot of faith. None of them had any idea where they were, as the cloud had deposited them in an even more remote corner of the vast desert, quite far away from where they'd first caught up with it.

They walked on for awhile, Radianne carrying Blink in her bag while helping lead Henrick with her free arm.

He was in a very unpleasant mood, which she was used to by now. Thomas was also in poor spirits and Blink had grown very solemn.

As night fell once more, they found a place to settle. Thomas scowled as he built a fire. He was not enjoying the constant complaining of Henrick.

Radianne didn't know how to cope with the grumpiness of her travel companions. Her main concern at the moment was for Blink, who continued to look ever-more sickly with each ticking hour. She grew increasingly worried about her friend.

He sat near the fire, his points very stiff, his face looking stony. She settled down next to him and gave him a gentle pat.

"Are you alright, my dear friend?" she asked him softly. "It shouldn't be long now until we reach our destination." She didn't know what other comfort she could give.

The star slowly looked at her, then turned his eyes up toward the sky, where he often gazed when deep in thought. "To tell you the truth, I don't feel quite right," he said. "In all seriousness I feel like I'm fading away. Losing something."

Emotion welled up in Radianne's throat but she forced it back down. She knew she had to be brave.

"I'm sorry you are feeling out of sorts. But I do have faith this journey will come to an end soon and you will be back to your normal self. You have to just hold on a little while longer…"

Blink nodded. "I will certainly try."

They talked a bit more, until Blink drifted off to sleep. Radianne then stood and walked over to Henrick, who lay sprawled out on his back with his eyes still closed tight. He wasn't fooling her. She knew he was awake because of the deep frown he kept working.

"Things will not get better by staying eternally angry," she advised, settling down next to him on the sand.

"And how would you know?" Henrick retorted. "I've been directing your path on this journey the whole time, taking the brunt of the misfortunes. You certainly wouldn't have made it this far if it hadn't been for me. So don't tell me when and how things will get better."

His arrogant words stung. Radianne felt as if she'd been slapped.

"That's a rotten thing to say. I think it is Blink who has suffered the most. And you're the one who insisted you follow ME on this journey."

"Maybe I shouldn't have. In a multitude of ways, this adventure has left me worse for the wear. Perhaps I would have been better off if I'd just kept walking that day."

Radianne's heart sank further at his words.

Henrick turned his head back toward the fire. He knew he'd hurt her but he was hurting himself by becoming so involved, and didn't know how to handle things.

Radianne was very disappointed that he thought nothing of his choice of words or the deep impact they had on her. Perhaps she'd been wrong about the feelings she'd thought they'd shared together... she stood up, moving away from him.

She told herself once again to remember he was a Wanderer, after all, and would be tied down to no person or place. He was a very egotistical and unstable Wanderer at that, she thought.

She decided then and there that she should no longer waste her time pining for something that would never be. Or someone who thought so little of her.

At that moment, she caught Thomas staring staring at her with sympathy. Embarrassed he'd heard their conversation, she returned to Blink. She lay down next to the star and turned her head away from the two men, trying to shut the thought of them out. Time with the both of them had been extremely draining.

No sooner had she closed her eyes than she heard their loud voices bickering. Her eyes popped open and she listened.

Thomas, apparently tired of Henrick's foul attitude, was trying to get him to open his own eyes instead of feeling sorry for himself again. Henrick of course, was objecting.

"Just leave me alone and mind your business," he snarled. "I know what I'm doing."

"Oh yeah?" Thomas countered. "It sure doesn't seem like it. Again you were almost killed by a Desert Dog, then imprisoned by the Snorgs, then blinded by sand... it sure doesn't seem like you know very much about survival in the wilderness at all. How you've managed to be a Wanderer all these years is a great mystery. And your attitude toward Radianne stinks."

"I'm not the one who ran off to the desert and hid away for years like a recluse," Henrick shot back. "Like a scared little boy. And leave Radianne out of this, you don't even know her."

"My family was killed, I needed time to think," Thomas said angrily.

"My family was killed too, but I didn't hole up in some desert and just try to forget."

"Nah, you just turned yourself into a heartless Wanderer who thinks he knows everything but actually knows VERY LITTLE. Especially when it comes to women…"

Radianne stood up. She'd heard enough. "I think both of you need to stop this childish behavior, right now!"

Thomas and Henrick were both standing by that point, fists clenched at their sides.

"No one forced you to come along with us," Henrick said to Thomas. "You could have stayed in your cave and continued to shut out the world."

"And if I hadn't come along, you'd be dead."

"You two are ridiculous, I'm going for a walk," Radianne announced. She turned on her heel and began to walk away into the night. The act was becoming all too familiar for her.

"Don't do that, you don't have a map," Henrick called out after her. "You might get lost."

Radianne stalked away from the bickering men. She wanted to grab Blink right then and leave them behind... maybe she would, she thought. Maybe she'd go back to the camp, pick up Blink, and tell those two good riddance. They were bringing her nothing but trouble and heartache. They only cared about themselves and their egos and not the present mission at hand.

She fumed over how much Henrick managed to get to her. It frustrated her that she'd let him and that his words had the ability to cause such terrible reactions. He had turned everything topsy-turvy throughout their travels.

She had gone back to rescue him and then all this had happened...

If he was so miserable with her and Thomas, she wondered, why was he still there? Why hadn't he stayed with his sister?

Was it all done out of boredom? Was it something Wanderers just did for fun?

Just then, caught in the wasteland between worlds, Radianne was more confused than ever before. Where was Shondalina? How much longer would it take to find the key to Blink's freedom?

Focus, she told herself. Her focus had to be sharp and she had to stay calm. She looked up at the stars, imagining Blink's mother was looking down at her.

"I'm bringing your son back," she whispered. "I promise, I will."

Returning Blink home was vital. Once he was safely home, she would go back to Eugladia and forget about Henrick and Thomas. She'd then set out again on her own to rescue the Floppersnogs. This time, it would be all on her own. She would be better prepared and knew she had gained the confidence. Even if Henrick didn't believe in her capabilities.

She turned back to camp.

****

Sometime during the night, the swelling in Henrick's eyes miraculously went down and the sand worked its way out. In the morning light, he announced that he could see again, though his vision was blurry.

"That's good to hear," Radianne acknowledged, politely, as she gathered Blink up in her arms. She would carry the star for the remainder of the trip, as he had no movement left in his poor little body. "With that being said, there is no time to waste," she continued. "As you can see, though neither of you may have noticed, Blink is deteriorating quite rapidly now and we have to get to Shondalina as soon as possible. We're leaving now and we are going to find a way. With or without you."

Thomas and Henrick looked taken aback, but she didn't care. It wasn't about them or their hurt feelings, wounded egos. It was not about her either, and her thirst for adventure and need for change. She realized she'd been selfish, thinking and brooding about nonsense for much of the journey.

This was about saving a life. A life that was fading in her arms. And it was her responsibility now to do what she had first set out to do and help her friend get back to where he belonged.

She didn't look at the two men as she left. She was done caring. She just held Blink close and let her heart guide her, pulling her forward along an unknown path.

Her eyes filled with tears as she walked. She thought again of her selfishness on the journey, always thinking of her feelings for Henrick too many times to count. Perhaps she hadn't taken Blink's predicament as seriously as she should have. At the moment, the situation was grave.

She hoped that she'd still be able to save Blink, or she didn't know how she would ever forgive herself for not being able to fully devote her attention to him and his needs.

So she walked. And she pressed on, even when her knees felt like they would buckle under her. She grew thirsty and tired. But she had a feeling, deep down, that she was being guided.

She felt the despair slip away. A warm glow filled her spirit, and she knew then that it came from within. Throughout the journey, she'd slowly been transforming. The naive girl of yesterday was gone. In her place was a young woman with ambition... with purpose... with hope.

And then, there it was. What she saw made her heart skip a beat. The desert had finally come to an end.

A path of lush green grass stretched out just ahead, beyond a foggy cloud of sand, in a sort of winding road running into a meadow surrounded by light. Just when it felt as if she and Blink could go on no longer, she had arrived. She knew then that the sand funnel had been sent by The Creator to help speed things along, so they'd make it in time. She knew He had led her there, in the final hours.

Tears streaming down her face, Radianne stepped forward. She walked onto the path that led into the meadow and collapsed in the soft grass, too tired to go further at the moment, even though she knew she must.

"We've made it Blink," she whispered. "We've made it to Shondalina."

-22-
Last Hope

Radianne realized that many places throughout the journey had been beautiful, but she was quite certain Shondalina had to be the most extraordinary she'd ever laid eyes on or ever would, at least outside of Heaven.

Pale purple mountains surrounded the meadow from all angles, their peaks jutting up into beds of puffy white clouds scattered across a serene blue sky. Blades of wispy grass in all hues of green blanketed the gently undulating hills of Shondalina's countryside, which was dotted with bright and glorious smelling wildflowers.

A river snaked its way through little valleys between and over the hills, seemingly stretching for miles beyond what the eye could see.

And then there were the butterflies.

These were not of the Gentle Giant variety; they were just normal, but beautiful, shimmering butterflies. There were a great number of them and they seemed to dance everywhere at once, as if in celebration of their lives and the fact they lived in such a pristine and wonderful paradise.

Though time was of the essence, Radianne just had to sit there for a few moments and revel in the remarkable beauty of it all. As she looked down at Blink cradled in her arms, she noticed he too was taking in the lovely scenery.

"We've finally arrived Blink," she whispered to him again. "We've made it. You are that much closer to home now."

"Yes," the feeble star said weakly. "We've finally arrived."

Radianne turned her head and watched as Henrick and Thomas slowly trailed in. They had apparently followed her, being sure to keep a good distance behind. She supposed she hadn't expected them to do anything else anyway, and admittedly, would have been put off if they hadn't.

It was a wise decision on their part, she thought as she took in their guilt-ridden faces as they approached.

As the two came forward, Thomas bent down and, in one sweeping gesture, plucked up a beautiful white flower from a cluster of the wispy green grass. Bowing, he took a few steps closer and presented it to Radianne, as if handing her a peace offering.

"A beautiful flower, for a wise gem of a lady," he said, blushing and suddenly seemingly shy.

Radianne raised an eyebrow. She wanted to stay irritated with them both, but things had changed so much for the better that she could not bring herself to do so. She giggled, taking the lovely flower in her hands and sniffing its petals.

"Thank you."

With a casual glance she noted that Henrick took in the exchange without a word or change of expression. His face was blank. He didn't say anything to her and she actually didn't mind. She did not want his sourness to ruin her wonderful mood.

Besides, there was no time to waste thinking about such things. It was time to get moving.

Though the sun shone brightly in Shondalina, the heat was not scorching hot like the desert had been. A gentle breeze blew as the group walked.

Radianne wondered how to find the Queen of the Pegasus. She didn't have to wait long. Winged horses began to appear.

"Look!" she said, delighted, pointing to a nearby field where the horses grazed. "Aren't they stunning?" The horses had long, silky flowing manes and glorious wings graced with various hues of the rainbow. Some of them also had foals nuzzling their sides.

The lovely creatures looked up as the group passed, several stopping to stare and others moving in close together in a huddle as they whispered about the newcomers in their midst.

A large blue Pegasus suddenly galloped forward, stopping the newcomers in their tracks.

"Greetings!" the horse said. His voice held an air of nobility and authority. He wasted no further time with pleasantries and got right to the point. "I am one of the Queen's Watchers. May I ask what your business in Shondalina is?"

"We are here to see Her Majesty," Radianne said shyly. "On a matter of very important, private business."

The blue horse glanced at a few other Pegasus standing nearby. They exchanged a knowing look before he turned back and grunted his approval.

"Of course. I will take you to her at once. All you have to do now is just climb aboard."

Radianne's heart pounded at the thought of meeting the Queen. She gestured to her friends and hoped she wasn't being too rude or bold.

"If you don't mind, my friends must accompany me as well," she said. "And, well… we can't all fit on your back…"

"Of course." The blue Pegasus laughed. He whinnied and two more of his stately brethren arrived on the scene, ready to cart the group off.

He bowed down low and Radianne climbed up, holding Blink firmly tucked inside one arm and wrapping the other around the soft neck of the horse. Henrick and Thomas followed suit on the other two Pegasus. When all were situated comfortably, the winged horses took off at a slow gallop and soon soared into the sky.

"Whheeee," Blink said softly as they ascended, smiling. "My, but it does feel good to be up in the air again."

"Soon you'll be home and back in the air permanently," Radianne said softly. Her heart fell a little at her own words. While she indeed wanted Blink home in his rightful place and she had known all along her friend would be leaving her, she hadn't realized just how much the reality of him leaving actually hurt.

The horses flew through the clouds for some time until they began to circle around an elegant white castle set atop an enormous expanse of solid looking cloud. The Pegasus descended with a gentle landing and then bowed down low to let the riders slide off their backs with ease.

On one side of the marvelous castle sat a small forest of blue pine trees. Two of the winged horses immediately trotted off toward it.

"The Queen likes to spend her days reflecting and planning in these trees," the blue horse explained. "I will also go to her at once and tell her of your arrival."

Radianne, Henrick, and Thomas waited quietly on the cloud, examining their surroundings with wonder, amazed that a cloud could be as solid as the ground.

Radianne, in particular, was so engrossed with the marvel of it that she didn't hear the small gasping sound at first. But when she finally heard it, she looked down with horror and all color drained from her face.

Blink appeared to be choking. He stared up at her and his eyes were wide with alarm – eyes that were for the first time since she'd met him, full of extreme fear.

"What is it Blink?!" she cried, kneeling down and gently cradling her friend in her arms.

And then she saw. And she screamed.

Blink's mouth had disappeared. In its place was a line of solid rock, the same sort of texture his points had transformed into.

The only body parts he could move were his terror-filled eyes.

"No! No! No!" Radianne cried. Tears slid down her cheeks and fell onto her friend in little splashes. They had come so far, they were so close! He could not leave her now.

"Hold on Blink! We are almost there!"

Henrick and Thomas kneeled down next to her, and tried to console both the girl and star. Henrick was especially alarmed, but was trying to remain calm.

"He's tough, Radianne. He will make it through this," he murmured, placing a reassuring hand on her back.

Radianne struggled not to shake him off. She felt like saying something cruel to him then, as she felt he had done several times on the journey, when he seemed to only care about himself and his brooding. However, such grievances were trivial in that moment.

She brushed away tears as she continued to stroke Blink. His eyes relaxed under her touch. She knew it was only a matter of time before the star turned to completely to rock.

Had it all been for nothing?

She had to remain hopeful. If they could only send him home soon, she was sure he would return to his true form. He had to.

"Hold on, my dear friend," she whispered.

The three Pegasus reappeared. Unaware of what had just transpired, they neighed loudly as they announced the arrival of the Queen.

"The Queen, Permeredia."

With that, they abruptly flew away, leaving Radianne and her friends standing alone on the cloud, waiting for the mysterious noble to arrive. Radianne's heart beat wildly in her chest. She felt so helpless as she prayed that Queen Permeredia would be able to save Blink in time.

So distraught was she, she didn't notice Henrick staring at her, taking in her scruffy clothing and appearance.

The three of them hadn't washed in days, but Henrick was thinking Radianne was the most beautiful woman he'd ever seen, and never more so than at that moment, when she was completely oblivious to anything but saving her friend. He was worried about Blink as well, and found himself frustrated at the direction his thoughts were going in such a dire time. But he could not help it… her love for the star was so evident. It was, and she was, beautiful.

The Queen emerged from the pine trees in silence, stepping out into the sunlight, revealing a coat a shimmery shade of lavender, her wings and mane a luminous and elegant silver. Her hooves were snow white, her eyes a wise sky blue.

As she approached, she nodded her head, as if she'd known all along they were coming.

"How do you do, weary travelers?" she asked in a soft sing-song voice. "Hello again, Henrick."

Henrick nodded his head. "Your Majesty."

Radianne and Thomas politely responded, not quite sure how to greet the lovely creature.

After the brief introduction, Radianne could not afford to stand on ceremony. She could not contain herself any longer. Not caring if she was being bold, she cleared her throat.

"We have come very far," she began, stepping toward the Queen with tear-filled eyes, holding Blink forward with outstretched arms.

Permeredia quickly, but kindly, cut her off. "I know you need my help, that much is clear," she said gently. "We do not get travelers from other parts of this world so much these days. I've heard whispers and rumors of your coming. I think I already know what it is you ask of me. But please, forgive my interruption. Continue."

Radianne went back to the beginning, and told the tale in a hurried tone. She told of how Blink had unexpectedly and miraculously fallen into her life. She spoke of their long journey, the brief encounter with the Snorgs and how poor Blink's state of being had become along the way. She spoke of her great love for the star, and how she wanted nothing more than to return him to where he rightfully belonged. She told the Queen how that had been the goal and the sole reason for the journey since the beginning, and she had to see it through.

The Queen listened quietly, shifting her gaze every now and again to Blink.

"We do not have long," Permeredia said when Radianne finished talking. She sighed. "It is difficult. This is the second time I've seen a star fall from above," she added, her thoughts suddenly seeming to drift far away as her eyes looked across the horizon, remembering. "There was a star that fell long ago in these parts, and befriended us. We did not know at that time what would happen if a star spent too much time below. This star assumed he would have an adventure, learn all he could about this world. He would then return to his own realm."

"What happened to him?" Radianne quietly asked.

The Queen lowered her head to Blink and squinted at him, then straightened and focused her attention on Radianne, her face very grave.

"The star didn't realize that a star that stayed too long below would soon become a rock. Sadly, that is what happened to our other friend, and he realized what was transpiring too late. His fate was secured. He is now a sad and lovely stone."

She shook her head and sighed again. "You haven't much time to help Blink, I'm afraid. His state is very poor. I can only hope there is enough time for the journey. I would bring him back today, but this kind of endeavor will take much of my strength." She paused. "After the tragedy with the first star, we realized if such a thing were to ever happen again, we had to figure out the best way to make a return possible. The way back is much too high and far. I must take special sustenance tonight to provide my body with the enormous amount of energy needed before our trip. The concoction will also speed us ahead. But I am afraid that we can't depart until morning."

She turned and walked toward the castle. "Come with me. Stay as my guests. I will take your star at the first rays of morning light. We cannot do more for him now. But I will do my best tomorrow."

-23-
Reflections

Radianne lay propped on one elbow on the soft bed. She looked down at Blink, who seemed seemed to be sound asleep at the moment.

After they'd been shown their rooms, they'd been treated to hot baths and a delicious-smelling dinner, though Radianne had hardly been able to eat due to all the anxiety she was feeling about Blink's deteriorating health and the mixed emotions she had about his impending departure. Queen Permeredia introduced the group to her three young children, all beautiful and delightful, frolicking creatures. They all had their mother's eyes.

The early evening had passed in a sort of blur. However, over dinner, Radianne had learned the sad tale of the Queen's husband, King Eurene. He had disappeared while on a "secret mission" the year before, and rumor had it that he had been killed by a band of Snorgs. The Queen, who preferred to stand at the head of the enormous dining table (instead of sitting on ornate cushions on the floor, like the other Pegasus present) simply said the Pegasus had underestimated the Snorgs and their growing power. It was one of the reasons they were laying low until "the time was right."

The Queen did not go into much detail. Radianne wondered what exactly had happened. She also wondered why she hadn't thought of the King before. She'd only always envisioned the Queen when she thought of Shondalina.

His death was another tragic loss due to those Snorg fiends, and she knew more deaths would be coming. Growing cold, she lay on her back and wrapped her arms around herself. If the Snorgs could take down the King of the Pegasus, what little hope was there for the rest of them?

Guiltily, she thought again of the Floppersnogs and hoped to find them alive when she went back for them.

She knew, however, that she had to focus on the task at hand at present. Her eyes welled up with tears for what seemed to be the tenth time that day as she gazed at her friend.

It seemed to her like only yesterday Blink had fallen into her life… but then again, it also seemed ages ago somehow. So much had changed since she'd left Eugladia. She knew she had been selfish at times, thinking more of herself, her "adventure," and her odd relationship with Henrick than about what her friend may have needed.

Yet, she'd also learned so much from Blink over the course of the journey. He taught her so much about taking things for granted. He taught her how to keep pressing on, how light and strength could be found in even the most dire of circumstances. She hoped she had the chance to tell him how much his arrival into her world had changed her life. It had changed her, forever.

At that moment she knew he needed to rest. Tucking Blink gently under one corner of the silky blue blanket on the bed, Radianne stood up and walked quietly out of the room, closing the door softly behind her.

The Queen had given them leave to explore the grounds if they desired to do so, and Radianne certainly could use some time alone. She shook her head as she walked. Always had to analyze things.

As she wandered through a long and elegant white corridor of floors that seemed to be made from pearls – they shimmered so beautifully – she gazed up at the portraits of generations of Pegasus royalty and warriors.

She wondered about the lives they had lived and what they may have been like. Some of the paintings were centuries old. She could not believe at that moment she was walking around in a place she could only dream about as a child. She remembered she used to wonder if Shondalina were even real or just a story adults told children to keep them entertained.

If only her heart weren't so heavy, she thought, she would treasure the experience of being in Shondalina so much more…

There was a door that led outside. As she stepped out into the early evening air, she caught the first glimpses of the sun going down. The sky was streaked with a glorious array of colors – pinks, reds, purples and gold, all mixed together brilliantly. The sight was painful, somehow.

Walking around the side of the castle, she spotted a still pond. It had a large boulder that seemed made for thinking, ironically. She as was taken back to where it all started, sitting on a rock one evening at home.

Her heart skipped a beat. It was in some ways eerie.

She shivered and walked over to the boulder and sat down. Sighing, she closed her eyes. She decided to let herself let go of time and just get lost in the moment. Get lost in reflections of where the journey had taken her and where life would lead her next...

"Beautiful night, isn't it?"

The voice broke into her thoughts.

Radianne's eyes popped open. Thomas was suddenly there beside her on the boulder, his eyes lifted up toward the fading sun.

"Though I have to say, nothing compares to the beauty of a sunset in the desert," he mused, his face a little sad as he said the words. "I think my heart remains there and always shall."

He turned to Radianne and stared at her with an odd intensity. "Never mind that though. How are you feeling?"

Radianne shivered again. It could have been from the slight breeze blowing, but there was something else. It was something about the way Thomas was looking at her.

As the last rays of setting sun alighted on his long dark hair and illuminated his face, her heart fluttered a little. His beautiful blue eyes showed concern for her – he actually seemed to care about her well-being – and she thought that was quite flattering.

Though she knew should be thinking about Blink, at that precise moment all she could focus on was Thomas's gaze.

Henrick had never really seemed to care all that much how she was feeling, though she cared too much for him. Though there were times she'd thought he'd felt the same way, he'd also seemed too lost in his own head most of the time...

She remembered Thomas had asked a question. She cleared her throat. "I'll be OK," she whispered. "It's been one wild journey and I'm worried about Blink. I just hope we can get him home in time."

Pain filled her heart as she thought again of her friend back in the room, under the blue blanket, his body mostly gone to stone. She thought of the Floppersnogs, trapped in that horrible place. It had all become too much. For the first time since embarking on the journey, she began to weep. To really, deeply weep.

Embarrassed, her hands found their way up over her face, in a feeble attempt to shield her raw emotions. They came pouring out anyway. She couldn't control the flow.

"Shhh," Thomas whispered, wrapping a comforting arm around her as he pulled her close to his side. He didn't offer any other words of consolation, but instead just held her and allowed her to her cry until no tears were left.

It was exactly what she needed.

Then they sat silent for some time, watching as the sun vanished on the horizon, waiting until the stars began to come out one by one. Feeling completely caught up in the moment, Radianne lowered her head to Thomas's shoulder.

"Blink will be alright you know, you'll see," Thomas murmured into her ear. "Things have a way of turning around and turning out exactly as they should, in the end."

With his free arm, he gently turned Radianne's face toward his. "And you know what else? I'm starting to feel like this is how things should be too."

He lowered his lips to hers.

For a moment, Radianne's world spun out of control and she was lost in Thomas's embrace. She had to admit that she did enjoy the kiss, though it left her a little confused.

Thomas was a good person, exotic, charming. Yet as she sat there and kissed him – her heart a jumble of emotions amid its rapid beating – the face of another flashed to her mind. She knew she couldn't ignore the fact that for whatever reason, her feelings for that man were undeniably stronger.

"Thomas," she whispered, as she pulled back slowly.

"Radianne," he whispered back, touching her face. "From the moment I saw you out there in the desert moonlight, looking like a wild sand fairy, you have managed to capture my heart. You are such a strong and good young woman, stronger than you believe. Did you know that when you came along, you saved me from myself out there? I think our paths were meant to cross, and I do believe this could be meant to be. Or, at the very least, we could try to figure it out."

Radianne let his words sink in for a moment. She was just learning about the strange and many faceted aspects of love, and was not entirely sure she even understood any of it. But she suspected "could be meant to be" probably was not enough. Was it meant to be if you weren't exactly sure? Though she suspected that sometimes love did grow with time.

However, she knew she couldn't deny those feelings she had for Henrick at the moment. Everything was confusing and her emotions were obviously not functioning properly. Henrick had been such a horrible person at times... and Thomas was so kind and so very handsome... she looked at him again.

She realized she had to be true to her heart. At least to what it was telling her then.

"After we get Blink home safely, come away with me," Thomas pressed. "Come back to the desert with me. Maybe we can marry? We can have a nice life there together, but far enough away from the Snorg's lair. I've decided I need to go back. You can help me plot my revenge against the Snorgs..." he trailed off, eager at first, but then, as he noticed Radianne's sympathetic expression, he realized his pleading and dreaming would probably prove useless.

"I can't, Thomas," Radianne said gently, touched at his words and a little shocked at what seemed to be her first marriage proposal. But she would think about that later, she told herself.

"I don't know what I'm going to do exactly, though I plan on going back for the Floppersnogs as soon as possible. I also know I must go home and see my family first before I set out on that quest. I've missed them... I actually miss Eugladia too."

She couldn't believe it was true but she desperately missed home. She hadn't realized just how much she would miss it, but there it was. She had taken her mundane life for granted. She had taken the people in it for granted. There was an ache for them now.

"Why don't you come back with me, as my good friend?" she asked Thomas. "You could meet some new Eugladians there, we could possibly find some recruits..."

"I know what this is about," Thomas cut her off, his downcast expression giving away his disappointment. "It's about Henrick, isn't it? Well, let me tell you something about him." He narrowed his eyes. "He doesn't deserve you Radianne. He's jealous, hot-headed, and very inconsiderate. His moods are outrageous, he whines a lot, and I don't think he believes in you like I do. I'm not even sure what he believes in, exactly. He's too busy brooding all the time."

Thomas turned his head then, looking out toward the water, frowning.

His words hit hard. The two sat in an uncomfortable silence for several moments.

Radianne remembered how angry she'd been the day she met Henrick. He had indeed seemed rude and self-serving and, as she'd thought even moments before, as if he didn't even care at times. But she also had to be honest with herself and remember the rest.

There were those undeniable moments when Henrick had helped her find her way, even when she hadn't wanted his help at first. How he'd fended off monstrous creatures, how they'd met the Floppersnogs together, that kiss by the waterfall... he seemed to care for Blink as much as she did.

Henrick had his own set of warts and quirks, but, she supposed, didn't they all? She did not believe for one moment he was as bad as Thomas implied, though she knew he definitely wasn't without imperfections and she herself had questioned his motives on many occasions. In fact, she wasn't so sure she even wanted to be with him, but she knew she did care for him. Possibly even more than care...

"He isn't that awful, Thomas," Radianne said quietly. "He actually has a lot of good character traits, when he lets his guard down, and gets over himself, of course."

Thomas snorted and shook his head. "I fail to see as you do. But then again, I suppose I haven't known him as long as you have."

He sighed then and touched her face. "Ahh well. You are pretty amazing," he said, as his expression softened. "Maybe one day you'll change your mind. And know that if you do, the desert will be waiting, and so will I. There will come a time when you get tired of him. And his mood swings."

Radianne smiled. "You probably think I'm pretty amazing because I'm the first woman you've seen in years, stuck in that cave of yours," she said with a laugh as his face flushed. "And anyway," she continued, "I honestly don't expect to be with Henrick. As I said, family, then Floppersnogs. I do believe he is on his own path. And so am I."

Adventure would always be there, she knew now. Maybe romance too, later. But some other precious things might not. She had to see her family soon. And first, there was Blink.

She again thought of his dire predicament, and of home, and the Floppersnogs and the promise she'd made to their mother. Her smile faded. She prayed to The Creator that both she and Blink would find their way in the days to come.

****

Henrick had seen the whole thing unfold as he stood behind a tree in the little forest. He had been taking a walk when he saw her. And then he decided to watch her, as he had that first day he'd met her, dealing with mixed emotions as he thought of the right words to say before he approached. He was finally going to let Radianne know how he had been feeling. And apologize for his outlandish and inexcusable behavior. But then... Thomas had sat down. He'd missed his chance.

The cave dweller had come and swept the only woman he'd ever loved off her feet and there was nothing he could do now but watch the whole sordid affair unfold before his very eyes. Even so, as he'd watched Thomas kiss Radianne, the fury he would have normally felt wasn't there.

Instead, there was a deep ache. An ache for things that had been and things that could have been and things that would never be. He had brought it on himself, he knew. His behavior had been horrendous at times and he supposed he deserved it.

His new friends were slipping from his grasp and soon he would be alone again. The Floppersnogs had been taken hostage. Blink would be gone tomorrow, hopefully, back to where he rightfully belonged. And most of all there was Radianne – who, it was obvious from the kiss, had fallen for Thomas's odd charms. She would no doubt join up with him when all was finished.

Squaring his shoulders, he told himself to be stronger for once in his life. To stop whining and stop being negative. To be confident and positive. Like he used to be. Though it seemed that was so very long ago...

There was no time for self-pity or acting like an infant, he decided.

He would get through the disappointment, as he had for years. As always, he would go it alone, in the end. He knew he had a purpose and part of that purpose was avenging the death of his family and rescuing his sister and the Floppersnogs. That should and would be his real focus. He had to save them.

When it came to Radianne he would just accept things as they were, he told himself as he walked back to the castle. He realized that perhaps she had ultimately come into his life to help lead him to his sister. And that was a very good thing.

And yet – as he walked down the hallway to his quarters, he couldn't deny the deep sadness he felt in his heart at the idea that there was nothing more.

-24-
Until We Meet Again

In the middle of the night, Radianne woke with a start. Her heart beat quickly. She felt anxious and her skin was clammy, and she knew that although Blink still lived, his time was drawing precariously to a close. Attempting to go back to sleep just then would be futile. In the shadows, she saw that Blink was sleeping. Distraction would be good. She hoped the Queen wouldn't mind her taking a stroll at the late hour.

Quietly climbing out of bed, she left the room and headed down the hallway. She walked down the corridor of Pegasus ancestors, passing their watchful eyes, and through several white halls that seemed to go everywhere and nowhere at the same time. It seemed the castle could go on forever in such a maze-like fashion. She lost track of time and of where she was going.

After a while, she found herself standing in a great hall with a shining silver door located at the rear. Two pearly white doors stood on opposite sides of the room. Radianne looked around quizzically. How odd, she thought. She felt as if she shouldn't be in this particular place and had suspicions it was off-limits. Perhaps she should turn around and go back to her room. The only problem was, she realized, she now felt lost. Looking back the way she'd come, it seemed to be a jumble of corridors and dizziness rose up in her head at the thought of trying to make her way through the maze again.

The room spun just then. She focused on the silver door. As she concentrated, the dizziness cleared and a pull led her toward that door with an insatiable curiosity. Just what was behind it? Where would it lead?

As if in a dream, Radianne put one foot in front of the other and made her way to the door, looking around guiltily as she did so. It wouldn't hurt just to take one peek, she reasoned with herself.

She paused when she reached it. There were no knobs or handles, as Pegasus had no use for such things. Taking a deep breath, she leaned forward and gently pressed on its shiny surface, wondering if it would even open. To her surprise, it gave way quite easily, with barely a creak.

Radianne stepped inside the mysterious room. The door immediately closed behind her and she hoped she would be able to get back out again.

A sort of white fog covered everything so it was difficult to see much in the room. Very strange, she thought. She could see, however, that the walls and floor were all silver.

As her gaze continued to sweep over the chamber, her eyes came to rest on an ornate silver table placed directly in the middle of the room. The table appeared be covered with a glass dome, and she walked toward it, intrigued. An object was housed inside the glass. Radianne peered at the dome's contents for only a moment or so before full understanding registered. Covering her mouth, she stifled a scream.

It was the star. The star that had turned to rock. A chill coursed through her body and she backed away from the table, stumbling once. She had to get out of there! She shouldn't have come. She needed to get back to Blink, to spend what little time she had left with him. With horror, she realized she just might have glimpsed his future.

As she turned to leave, a voice spoke to her from somewhere in the fog.

"Don't leave. Please stay."

Radianne spun around. Queen Permeredia showed herself.

"Oh! Your Majesty," Radianne said nervously, lowering her eyes and head in shame. "I'm very sorry. Forgive me, I have no right to be here. I should not have intruded."

The Queen shook her mane and spoke softly. "All is well. I wanted you to come," she said. "In fact, I opened the door, which is usually sealed shut. Don't fret, child. You've entered my Silver Room of Secrets. You are welcome here." Turning from Radianne, she walked around the domed table, gazing down at the star.

"Though you must understand that there are hidden things in our midst I cannot show you," she said. "However, I thought you would want to see Blaze, as unfortunate as his tragic tale, and the timing, is."

"Blaze," Radianne whispered. She slowly walked back to the table and looked at the poor star that had turned to rock. She did not understand why the Queen would think she'd want to see him. The tragic sight just made her more fearful for Blink by the minute.

"Blaze was his name. Our dear friend." The Queen lifted her head and stared at Radianne with sadness and an intensity in her eyes. "Truth be told, there is always a chance that your friend will meet this fate," she said quietly. "But it may be that the crossing of your paths has prevented this."

She looked down at Blaze once more. "Many fond memories I

have of our time together. He has a treasured spot in this room and always will. Aside from that…" she trailed off and walked around the table, coming face to face with Radianne.

The Queen stepped into the fog and came back out with a vial with her teeth. She presented it to Radianne.

"Blaze left behind a trail of stardust. We have studied it a bit, and know that it has unique properties. I give it to you now, in hopes that you may find some use for it."

Radianne held the vial up to get a better look. The glass tube contained a shimmering sort of golden powder. It was like light in a bottle. She experienced that odd tingling sensation she felt with Blink as she held it in her hand.

"Thank you… thank you very much. I'm honored you would give it to me."

The Queen smiled sadly. "Blaze leaving the stardust behind is a good reminder that beauty and light can still remain after all hope seems lost. Come now, why don't I lead you back to your room so you can rest. We have a big journey ahead tomorrow."

****

The strange part was, the Queen said she would have to fly back to the place where Blink first fell and ascend from there. Something about being limited in how long she could feasibly remain in The Outer Space. Radianne was shocked and nearly wept again when the Queen told her the plan the next morning, as she thought there would be no time to travel that far in the short time Blink had left.

"My dear, this is the way things must be done," the Queen assured her. "And you know little of Pegasus magic. We will make it back to Eugladia faster than you think."

At the first sign of morning light, Radianne climbed onto her back, Blink wrapped tightly against her chest. When learning of the power and speed of Pegasus flight – and assured they would be taken wherever they wished when the mission was complete – Thomas and Henrick both insisted they accompany Radianne and Blink on the journey. Two more Pegasus were summoned to fly with the Queen.

Radianne felt dizzy at the thought of traveling so far in such a short amount of time. They'd retrace their path back to Eugladia, through all the lands and days and weeks she and Blink and Henrick had traveled together. How very far they'd come. She didn't voice her concerns, but as if reading her thoughts, Queen Permeredia laughed.

"Don't fret Radianne," she said. "It will be quite the swift journey, you'll see."

And how true those words were.

The Pegasus' flight was like the wind, as the Queen rapidly backtracked over all the lands Radianne had explored. The treacherous Ongoing Desert, The Jungle of Vancor. The Land of Sandalia – with its giant and unforgettable hermits. The barren and vibrant sections of Eustasia – over the very same spot she and Henrick first met. Many days worth of travel were covered in less than a day's time due to the impressive and magic speed of the Pegasus.

There were moments during the flight when Radianne had to simply close her eyes, because everything was whirring by her line of vision so quickly. It was almost as if she were in a bizarre dream, floating out of time and space.

Radianne could hardly believe her eyes when they touched down in the field near her Eugladian home in the evening. The once familiar land now seemed so completely foreign to her, and she climbed off

Permeredia's back with shaky legs, feeling shocked, cradling Blink close to her chest.

She couldn't believe the time had come. She couldn't believe she was home.

So much had changed, she thought as she looked down at her friend, who was staring up at her with wide eyes. They seemed glazed over, as if they were focused on a far-off place only he could see.

"We're here Blink," she whispered. "Back to where it all began."

The group gathered round. Though everyone was tired, Queen Permeredia said there was no time to waste and insisted it would be best to begin the ascent to the stars immediately. Radianne agreed, with one condition.

"Can I just have a moment?" She looked at all her newfound friends. "I need to speak to him privately for a moment. I only wish he could also talk to me one last time."

As they somberly watched, she left the group and walked over to her boulder, her favorite thinking spot. It seemed as if it had been an eternity since she'd sat there.

As she settled onto it, she looked down at the friend who had changed her life forever. His glow and mouth were gone. His eyes still held that vacant stare. If one wasn't looking hard enough, it would seem as if she simply held a rock in her two hands. Her eyes filled with tears.

"I just want you to know Blink, you have been a wonderful surprise," she whispered, trailing one finger above his eyes. "You have brought excitement into my life, but so much more. You've taught me to appreciate the things I have and not take home or my many blessings for granted. You've taught me how to be a better friend… how to have faith that things will work out in the end…" she trailed off and a tear rolled down her cheek, landing on him.

Oh, how she wished the two of them could talk again. As she

thought about it, she felt that odd, now familiar tingling sensation run through her body. But it couldn't be Blink... could it? As understanding dawned, she pulled the vial of stardust out from a hiding place in her tunic and held it up. The tingling rushed through her fingers, traveling down her arm. The stardust shimmered in the glass vial. Though it was a sad reminder of Blaze, it was also one of hope. The glow reminded her what Blink was really made of and where he truly belonged. *Up there in that world of light.*

Would the stardust help him now? It was worth a try. Radianne gently opened the lid and pinched a bit of the shimmery dust between her fingers. She sprinkled it over Blink.

His own eyes filled with star tears as she spoke again. "I love you very much and I will never, ever forget you."

She lifted him from her chest and held him up as she stared at the sky, waiting and hoping for something to happen.

"Tonight you'll go home. And you'll see your mother and tell her about all the things you've seen down here. About your long journey. And your heroism. And I hope you will tell her about me..."

Radianne lowered him and cradled him in her arms once more. "Just so you know, whenever I see a star blinking in the sky, I will think of you. And I'll hope that it's you shining down on me." She sighed. "And now... now I suppose it is time to say goodbye, my sweet star friend."

"I love you too, Radianne."

She looked down in shock. Blink's mouth had reappeared, and with it, a faint glow had returned to his body. The stardust had worked! His voice was tiny and weak, but Blink was speaking again! They both began to cry.

The girl and star held each other for a time. It was such a bittersweet moment... the ending of something special, but also the beginning of something new. New experiences awaited them both, although they of course could not possibly know what, when, and where.

As she clutched him one last time, she felt the familiar light and strength course through her body. Yet in that moment, she realized again that it wasn't only Blink's light making her strong. His light had helped her tune in to the light and strength she also had within, the light The Creator had also given her – the light she'd found when she'd been lost at the edge of the desert.

A hope and maturity Radianne hadn't felt before suddenly filled her being. She knew then, how much she had changed for the better. And much of it was thanks to Blink, a brilliant soul, who reminded her of all she was – and all that she could be.

"I'll miss you," Blink whispered, staring at her with shining eyes. "Thank you for everything. Thank you for this adventure and for saving me and for being my friend. I will never stop thinking of you or this time we've spent together. You are a wonderful young lady Radianne. Never forget that."

"No, thank you, my dear Blink," Radianne said softly. "You've changed my life more than you'll ever know."

"You will see me from Eugladia," Blink whispered. "I will shine my brightest just for you. From now on, I'll make sure to give off an extra twinkle, just so you know exactly where I am. "

Radianne sniffed. "But you won't see me, not really."

"I'll always see you in my heart," he said, and she kissed him.

For the first time, he kissed her back. It was like a thousand sparkles filled her spirit, the light and love welled up and overflowed inside.

"You remember too, Radianne," he whispered. "Shine where you are planted. You have a light all your own inside, no matter where you go or who you go there with."

Radianne nodded as tears streamed down her cheeks. She slowly stood and placed Blink on her shoulder one last time, as she had done so many times before. Then she walked back to the Queen and the others.

After Henrick and Thomas said their goodbyes, Radianne attached Blink securely to the Queen's hair and bid him a final farewell.

"Until we meet again," she whispered, her voice trembling. "Shine bright, dear one."

"Yes. Until we meet again, I'll sparkle just for you. And whenever you see a star wink three times, you'll know it's me," Blink whispered back.

The Queen ascended.

And he was gone.

-25-
Home

The Queen had announced before her departure that the special "sustenance" she'd partaken of would give her enough energy to fly Blink home and then she would immediately take herself back to her kingdom, as she didn't want to spend much time away. The group thanked her for her help before she'd left with Blink and were not expecting her to return.

The other winged horses and Henrick and Thomas, however, were quite tired. Radianne knew they would need time to rest.

Home was just over the bridge, over the laughing river. But as Radianne stood there, at a crossroads of sorts, she wasn't ready to go yet.

No, she decided. She would spend one last night under the stars. She had to. She needed a sign Blink had arrived home safely. And as eager as she was to see them, she knew she was not yet ready to deal with the wrath of her family. The reunion would wait until morning.

She sat down on the thinking boulder and her friends came and settled close by. All were quiet as they stared at the stars, waiting for something, though they weren't exactly sure what they were searching for.

Soon, the temptation to sleep won out. The observers all found comfortable spots on the grass and curled up for the night. The hours passed and eventually Radianne also found herself on the grass and drifting off to sleep. But then – suddenly, something startled her awake.

Two bright lights appeared overhead; two stars spinning in circles and flashing brilliantly against the velvet night sky. The lights were dancing. It seemed like a vision out of a dream, but she was certain it wasn't.

Radianne smiled in the darkness. Blink had reunited with his mother. He'd made it home.

****

They woke early with the first subtle rays of morning light. The Pegasus went off to one side of the field to graze for a bit before their departure. Henrick and Thomas would fly with them to destinations of their choosing.

Radianne was a little worried that someone she knew would soon be up and about and take notice. As eager as she was to see her family and friends again, there were matters she had to see to first.

Her eyes slowly drifted over to the two of them. Those two ruggedly handsome companions, two opposite men that had both had left impressions on her in one way or another.

They stood a little ways off and seemed uncomfortable and unsure of what to say to her, or to each other for that matter.

Radianne's heart began to beat a little faster and ache in an odd way at the thought of saying goodbye to them – admittedly, they'd both become her friends even though they'd infuriated her at times.

She'd developed a special fondness for Thomas, but she was dreading saying farewell to Henrick. And even at that moment the reason why didn't make much sense to her...

Shyness took hold. Her cheeks flamed and she fidgeted. She felt nearly as embarrassed as the day Henrick had caught her bathing nude in the river. Almost.

Thomas, gallant soul that he was, decided to make the first move. "Well," he said, scratching at his long black hair a little nervously as he took a few steps toward her and held out his hand. "What I said before still stands, Radianne. I'll leave that decision up to you," he winked. "For now though, I guess it's goodbye. I have things I must attend to."

Radianne wondered what things he was referring to but had no time to ask. Thomas moved forward then and embraced her, kissing her cheek, darting a mischievous look at Henrick as he did so. He smiled as he noticed Henrick watching the exchange with an unpleasant expression on his face.

"The desert is waiting," Thomas whispered in Radianne's ear, out of Henrick's range of hearing. "And I will be too. Always."

Radianne smiled softly as she hugged him back. "Thank you for everything Thomas. Stay safe and alert! I'm sure Elin has it out for you even more now. I'm also sure we will meet again one day, possibly sooner than we think. We have another mission, after all."

Thomas nodded and pulled back. "Until then. Take care."

Slowly, he turned around to face Henrick and cleared his throat. "I know things haven't been great between us," he told him. "But in truth, if you're ever looking for someone to help you organize an army against the Snorgs, I will be happy to fight beside you."

Henrick, though his eyes were slightly steely, gave a curt nod. "I appreciate that." To Radianne's surprise, the two men proceeded to shake hands.

Thomas waved one last time to Radianne and set off to join the Pegasus. Sadness began to well up inside her again as Radianne watched him walk away and she thought of the journey coming to an end. While she had indeed grown to appreciate home and family more than ever before, life in Eugladia would never be the same now, she knew. Despite the ache she felt for it all. Her own path and story had been forged, and it was only the beginning.

She felt Henrick's eyes on her as she stood there under the warm rays of early morning sunlight. *The moment had come at last.*

Slowly, she raised her eyes to meet his. Her heart skipped a beat. His eyes were now stormy, his hair looked like strands of spun gold in the sunlight.

"Well, this has been quite the journey," he said slowly, as he kept his gaze locked on hers.

"It certainly has." Radianne shifted from one foot to the other. She thought about how much she'd hated him at first. His arrogance... how he had seemed to want to sabotage her adventure... how he seemed to know everything.

He cautiously took a step closer. "We've both come far, I think."

"True. In more ways than one."

"Where does this journey lead now?" He raised an eyebrow.

"I think I need a little time to figure this all out..." Radianne paused for a moment, before continuing. "I want to go back for the Floppersnogs as soon as possible. Maybe with the help of a Pegasus this time though," she added, with a small laugh.

Conveniently, the Queen had given her a special device, which would call on the Pegasus when the time came to rescue the Floppersnogs. It would save her quite a bit of mileage on the return journey.

Henrick nodded. "I see."

He cleared his throat and looked over to where Thomas was standing, just about ready to take off with the winged horses.

"So... I have to ask... what was that Thomas was talking about? What he said before still 'stands'?"

Radianne's lips cracked into a hint of a smile. Was that a bit of jealousy? Henrick seemed to be worried that something romantic may have happened, or might in the future happen, between her and Thomas. Interesting, she thought.

"Oh. He asked me to join him in the desert. I said I'd maybe see him sometime soon." Radianne said the words nonchalantly, trying to keep her voice level and devoid of any emotion. She watched closely to see how Henrick would react. He looked confused.

"I'm surprised you didn't say you would join him," he said with a frown. "I know you want to see your family and all... but I at least thought you'd ask him to stay or say you would join up with him later?"

"Why would I do that?" It was Radianne's turn to raise an eyebrow. And then, feeling a little bold, she took a step toward Henrick, tired of feeling intimidated or made foolish by him.

Henrick flushed. "Well..." he stumbled over his next words. "I, er, uh. I guess you could say I did happen to see you two together, back at the castle."

"Spying again." Radianne shook her head and sighed. "And?"

Henrick averted his eyes. "I guess it's just hard to read your feelings, that's all. You two seem quite taken with each other."

Radianne was quiet for a few moments as they both fought with their emotions and tried to figure out how to put everything they were feeling into words.

Her feelings for Henrick had gone up and down, this way and that way, since the day she'd met him. But in that moment she knew she had to do one thing, even though pride nearly prevented her from doing so.

She cleared her throat.

"Henrick, I honestly never thought I would be saying this," she said sheepishly as she looked up at him. "But I just want to tell you that now, in the end, I am grateful you came along when you did. I admit I was a bit naive at the beginning of the quest."

She paused and shifted her feet around. "Though pride almost prevents me from doing so – and if the truth be told, you have indeed completely infuriated me at times – I will be the first to admit that I don't know how I could have done it all without you. Blink would say the same, I'm sure."

She stopped talking a moment to take in his surprised expression.

"Although," she continued, a glint forming in her eye, "I know I'll be quite capable of handling the next quest presented to me on my own. Without your help or, should I say, hijacking. It will be completely my adventure, on my terms."

Henrick smiled. "I'm sure it will be."

Then, in typical Henrick fashion, his expression sobered and he looked pensive. His next words surprised her.

"You are stronger than you know," he said. "And I'm going to say I am sorry if I've been a horrible friend at times and didn't reassure you of that… if I ever made you doubt yourself or feel bad. You have every reason to feel proud. I have been cantankerous and moody at times, I'm well aware of that fact. You are truly an amazing woman Radianne. And I believe I got what was coming to me many times on this journey, especially in recent days."

He took another step closer. "But all that aside, it has been worth every second. There's something else I have to tell you too."

Radianne's heart quickened.

"Yes?"

Henrick reached out slowly, gently taking one of her hands in his, lacing his fingers in her own.

"You have changed my life more than you know," he whispered. "You have given me something to fight for, something to hope for again. You never really gave up on me or pushed me away. You made me realize the power of my own inner strength, when for years I've felt like a failure. Finishing this journey with you showed me that. Last night I reflected deeply on it. I know I may have been somewhat of a moody beast on this adventure, and I will understand if you want to walk out of my life forever..." he trailed off.

"And I know it may be too late, and Thomas may have very well swept you off your feet, and you might very well have plans to meet up with him again sometime soon. But..." He hesitated, looking deeply into her eyes. "I will have no regrets. I just have to tell you... I want to tell you... I love you Radianne. Even if I acted like a child at times and couldn't treat you the way you needed to be treated. I love you."

"There," he breathed, with a very flushed face. "I've babbled quite a bit but I've said it. And I suppose it can't be undone."

Radianne's heart soared. "No, it can't," she agreed.

In that moment, when she had confirmation Henrick felt the same crazy way she did, she felt as if she could soar all the way to the stars and dance with Blink and his mother – her spirit felt so light. As she stood there looking at Henrick's face, she knew she also had to be truthful.

"I might as well say it... just so you know, I turned Thomas down," she said with a smile. "I turned him down because there is only one man my heart can belong to. And despite your beastliness, I do believe that man is you... I love you too, Henrick."

The two weary wanderers stepped forward and embraced. Then

they held one another close for some time in the early morning light.

****

Radianne sat on her thinking boulder and stared up at the sky, searching the stars for any sign of Blink. The day had been a busy one and the reunion with her family had been emotional.

However, she'd not encountered the wrath she'd been expecting. Her parents and brother had been overjoyed to see her and were quite overcome with emotion, though they did eventually give her a good talking to about never disappearing like that again without proper notice.

No matter how old she was, her parents told her, she would always be their daughter and they would always worry. And as the day wore on, they must have sensed how the journey had profoundly changed their girl too. They both commented how their daughter had grown into a remarkable woman during her short time away. Even her brother seemed impressed. They no longer treated her like a child.

As for Henrick...

Soon, she would join up with him and figure out how to rescue the Floppersnogs and save his sister.

Before she'd gone home, they'd walked in the woods for a while. He told her he wanted to give her time to spend with her family, but would soon return to properly introduce himself to her parents before the next quest. Which they would happily be embarking on – together.

Where Henrick would go in the meantime, Radianne wasn't sure. But she now knew Wanderers had a multitude of secret hideaways and he would be fine.

"Until we meet again," he'd whispered as he kissed her goodbye and walked away in the early morning sunlight.

As she finished reflecting on the day's events, Radianne began to fervently search the sky once more. A lump formed in her throat as she wondered what Blink was doing at the moment. Was he telling his family and friends stories about their travels together? Did he miss her as much as she already missed him?

As she fretted, her fingers brushed against the necklace still hanging at her throat, and she smiled. The mermaid's pearls had certainly brought her and her friends luck, in the end. She had to believe that same luck would continue in the future. By The Creator's grace, it would.

The wind picked up and it seemed a storm was looming on the horizon. The stars suddenly were blocked by oncoming clouds. Radianne knew she would have to leave soon or get caught in the downpour.

Disappointed, she scanned the sky once more for any sign of her friend. She was just about to give up when... there!

She spotted him in a sudden clear patch of sky. It was as if the clouds parted just for her. The one lone star, twinkling and winking three times, then zooming around. She knew it was Blink, and, as promised, he was putting on a show just for her.

She waved and blew him a kiss, knowing that even if he couldn't physically see it, he would sense it. They were connected that way, forever. She knew he'd always be there, looking out for her. Just as she'd look out for him, all the rest of her days. He'd been a light that had miraculously come into her life and she'd never forget the inner light he'd helped her find.

With a smile on her face and that familiar warm glow filling up her spirit, she stood, turning toward the laughing river.

And headed home.

About The Author

R.M. Anderson grew up in Illinois with a love for reading, writing, fantasy and imagining worlds populated by talking animals and magical creatures. After graduating from Northern Illinois University, she worked for two years as an English teacher in Taiwan, traveling through several other Asian countries while living there. She considers those few years to be dear and transformative chapters in her own life story. Her faith is an important part of who she is, and is often an inspiration in her writing. She currently lives in a renovated 1800s farmhouse in northern Illinois with her husband, her daughter, and their husky – who may never be a sled dog, but is an expert chowhound.

More at www.rmandersonbooks.com

Made in the USA
Lexington, KY
16 July 2018